The Letter Writer

by

Sharon Carr

Front cover illustrated by: Patti Rule

CHAPTER 1

Eggsactly!   The cute little coffee shop is Susan's standing Tuesday and Thursday morning breakfast stop.   She orders the same thing each week- English muffin, cup of fruit, cottage cheese and hot tea- chamomile.   She sits in the same spot each week- at the counter- right smack in the middle.   The owner, Rose, threatens weekly to put a reserved sign with Susan's name on it between the hours of 9-11 a.m. on Tuesdays and Thursdays.   No need.   Susan doesn't mind waiting if someone is already sitting there when she arrives.   She has no where to go until 1:00 p.m. when she has to pick up Myles from Kindergarten. She loves this little coffee shop.   It isn't as trendy as the other diners on San Vicente, but it's cozy and warm.   And Susan loves the name.   That's what drew her here in the first place.   The name is just how Susan feels.   She is exactly/eggsactly where she wants to be.

Susan has been coming here for 8 years.   She discovered it when Jessica started Kindergarten.   She had dropped Jess off at school and was heading to her yoga class when she saw the sign-   a big friendly yellow sign with the Gs made to look like eggs over easy.   She decided she would come back after yoga. And she did.   Since then her Tuesday and Thursday mornings have been the same- drop the kids off at school, go to yoga, go to breakfast at Eggsactly, go volunteer at the animal shelter, if she has time (i.e. no one was sitting in her spot at the diner and made her wait), pick up kids from school.

It's odd but Susan feels as if this place is her retreat away from home where she can get special alone time. The place has a very homey feeling. Seven yellow covered stools line the counter top. Ten tables occupy the dining room- four two-tops along the wall and six four-tops in the center. On the sidewalk are four tables for when the weather is nice which is almost always in sunny Los Angeles. Inside is decorated in country chic- frilly lace curtains, yellow and white flowery upholstered covered chairs and vases filled with daisies.

In all of the years she has been coming here, she has only come here with someone else on three occasions. The first time she brought Sammy when he announced when he got to school that he wasn't feeling all that great. So instead of dropping him off at school, she brought him with her to the diner thinking it would make him feel better. No such luck. Sammy whined the whole time, and then shot a spitwad through his straw at Bobby, the busboy. They left immediately. Poor Bobby had just started working at Eggsactly! What a welcoming!

The next time she brought Sophie. Susan and Sophie were on a special mother/daughter day for Sophie's 13th birthday. Susan had planned they would have breakfast and then go shopping along San Vicente to look for a special piece of jewelry for Sophie's birthday. Sophie wasn't hungry as she was on one of her infamous diets, not that she needed to be on one, especially at 13, but she was. Sophie was in a hurry to go shopping to find her gem. She was not in the mood to sit in "this outdated diner" especially when

2

they could be eating at one of the trendier places on the street where "everyone else goes."

The third time Susan brought Jack here. He had actually taken a day off work because he was exhausted. Susan convinced him to go out to breakfast. He was grumpy and just wanted to hit the greens to take off the stress. Once again -another unsuccessful trip to the diner with company.

Three strikes and you're out!!! Susan vowed never to bring anyone else here again.

She loves it here and doesn't want anyone else to ruin the good feeling she has when she comes. Eating alone is fun. She loves to people watch. When she's alone she can be free to stare and listen to other customers as much as she wants without being scolded by her kids or her husband.

Susan knows many of the regulars by now as well as the staff. White haired Drew and Marion are in their 80s and have been coming here for about 4 years since they moved into a townhome down the road. They have 3 daughters, 6 grandchildren (each daughter has two children) and 4 great-grandchildren. They all live close and see each other often. Drew retired from the film industry as a sound editor ten years ago. He has one academy award which he talks about proudly and frequently. Marion was a model in her youth, then a stay at home mom. She makes apple head dolls for family and friends. They are actually quite good. Everyone tells her she should sell them on QVC, but she just enjoys doing them for fun and doesn't need the money.

Both Drew and Marion are still very attractive

and regal looking. Drew stands just shy of six feet with a slender firm frame which he keeps in shape by playing tennis three times a week. His chiseled olive skinned face has barely a wrinkle and his piercing blues eyes look like gemstones. Marion stands five foot ten with her perfect posture and long regal Audrey Hepburn neck. Her tiny delicate facial features and sapphire colored eyes make her look like royalty.

Eddie, 32 years old with the body of a boxer and a friendly always smiling face, is a single father whose wife left him for his best friend, an aspiring actor. Eddie loves his 8 year old son, Tyler, and spends most of his time with him, but is now ready to get back into the dating scene. Eddie is the Physical Education coach at Tyler's elementary school around the corner, the same school where Susan's kids attend. In fact Tyler and Sammy are in the same class. Eddie stops into the diner to pick up muffins for the teams during his morning break. He is always friendly and says "hello" to everyone.

Cherise, not her real name, is an aspiring model/actress/singer/dancer/writer/producer. She moved to Los Angeles from Minnesota 2 years ago and is still waiting for her big break. In the meantime, she works for a catering company that does Hollywood events. She really is strikingly beautiful- 5'10", long deep auburn colored hair, big milk chocolate colored eyes with glimmering golden specks, high cheek bones, naturally arched brows, firm rounded breasts and bottom, small waist, perfectly flat stomach, creamy caramel skin.

Susan is actually very surprised that she hasn't been "discovered" yet, but Cherise is only 20 years old, so she has plenty of time. Cherise comes into the diner often to rehearse her lines from her skits in her acting classes. Sometimes Susan reads lines with her when no one else is in the diner. They move some of the center tables to the side, so they can rehearse the scene with Rose, Bobby and Nico, the cook, as their audience.

A few times Susan thought of fixing Cherise and Eddie up, but decided the age difference was too much. But who knows, maybe… Cherise is incredibly sweet, so maybe the age gap wouldn't matter.

Rose a robust red-headed 68 year old owns and runs Eggsactly. Sometimes her retired husband, Saul, comes in to help out. They don't have any children of their own, so they treat all of the guests like family. They are the kind of people everyone wishes they had as grandparents.

Bobby is Rose's 20 year old grand-nephew. He's been helping out as a busboy for three years to help put himself through college at UCLA where he is a junior. He is majoring in history and hoping to go right into law school after graduating next year. He is classically handsome- 6'3", broad shoulders, light brown hair with blond highlights, tan skin from many years of playing volleyball, green eyes, a firm jaw and a killer smile.

Nico, born in Sicily, has only been in the states for 3 years having come to open up his own authentic Italian restaurant. He's been putting his money away to do that while working as a cook at Eggsactly. At twenty-one, he has a lot of energy and charisma. He's a real Italian Stallion - 5'10", olive skin, dark wavy hair, black sexy eyes, long elegant fingers and luscious full lips. From ages one to hundred, all of the ladies love Nico.

Even though the outings with her family to Eggsactly haven't been Eggsactly perfect, Susan feels her life is. Her life has turned out Eggsactly as she hoped and planned.

Susan grew up in the Palisades, a posh town in between Santa Monica and Malibu. Her dad, Dr. Eli Klein, is a very successful orthodontist. In fact, most of her friends growing up went to him. And now their children go to him. Susan always contributed her dad's success to the fact that at the end of his examinations he gave the children candy: caramels, suckers, jelly beans, anything sweet enough and sticky enough to insure a return visit, as a cavity or a broken tooth was definitely in sight. Her mom, Shirley, was a stay at home mom. As a result, she and her mom have always been very close. Mrs. Klein was always the classroom mom and field trip chaperone for all of the Klein children of which there are 3: Susan, her older sister, Barbara, and her older brother, Michael.

Barbara six years older than Susan was and is the brain of the family. Average looks, but extremely high intelligence. She's a pediatrician with her own practice in Beverly Hills. A lot of her clients are children of celebrities. Her husband, Carl, is a heart surgeon. They met when they were med students at Stanford. Their 16 year old son, Patrick, will be graduating a year early and going to Harvard. Their 13 year old daughter, Piper, already has published a collection of children's stories.

Michael, three years older than Susan, is a successful Hollywood agent. His wife, Rachel, is a jewelry designer. Their thirteen year old twin boys, Justin and Dustin, have formed their own rock band, "Just in the Dust."

Susan was always an average student, but one of the most popular because of her upbeat, caring and kind personality. Her good looks didn't hurt either. She's always looked like the typical California beach girl- blonde hair, big blue eyes, tanned fit body, cute little button nose. She attended UCLA (how she got in- to this day no one knows!) just to pass time until she got married. She majored in liberal arts and then got her teaching credential. It was her last year of college when she met Jack Martinelli.

She and one of her sorority sisters, Debbie, were at a fraternity party in Holmby Hills. The home belonged to the parents of one of the frat boys. The girls were surrounded by a bunch of guys when Dave stepped in to introduce his cousin, Jack, from Chicago to the group.

WOW!!!! That's the only word that came into Susan's head. Jack was so hot and so different from the rest of the California UCLA guys. He had that mid-western appeal- manly and solid, none of the "want to be actor" thing going on. Jack stood 6 feet tall with wavy dark hair, chiseled features and a rock solid body with incredible abs, not too bulky, just perfectly ripped and piercing deep-set blue eyes.

(Susan didn't actually get to see his abs until later
that evening when the party turned into a pool party
and everyone jumped into the pool in whatever little
bit of clothing they could get away with.)

Jack was four years older than Susan. He had
completed the graduate program in architecture at the
University of Illinois 2 years prior and had just
moved out to Los Angeles to start working at an up and
coming architectural firm.   An architect, Susan
thought- how Mike Brady sexy-like!   An architect-
what a perfect match of the left and right brains. On
one hand, one needs to be mathematical and analytical
to create a perfect structure, yet on the other hand,
one also needs to be creative to create something
visually appealing. What a perfect profession for a
husband, Susan thought!   Not to mention his athletic
body.   In fact, Jack participated on the soccer team,
baseball team and water polo team.   Soccer defined
his legs. Baseball defined his arms. Swimming
defined his back and gave him lots of endurance for
many other things of which Susan soon found out!

Jack was immediately smitten with Susan as well.
Who wasn't?! Just what a Chicago boy wanted- the
peppy, cute California beach babe.

"Hi, I'm Susan."   Susan offered her hand to Jack
in a cutesy girlie manner.

"Hey. I'm Jack." Jack took Susan's hand and
just held it for a couple of seconds.

"So, I could totally tell you were from Chicago."

"Oh yeah, how?"

"Well, you look all windblown as if the wind just
blew you in. You know being from Chicago and all."

Susan winked with a flirty smile.

"Well, I could totally tell you are a true California girl."

"Oh yeah, how?"

"You look all beachy, blonde and tan- a real LA girl."   Jack returned the wink and flirty smile.

"I guess I am a real LA girl. Born and bred. Have you been to California before?"

"Once, when I was six. My parents brought me, my sister and my brother here to go to Disneyland."

"Fun!   Hey I have a brother and sister too. Where are you in the line-up? I'm the youngest."

"I'm the youngest, too,"

"I guess it's destiny."   Flirty smile.

"Must be."   Flirty smile back at ya.

"So, what places have you visited since you've been here?"

"Not many really. I am staying with my cousin, Dave, but he is at school most of the day. I'm at work during the day, and then on the weekends I am looking for an apartment."

"Well then, you need a personal tour guide to show you all of the LA hot spots."

"Know anyone?"

"As a matter of fact, I do.   Your personal Welcome to LA tour guide at your service! Free of charge."   Susan gave a little curtsy and a wink.

"When can we start?"

"Right now, Chicago boy. But you have to take my hand. I don't want you to get lost on our first day!" Smile. Smile. Wink. Wink.

"Not a problem at all, LA girl."   He took her

hand and didn't let go for the rest of the evening.

The two of them soon became inseparable. From that night on they endearingly called each other CB (Chicago Boy) and LG (LA Girl). The morning after the frat party Jack picked up Susan to begin his personal tour of LA. They started with breakfast at a little café on the boardwalk in Venice. Jack loved seeing the eclectic crowd from pierced tattooed skateboarders to gold wearing rappers to singing roller skaters. After breakfast they just strolled up and down the boardwalk and got henna tattoos. Susan's said "LA Girl." Jack's said "Chicago Boy."

Afterwards they took a drive north, up the coast. They picked up sandwiches and had a picnic on the beach at Point Dume where they watched the sunset. They walked in the water and played tic-tac-toe in the sand with their fingertips as pencils. Just as the sun was setting Jack leaned in and gave Susan a kiss. Not a "you're so hot I want to have sex with you" kiss (although Jack certainly did want to have sex with Susan), but a "I really like you" kiss. It was slow and sweet and soft. A real stomach fluttering kiss. Susan smiled and beamed with happiness. Jack was equally beaming.

They saw each almost every day after that. Jack moved into an apartment in Brentwood. Susan continued to live in the sorority house, but often stayed over at Jack's. It was a month before they made love for the first time. The longest Jack had ever waited since he started having sex at 15. Jack wanted to wait because Susan was special, and so he wanted the first time to be equally as special.

On their month anniversary, Jack recreated their first date and took Susan back to Venice Beach for breakfast and then the drive up the coast. They stopped at the same spot where they had first kissed and again watched the sunset. Afterwards Jack surprised Susan by pulling into a hotel, in Malibu overlooking the ocean, where he had reserved a room. Dinner was waiting for them when they got into the room. By now Jack knew all of Susan's favorite foods- basically an all carbs diet- bread, pasta and chocolate. They ate dinner with the French doors open looking out over the ocean. Soft music played. They were both nervous but excited. After dinner Jack took Susan's hand and they swayed to the music. Jack began kissing Susan and then like their first kiss they made love, slow and sweet and soft (well mostly soft, soft in the right places).

They loved just being together. For the next year, Susan made good on her promise to be Jack's personal tour guide and introduced him to everything Southern California- dining and people watching on Melrose Avenue, shopping and Christmas lights in Beverly Hills, dancing at trendy Hollywood clubs, hiking in the Santa Monica Mountains, weekend vacationing in Palm Springs and Santa Barbara, skiing in Big Bear, kayaking in Malibu, volleyball watching in Manhattan Beach, rollerblading along the beach boardwalks, watching movies at The Grove.

Susan graduated and then began the teaching credential graduate program at UCLA. For appearances, she moved back in with her parents, but mostly stayed with Jack. Susan's family adored Jack. He was polite, well-mannered and educated. Susan completed the graduate program and began teaching kindergarten at the same school where her sons, Myles and Sammy, go now, and her daughters, Jessie and Sophie, went before them. On the year anniversary of their frat party meeting, Jack proposed.

Jack created a treasure hunt for Susan. Each clue led her someplace they had visited over the last year. The first clue led them to the spot where they had first met- the frat boy's parents' home in Holmby Hills. Jack had gone back there and explained to the parents that he was going to propose and asked if they minded if they returned to their pool.   The parents were agreeable, although a bit surprised, as they never knew their son had thrown a party at their home. (Clean-up must have been darn good!)   They each drank a beer and took a dip in the pool before heading off to the next spot- the spot on the beach where they first kissed. Here Jack had a picnic waiting for them (with the help of his cousin, Dave). From there they drove all over the city to different little spots that had meaning- Bloomingdale's where Susan first helped Jack pick out bedding for his new apartment, Lucky Strike bowling alley, where Jack showed off his bowling talents, Rancho Park where Jack first taught Susan to golf, Sushi on Sunset where Susan introduced Jack to sushi, finally they ended up back at the Malibu hotel where they first made love. Of course, Susan had an idea of what was going on, but played along without giving anything away. The ring was under the covers on Susan's side of the bed (Susan always had the left side). When Susan pulled back the covers, she screamed with excitement and then began crying as Jack got down on his knee and proposed to his "LA Girl". The ring was exactly what Susan wanted. A platinum antique-y feeling band with little diamonds all over and a 2 carat center diamond. Susan did not hesitate to say "yes" to her "Chicago Boy".

Susan spent the next year planning the "wedding of the century."

The wedding and reception were held in an estate overlooking the Pacific Ocean in Malibu. Susan had 7 bridesmaids, including her sister as maid of honor, Jack's sister, Eleanor (Ellie), her sister in law, Rachel, and Debbie, her friend from college. Jack also had 7 groomsmen, including Susan's brother, Michael, his own brother, Mark, and his cousin Dave, as the best man, as he without necessarily meaning to, introduced the two. Susan was driven by a horse-drawn carriage from the main house to the garden where the wedding ceremony took place. After the ceremony the horse-drawn carriage took Jack and Susan around the property for their first ride as husband and wife. Champagne, caviar, chocolate covered strawberries flowed all night long. A band played all of the couple's favorite songs. The figurines on the wedding cake had the initials CB and LG engraved on them. The final guests did not leave until after 4 a.m. The newlyweds took off the next day for a two week honeymoon in Tahiti, Fiji and Bora Bora.

Jack and Susan moved into a house in the Palisades near Susan's parents when they got back from their honeymoon. It was a one-story three bedroom

home with a swimming pool.   Jack was already doing
quite well at the architectural firm.   He had only
been there two years and was already promoted 3 times.

Three months later Susan was pregnant with the
soon-to-be Sophia Isabella.

A month before Sophia was born, Susan left her
teaching job so she could stay home with the baby.
Sophia soon became Sophie.   Sophie from the beginning
was a very strong-minded, serious, intelligent person.
She has always known what she wanted and how to get
it.   She has always been the light in her father's
eye.   Even as a baby, she was stunning with her dark
hair and light eyes.   Barbara was pregnant with
Patrick at the same time.   Sophie was born one month
after Patrick.

Three years after Sophie was born came Jessica
Rose.   She is the spitting image of her mom- blonde
hair, blue eyes and bubbly personality.   Jessica has
always made everyone feel good with her kind words and
caring nature.   She is the animal lover, always
bringing in strays and nursing the injured back to
health.   She's the nurturing one.   Coincidentally
Barbara was also pregnant again with Piper, as was
Michael's wife, Rachel, with the twins.

Barbara and Carl and Michael and Rachel all
thought two kids were enough, not Susan and Jack.

When Sophie was 5 and Jessica 2, the family moved
to a bigger home Jack designed, in Holmby Hills, not
too far from the home where they first met at the Frat
party.

Five years after Jessica came Samuel Ford, the
spitting image of his father- dark hair, light eyes,

14

warm friendliness, natural athlete, a real people pleaser (except of course when he is not feeling well and throwing spit wads at busboys, but everyone has their off days!)

Three years later came Myles Stone, the cut up. No one can be sad around Myles. He's the funny one, always making everyone laugh. His mood is always lighthearted as are his looks- blonde hair and blue eyes.   Myles is also the sensitive one.

Like Susan's mom, Susan became a stay at home mom. She is always the room mother and field trip chaperone.

Life is Eggsactly how Susan imagined- a loving husband, wonderful kids, beautiful home and close family.

But all this changes on the day She walks into Eggsactly.

CHAPTER 2

Susan walks into Eggsactly all sweaty after yoga
that Tuesday morning, as usual. Her spot is open, so
she sits right down. Both seats on either side of her
are free as well. Susan has just been served her tea
when She walks in.

She sits on the stool on Susan's left side. She
carries a Go Green tote bag. She takes out a pink,
rhinestoned pen and stationary. That's what catches
Susan's eye. No one ever writes on stationary
anymore. It's always texting, e-mailing, IM-ing now-a-
days. The stationary is cute, too. It looks like
it's made out of recycled paper. The paper is sepia
toned with burnt edges with old fashioned squiggly
lines on the borders. It looks like writing paper
from a long time ago.

Gosh, Susan remembers when she was in elementary
school and she and her best friend, Kelly, used to
write letters to each other. Sometimes they would
just hand deliver them to each other, other times they
would have another one of their friends deliver them
to each other and then sometimes they would actually
mail them. Oh how fun it was to receive a letter in
the mail! You tried to guess who it was from by the
handwriting without looking at the return address. Of
course, Susan always knew Kelly's writing. Kelly had
that perfect handwriting even as a child, the kind
that teachers have. In fact, Kelly now is a teacher.

Susan's and Kelly's letters were always so fun.
They talked about everything that went on that day,
even though they had spent all day together. They

16

talked about their secret crushes, made fun of the
mean girls and made up games for each other- quizzes,
word searches, "put these people in order from your
favorite to your least favorite." Of course, Susan
and Kelly were always on top of each other's favorite
list. They used different colored pens throughout the
letter to make them prettier. Sometimes they would
write sentences in circles or around the edges of the
paper. On the envelopes they would always put some
cute saying over the sealed part- a favorite was, "If
this letter gets lost, please send to heaven because
it's for an angel." Sometimes if they were feeling
naughty they'd put the reverse, "If this letter gets
lost, please send to hell because it's for a devil."

Susan still has many of those letters packed away
in a box in the attic. They always bring back such
pleasant memories of her childhood when she re-reads
them. How sad that most people don't know the beauty
of a handwritten letter.

Apparently She knows the beauty.

Once She gets settled with her pen and
stationary, She looks over the menu. She orders a
very hearty breakfast, especially for someone her
size- a veggie omelet, country potatoes, cinnamon
roll, turkey bacon, a double latte with extra whipped
cream. She looks at Susan and smiles. Susan smiles
back.

Susan notices that she is quite extraordinary
looking. She is strikingly tall, 5'10" with long
exotic black hair, swept up into a loose bun with
wisps framing her face, huge Elizabeth Taylor violet
eyes, fiery red full lipped mouth, huge breasts

testing the strength of her cotton t-shirt, tiny waist, long shapely legs coming out of her denim shorts and the finest porcelain skin. She looks to be in her early 20s. In fact she is 28.

Once She gives her breakfast order, She begins writing. Susan can't help herself from glancing over and reading what She is writing. Writing a real letter seems so foreign in this day and age. It is just intriguing. Who could She be writing to? What is so important that She actually takes the time to handwrite a letter? Why is She using such exquisite paper?

Dear Molly,

How are you? How is Jerry? I know I just talked to you this morning, but I didn't know how else to begin the letter! ☺ Did you get the kids off to school okay with the weather? Since we didn't really get a chance to talk this morning I decided to write you a letter and tell you about my experience here in Los Angeles so far.

Latte is served. Pen down. Sip of Latte. Pen up.

It's exciting here but kind of scary- small-town-girl-in-a-big-city syndrome. I rented this awesome apartment in Santa Monica. It's in this chichi area off of a street named San Vicente. It's incredibly expensive, so I am going to have to get a roommate, but that will be cool, then I won't be all alone. It's only 6 blocks from the beach.

Pen down. Another sip of Latte.

My first day of work was great. I can't believe I got this internship. It is such an awesome architectural firm. Thank goodness Tommy had connections out here; otherwise, I would still be looking for a job. I work all day Mondays, Wednesdays and Fridays and afternoons Tuesdays and Thursdays. That's why I can sit here in this cute little diner near my home eating breakfast on a Tuesday morning. It's called "Eggsactly." Isn't that cute?

The people at work are really nice, not stuffy at all. Very laid back, so LA. The man Tommy hooked me up with is especially nice and so helpful. Oh, did I mention hot? Too bad he's married. With kids. Cute ones, too. He has pictures of them all over his office. His wife looks cute, too. Bummer!!! Although I couldn't really see her as the one picture I saw of her was taken from a distance. But, I asked a co-worker and she said she is cute. Shucks!! And she's sweet apparently too! Double shucks!

A married architect with cute kids and wife- what a coincidence, thinks Susan.

Food arrives. Takes a few bites.

Too bad we didn't meet when we were both living back there. But I guess I would have been about 10 years old then (he told me he has been living here for about 18 years). Too young to start any serious romances I guess!! ☺

I am really excited about my new life here! But, I do miss you a lot already! And Jerry and Billie and Sarah and Mom and Dad!!! ☹

Hope you will come visit soon.

I'll write again soon. Thanks for the stationary by the way. It's really fun actually writing a letter. It's kind of like having a journal!

Love,

Your little sister in the big city, Maggie

Pen down. Places letter in matching envelope. Seals it. Puts it in her tote bag. Digs into food.

Note to self- must ask Jack if he hired a beautiful new intern.

Susan's neck is hurting from taking glances over at Maggie's letter and trying not to get caught.

Hope she makes it here in this city. She seems sweet. Maybe I should introduce myself and invite her out to lunch or somewhere. On second thought, better not. Then she will know I was spying on her letter writing.

Susan finishes her breakfast and doesn't engage in conversation, not wanting to be thought of as nosy.

Oh, but wouldn't she be perfect for Eddie! Hopefully he'll pop in before she leaves.

She finishes her breakfast, pays her bill and leaves.

Unfortunately no sight of Eddie.

"Yowza, Yowza, Yowza!" This from Nico, the cook, as She leaves. "She is one hot mama!"

Even as a completely heterosexual, happily married female, Susan agrees.

Susan leaves. It's too late to volunteer, so she just window shops for a bit, then picks up Myles. By the time the family sits down for dinner, Susan has forgotten about the beautiful letter writer in Eggsactly.

CHAPTER 3

That weekend, the Martinellis do their usual things. Friday night, pizza, popcorn and video night. Both of the girls have sleepovers, so the boys get to choose the movie- Cloudy with a Chance of Meatballs 2.

Saturday morning, Jack, Susan and Myles go to Sammy's soccer game- a victory- thanks to Sammy who scored the only two goals!!! Yippee!!! Saturday night, Myles and Sammy spend the night at Aunt Barbara's while Jack and Susan go to dinner with Debbie, Susan's college roommate, now a successful real estate agent and her husband, Larry, a used car salesman.   Susan never could understand what Debbie saw in Larry. He is a bit of a chump!   Truly the stereotypical used car salesman type. You know the kind that ends every conversation by shooting you with his imaginary gun finger and clicking his tongue. But Susan loves Debbie, and so for the sake of their friendship, tolerates Larry.   Despite Larry, dinner is nice. They eat at the Grove, window shop and watch the dancing water fountain show. The music is "That's Amore!" As the song and show end, Jack takes Susan in his arms, dips her and gives her a big Old Hollywood kiss. A bit cheesy, but Susan loves it!

Sunday, the family goes for a morning bike ride at the beach and then have a BBQ at home for Susan's dad's birthday. The entire family comes- Barbara and Carl with Patrick and Piper, Michael and Rachel with Justin and Dustin and of course Dr. and Mrs. Klein. They all go swimming in the Olympic sized pool and

have a karaoke contest. Justin and Dustin are voted
the winners, but Jessica comes in second with her
rendition of "It's in His Kiss." It's a glorious
weekend!

CHAPTER 4

The following Tuesday, as Susan is in her seat at the diner, She walks in again. This time She sits two stools down from Susan's right which actually make reading her letter a little easier. Yes- she is writing another letter.

Like last time She settles in, takes out the same kind of stationary and pen and begins writing, right after ordering- again a very hearty meal- traditional ham and eggs, eggs over easy, white toast and coffee with lots of milk. Susan is already nibbling on her usual fare.

She doesn't even look at Susan. Doesn't even acknowledge that she had seen her there last time. Guess she is concentrating too hard on what she is going to write.

Dear Molly,

Life is amazing. Love it here. Went to the beach over the weekend. Actually got a little burnt- can you believe- sunny and warm in February! (Notice I didn't begin the letter with the "how do you dos"- LOL!)

I hung out with some co-workers on Saturday night. We went to a really nice dinner in Venice and then went to listen to some Jazz. Not like the Jazz at home, but it was fun! Mr. Married Boss Guy of course didn't come; although, I secretly hoped he would. I mentioned it to him as we were leaving on Friday, but he said he and his wife had plans. ☹

Food arrives. Digs in.

Yesterday Mr. Married Boss Guy and I went to check out our new site- a hospital somewhere between Beverly Hills and West Hollywood. Our firm is designing a new wing donated by some famous celebrity. I don't know who. It's all hush-hush until the big unveiling.

As we were heading back to the office, Mr. Married Boss Guy suggested we go get a hot dog since we were both from the hot dog capital of the world. He took me to this supposedly very famous hot dog stand "Pinks."

Of course I ordered mine loaded with onions and chili. He made some comment about how he hopes I don't have a date that night. I explained to him how lucky I am that food doesn't affect my weight or breath. I can eat whatever I want and not gain a pound or have bad breath. I just have naturally sweet smelling breath.

Sip of coffee. More bites of food.

For a second I thought (and hoped) he was going to lean in to take a whiff and test out my declaration. But no, he just changed the subject back to work.

 At one point I got chili on my cheek and he did wipe it off. Oh my god, his touch sent shivers up and down my spine. How awful is it that I am lusting after a married man?!

He talks about his wife all of the time. At first I thought it was so sweet to hear someone so in love with their wife, but then I got to thinking (and again maybe hoping) maybe he keeps talking about her so much, so he can remind himself that he is married when he is around me. You know how irresistible I am! ☺

Finishes food.

This girl at work, Lisa, said she is going to fix me up with one of her cousins. I hope I like him. I need to stop thinking about Mr. Married Boss Guy!

What's new with you? When are you coming? Any plans for Valentine's Day? Has Jerry made some special romantic date for you? Hope so!

Xo, M

Stuffs letter into matching envelope. Packs up. Pays. Leaves.

It's fun snooping on her letters. But maybe she is not such a sweet-new-girl-in-town. Definitely would need to know more about her before I would fix her up with Eddie. Who knows, maybe she won't ever come in here again! Oh, just enough time to go volunteer.

Susan also packs up and leaves, but not before saying "goodbye" and "thank you" to everyone.

CHAPTER 5

Thursday, She doesn't show up at the diner. The other regulars are there though. It's actually quite a fun day for Susan. Eddie comes to get his muffins, but he has an extra free period before he has to get back, so he sits down with Susan to talk for a while. He pours his heart out. He is having a hard time meeting women. Susan can't imagine why. He is so good looking, sweet and wholesome. He explains it's hard with a child. Most women don't want a ready-made family and all of the baggage of an ex-wife. Susan suggests internet dating while thinking thank god she never had to do that! Eddie says that's not for him. When he is at home he wants to give his full attention to Tyler and not be on the computer searching for women. Susan wonders if She is going to come into the diner today. Surely She will catch Eddie's eye. But She doesn't.

While Susan and Eddie are talking, Cherise comes in needing to rehearse a scene from "Hannah and Her Sisters". Susan introduces the two realizing they haven't met yet; although, they had seen each other on a couple of occasions. Susan offers to help Cherise rehearse, which they do while Eddie watches until he has to leave.

Drew and Marion come in as well for a quick breakfast before they have to head to their great-grandson's school for Grandparents' Day. They also watch Susan and Cherise rehearse. At the end of the scene, Eddie, Drew, Marion, Rose, Bobby and Nico give the girls a standing ovation. Everyone knows Cherise

26

is going to "make it."   She is too beautiful and too good of an actress to not.

As Susan leaves she realizes that tomorrow is Valentine's Day, so she heads over to 17th Street Jewelers to buy Jack a new watch.   She has the back engraved with "Every moment with you is Valentine's Day, CB, xo, LG."

Thank goodness she remembered Valentine's Day because even after all of these years Jack still does something romantic for her. Their first Valentine's Day together, Jack surprised her by taking her to a spa weekend in Santa Barbara where they got a couple's massage in their room overlooking the ocean. Once the professional masseuses left, they took over giving each other a personal massage that lasted all night long.   Wonder what he is going to do this year?!

Jack doesn't fail this year. He arranges for all of the kids to be away for the night. He takes the day off, and so right after the kids leave for school he whisks Susan off for a night away in Big Bear for skiing. At the end of the day, he has masseuses waiting at the cabin to give them a couple's massage like the first year. Like the first year, they continue the massages once the professionals leave. And again they last until the wee hours of the morning.   Jack loves the watch.   He gives Susan a Cartier Love bangle in rose gold.

The Valentine's Day celebration is perfect!

Sunday morning they have a family Valentine's brunch. Susan makes the entire family heart-shaped pancakes and chocolate covered strawberries. They make homemade Valentine's for each other out of cookie

dough and jelly beans and red hots. They read them
aloud. Lots of luv u's and hearts.

CHAPTER 6

That next week is rather uneventful at the diner. She doesn't show up. Susan feels kind of like she missed out on a soap opera episode. But then the following Thursday She shows up again.

She sits right next to Susan at the counter as the place is full.

Same routine.

Stationary out. Pen out. Orders huge breakfast. The Rose Special Omelette. Potatoes. Side of bacon. Cinnamon roll. Grand latte. Begins writing.

Dear Sis,

Work has been hectic- crazy. So much to do when designing a hospital wing. Never realized how complicated it is. Everything has to be so exact. Can you imagine what would happen if the outlets were too far away and a life saving machine couldn't reach it?

Luckily for the hospital and our firm, Mr. Married Boss Guy is a genius. He makes everything look so simple when I know it is not. He really is very talented.

Lisa fixed me up with her cousin, Ricky, this last weekend. What a nightmare!!! Of course he is a wanna-be actor. All he did all night long was stare at himself in whatever would reflect his reflection- knives, windows, mirrors, side view mirrors, my compact- Yes, in the middle of dinner he asked if I had a compact so he could check his hair! In between staring at himself, he just constantly talked about himself-all of the auditions he has been on, his acting classes, what celebrity he knew or ran into and on and on

29

and on. Never did ask anything about me. In fact, half way through the dinner he called me "Sally."   Couldn't even get my name straight!!!

Food arrives. Eats.

What a loser!!! How could Lisa set me up with him?   He was cute though. But not cute enough. The topper of the evening was when he divided the check in half and asked for my share! I was in shock!   I didn't have any cash, because I wasn't expecting to pay, so I had to give him my credit card. Get this- when the waiter came over to pick up the bill, only my card was in the check folder, and he let him take it without putting in his share. I didn't know what to do. When the check came back, he just handed it to me.   I must have had a baffled look on my face because he finally said he thought it would just be easier to pay with one card instead of two, so we could stop at the ATM on the way home and he would give me my share.

Sips coffee.

As we were getting close to my apartment I realized that he either had no intention of stopping at the ATM or had forgotten, so I asked him what bank does he need to go to- to subtly remind him. He got flustered then said, "Oh yeah, man you really want your money, huh?! What are you broke?"   Are you kidding me?!?!?! He tried to make me feel bad for not wanting to treat him to dinner.

So then he reluctantly stopped at an ATM and got some money, got back into the car and tossed forty dollars in my lap- mind you, the dinner with tip was $100.00 and he had 3 top shelf bourbons. I had one glass of house wine because I didn't want to take advantage. As he was tossing the

30

money to me he said that he didn't have a ten dollar bill because the machine only gave him twenties, and he thought I tipped too much anyway! What a jerk!!! I was so mad!!! But since he is a co-worker's cousin, I didn't say anything.

Oh and did I mention he kept talking about this hot chick in his acting class whose "ass he liked to tap?"

Finishes breakfast.

Oh and then did I mention when I was walking back to the table from the bathroom I saw him slip a piece of paper into the waitress' apron- I know it was his phone number. He'd been looking her up and down all night. Not that I care. It was just so rude.

Oh and then did I mention that as I was getting out of the car he leaned over to kiss me? Are you kidding me?! I backed away and said "good night." Then he said "Aren't you going to invite me in?" He must be nuts!!! As if...

Then I had to face Lisa on Monday. Obviously she hadn't talked to Ricky because she asked me how it went. I just said he didn't seem that interested in me. She apologized and said she would try to find someone else. No thank you!!!

Why is Mr. Married Boss Guy married?!!! Why are all the good ones married?

Got to go- meeting Mr. Married Boss Guy at the site.

Love, Your Perpetually Single Small town Girl in the Big City Little Sister

Packs up. Pays. Leaves.

Although this was now the third time she sat near Susan, She hadn't acknowledged her since the first time. No smile, nod, wink. She must be in her own world.

Gosh, come to think of it, didn't Jack say he had a new hospital project? I'll have to ask him.

Eddie pops in right after She leaves.

"Hey Eddie!"

"Hey Susan. Nico. Bobby. Rose."

"Hey Eddie" choruses Nico, Bobby and Rose.

"So did you have a hot Valentine's Date?" Nico, never too subtle, yells from the kitchen.

"Oh yeah it was hot alright. My son and I went out for some spicy Mexican food. Real hot!"

"I have a cousin I could fix you up with. Her English isn't great and she has 4 kids, but she is real sweet. And she makes a mean lasagna!"

"You know what- I'm good. But thanks for trying."

Susan smiles. Seems everyone has a cousin that needs to be fixed up. I wonder if Nico's cousin would be as bad as Miss Letter Writer's friend, Lisa's cousin.

"So Susan why did you have to go and get married before I met you?"

"Sorry Eddie! Anyway I am way too old for you."

"Are you kidding? You look like a teenager yourself."

"Thanks, Eddie." Still got it, smiles Susan.

"It'll happen Eddie. You just have to be patient!"

"If I wanted patience, I'd have been a doctor!"

"You're too much!   Trust me, a great catch like you will not be on the market for long."

"Yeah.   Yeah. Yeah.   That's what they all say. Don't you have an identical twin sister who isn't married?"

"Sorry.   My only sister is a married doctor with two kids."

"My bad luck."

Eddie gets his muffins.

"See you all next week.   Susan, let me know if that married thing doesn't work out for you."

"Will do, Eddie.   Until then I'll keep my eye out for a suitable match for you."

"Cool.   Later."

"Later."

Susan doesn't feel threatened at all by Eddie. She knows he is just kidding.   He is a real solid guy and would never have an affair, especially after what happened to him with his wife, but it always feels good to have a handsome man flirt with you.

Susan leaves just in time to make it to the shelter.

Again Susan forgets to ask Jack about the Letter Writer.

CHAPTER 7

Saturday night Susan and Jack celebrate the anniversary of the day they first met at the frat party, even though technically the anniversary isn't until Monday. Even after all of these years they still celebrate the day. Each year they alternate who plans the celebration. It's Susan's year.

Susan throws a "frat part." They dance to 80's music, swim, drink beer, eat pizza, chips and salsa. All of their friends come including Debbie and Dave who had actually been with them at that first frat party. The party is a complete blast!

Jack thanks Susan for a wonderful night and tells her she is still the sexiest co-ed around!

Sunday the whole family spends it together just hanging out by the pool and relaxing. Some of the kids' friends pop in throughout the day, but all in all it is just a peaceful family day.

On Monday, Jack hits the snooze button on the alarm just as it is starting to buzz at 5:30 a.m. Gosh, I don't want to get out of bed. It has been a fabulous weekend. Family, friends and fun. What a lucky guy I am! My beautiful wife is next to me sleeping like an angel. How does the alarm never seem to bother her? Mmmmmm, gosh I love snuggling with her! She feels so good. She is everything I ever wanted in a wife- sweet, kind, fun, beautiful, caring, funny, good mother, good friend. I am a lucky man! I really don't want to get out of bed. It is so warm and comfortable, and Susan feels so yummy.

You know what- what would it hurt if I just

played hooky for a day. Sure the first set of drafts on the hospital project is due on Friday by noon, but they are almost done anyway. No problem. I can finish by then even if I take the day off to play with my wife.

There is something about going to the office today that just doesn't appeal to me. Oh yeah, that intern said she was coming in early today to help me. I told her it wasn't necessary, but she insisted. Why does she make me feel so uncomfortable? Sure she is beautiful and nice and really helpful, almost too helpful, but the way she looks at me with those lustful, longing eyes makes me feel uneasy. And she is so obvious. Everyone at work is teasing me about it. Phil, my partner, is the worst. The way he refers to her as "Jack's Groupie." Phil's constant ribbing me about having a secret rendezvous with her has got to stop. Maybe if I were 10 years younger and single, I would ask her out, but I'm not. I am completely happy with my life and most importantly my wife!

Oh my God, I can't get that day I took her to look at the new site and then to get a hot dog out of my mind. I was just making a nice gesture by taking her to Pink's to get something to eat. She acted as if we were on a first date with her flirty comments and subtle gestures. The way she kept leaning in close to me and touching my leg and arm when she would talk was just over the top. And what was all that about that she could eat whatever she wanted and not gain any weight or have bad breath?

And then when I just instinctively wiped the gob

of chili off her cheek as I would do with any of my kids, she looked at me as if I had just made a first romantic move and touched one of her erogenous zones. It was kind of creepy.

Maybe she is part of the reason why I so don't want to go into work today.

Whatever the reason, I am staying home and spending the day with my wife!

I can never get enough of this snuggling. Mmmmmm…. "Want to play hooky with me today, LG? Today is our actual anniversary of the day we met."

"You've got yourself a date, CB! Keep whispering in my ear. I love it."

"Yes, ma'am!"

Although they want to stay in bed and make love all morning, Susan does need to get the kids off to school. By 8:00 a.m., the kids are gone and Susan and Jack have the whole day to themselves.

They make love, have breakfast, go for a bike ride by the beach, play in the sand and surf, make love again. That night, they take the kids to their favorite Italian restaurant in Brentwood and then get ice cream cones.

As they both get into bed that night, they both are thinking how lucky they are and what a glorious day it was!

"Good night, LG. I love you!"

"Night, CB. Love you, too!"

CHAPTER 8

Right after Susan sits down at the diner, She walks in. She plops down three seats down at the very end of the counter. Great, how I am going to read over her shoulder today!! Maybe I should scoot down a stool or two. I'm not settled in yet. No, that would be too obvious! I'll just have to figure something out. I can't miss out on my weekly dose of New to Town's soap opera life!

She only orders coffee and cinnamon roll "for now." She seems to be in a particularly foul mood.

Paper out. Pen out. Deep breath. Pen to paper.

Molly,

What a terrible weekend!!! I am never going to date again! It is miserable. What is wrong with these L.A. men?

So, Lisa said she felt awful that the date with her cousin didn't work out, so she promised me she had the perfect guy in mind for me. Do I mind older, she asked. No, I said. She told me she was fixing me up with one of the hottest bachelors in town, that he was a real hot ticket and only dated models and actresses. In fact, she said he usually doesn't go out on blind dates, but would do her a favor as she is the wife of his brother's best friend, and for the fact that she told him I was beautiful. This is all per Lisa. He is supposedly this renowned Beverly Hills plastic surgeon.

Anyway, when I open my door to him on Saturday night, I thought surely Lisa is playing a joke on me. There stands this fifty-something short and I mean short, his head barely reached the bottom of my boobs, Indian

37

guy who smells of curry wearing 3 thick gold chains prominently displayed on his hairy chest that is revealed because his shirt is unbuttoned to his navel and whose hair on top of his head is a cross between Donald Trump's and Don King's– it flips over his head yet somehow stands up in back as if he has just seen a ghost!

He introduces himself. I can't understand what he is saying. I ask him to repeat his name which he does, twice, but still I can't understand it. It sounded something like Salami. Lisa had told me his name, but I couldn't understand her either. I just called him Salami all night. He corrected me a couple of times, but I never got it right.

He holds out his hand to shake mine or so I thought, but instead he takes my hand and places a wet sloppy kiss on the back of it. I think my hand is still wet! Yuck!

We go to his car, a convertible Jaguar (at least better than Ricky's 1990 Hyundai with the missing hubcaps) where Salami tells me that I need to take off my shoes and put them in a plastic bag because he doesn't want the newly cleaned rugs to get dirty.

As we get in the car, Salami makes a comment that thank goodness Lisa was right and I was beautiful because he was afraid he was wasting his evening. Salami further explains that he only dates models and actresses, but he made an exception for Lisa because she is his brother's best friend's wife and after what she told him about me, he felt sorry for me. What did she tell him about me?

We did go to this really nice restaurant in Malibu, Geoffrey's, overlooking the ocean.   As soon as we get there, Salami starts barking

orders at the hostess and wait staff.   When we are seated Salami keeps

looking at me as if he is studying me. Salami finally says, "You really are

beautiful. There is almost nothing I would change."   I must have looked at

him with a baffled expression on my face (maybe the same one I had on

when Ricky paid the dinner bill with my credit card only) because he

explains, "The only thing I would do for you is give you an eyebrow lift. It

would really open up your eyes and make you not look so tired. But other

than that and a little lipo around your hips, you are perfect."   Salami looks

at me as if he is waiting for a "thank you." Are you kidding? My eyebrows

do not need to be lifted and there is not a drop of excess fat on my hips,

they are perfectly curvaceous!!! Thank you very much!!!

As we are ordering Salami tells me (in front of the waiter, mind you)

to go ahead and get whatever I want because he is picking up the tab-

money is no object.   Fine, I do. I order the most expensive bottle of

champagne and entrée and appetizer and salad and dessert!!! To which

Salami asks, "are you sure you want all of those calories?"   Yes, I am sure!

Thank you!!

Throughout dinner Salami talks about all of the famous women he has

dated.   Again Salami makes it clear that he made an exception to go out

with me, but it's okay because he is not having too bad of a time.

During dessert I feel something crawl up my leg. I scream because I

think it's a rat.   I look over and Salami is giving me this lascivious smile.   I

look under the table and see that the rat is actually Salami's stocking clad foot creeping up my leg. Salami had slipped off his Bruno Magli loafer (I knew it was a Magli, the same shoes OJ wore, because he told me, when he was giving me the run down of his whole famously labeled attire, including cost) and was rubbing his black socked foot up my calf.

"Feels good, yes?"

"Umm..."

"Speechless? That's how I leave all my women. I just wanted to give you a little taste of my pleasuring. I am quite good in the bed!"

"That's uh...great."

Not wanting to make a scene I just moved my legs out into the aisle. I actually tweaked my back out from trying to avoid his foot advances!

Bad enough yet? Not quite? There's more. After Salami pays the check, he goes to the restroom. I sneak a pick at his credit card receipt to see how much Mr. Big Shot tipped. The check was close to $300.00 and Salami left a measly $5.00 tip. I was so embarrassed. I didn't have any cash on me, so I just mouthed "I'm sorry" to the waiter as we were leaving. So embarrassing.

As we are walking to the valet, Salami asks if I would like to take a walk on the beach first before we head back. At that point, can't think of anything I'd like to do less!!! I feign tiredness and say, "I think I'll pass."

We get to my street. I open my car door before Salami even stops. Unfortunately, Salami parks and gets out to walk me to my door. At my door Salami asks if he should come in. I say no. Then Salami says "Oh, you are one of those 'rules girls'." I say, "No, just tired, but thank you for

dinner." He says "No big deal. Well, let me give you this as a bonus gift."
At this point, Salami takes a business card out of his wallet, writes something
on the back, hands it to me, says it was nice meeting me, and walks back to
his car.

I hurriedly dash into my apartment, double lock the door, turn on the
light and read the back of the card – "Good for 10 % off of an eyebrow lift
or liposuction – your choice"

Pen down. Deep breath. Breakfast arrives.
Looks at food. Adds a side of bacon.

Up to this point She hasn't put her pen down
once. She has been writing fast and furiously.
Cathartically. Susan has yet to read it because the
letter is too far from her sight. But, luckily for
Susan, after taking a sip of the coffee and a bite of
the cinnamon roll, She goes to the restroom and leaves
the letter out in the open. Susan leans over the two
empty seats pretending to get a bottle of ketchup and
reads as fast as she can. Susan finishes just as She
returns from the bathroom.

Hurray! No one saw me. Not so fast. Nico gives
Susan a conspiratorial smile from the kitchen. Susan
blushes at being caught, but then just shrugs with a
little laugh.

Bacon arrives. Dives in.

As if the weekend wasn't bad enough!!! Yesterday/Monday morning I
get to work two hours early because I told Mr. Married Boss Guy on Friday
that I would come in early to help him with his drafts that are due this
Friday, and lo and behold, Mr. Married Boss Guy has taken the day off of

work. He didn't even call me to tell me not to bother coming in early.   I was so mad.

Then I run into Lisa who I make promise that she will never set me up with another guy again.   She looked at me like there must be something wrong with me to have failed on two of her excellent set-up dates.

So frustrating.

I wonder if Mr. Married Boss Guy will be there today. I wonder if he will apologize. I definitely will let him know that I came in early to help him.

Anyway, what's new with you?

Love, Your Frustrated Sister

Pen down. Folds stationary.   Stuffs envelope. Finishes breakfast ravenously.

Poor Susan doesn't get to read the last bit of the letter.

She leaves in a hurried fashion.

"So Miss Susan, you are a little snoop, huh?"

"Come now, Nico.   Just taking a little peek."

Gosh, how much does it suck to be dating! Thank goodness I found Jack! I'd hate to be on the search. If a girl that beautiful can't find someone decent, then God help the rest!

CHAPTER 9

Wednesday, Susan's mom calls to let her know her grandma has fallen and sprained her ankle. Is there any way Susan could go out to Palms Springs for a couple of days to be with her while she is recovering? Mrs. Klein would do it herself, but she and Dr. Klein are scheduled to go to an orthodontist conference in Las Vegas this weekend where Dr. Klein is lecturing. Grandma Stern is going to be released late on Thursday. The hospital is keeping her overnight just for a safety measure given the fact that she is 92.

Sure, Susan can do it. Susan decides to let the kids take Friday off of school, so they can go with her. The kids love hanging out at their grandmother's condo in Palm Springs, and Grandma Stein loves seeing the kids. It will be good medicine for her.

Susan and all four kids drive out to Palm Springs when they get out of school on Thursday. Jack stays behind because he is swamped at work and a weekend alone is a perfect way for him to catch up.

CHAPTER 10

Jack stays at work late on Thursday and Friday night and is there for most of the day on Saturday. On Sunday he goes golfing with his partner, Phil and his cousin, Dave. He wins. As always!

When Susan and the kids return on Sunday night, everyone is bushed, so they all get into their Pjs, watch television and go to bed early.

In bed, Jack and Susan share what they did over the weekend. Susan tells Jack that the kids went swimming and played tennis all weekend while she and Grandma Stein just hung out and got caught up and that Grandma Stein did seem steadier by the time they left Sunday afternoon. Grandma Stein was very appreciative that they had come.

Jack tells Susan that although he missed her, it was a very productive weekend, he got a lot of work done and had a great game of golf that day. Why I didn't mention that Maggie stayed at work with me on Thursday and Friday night, I don't know. In fact why I haven't mentioned Maggie at all, I don't know. Maybe I'll tell Susan about Maggie tomorrow when I am not so tired.

"Good night, LG! I love you!"

"Good night, CB! I love you, too!"

CHAPTER 11

This uneasy feeling I have had about my intern,
Maggie, only increased over the weekend. I cannot
believe she insisted on staying late with me Thursday
and Friday night, even though I repeatedly insisted
she go home.   What was that with the way Maggie set
up a picnic with the take-out food on the floor in the
conference room with little tea-light candles for
"ambiance?" Where she found tea-light candles in the
office I have no idea.   I told her it wasn't
necessary to go to any trouble that I usually just
plow through taking bites here and there, but she
insisted I take a break.   Her declaration that while
my wife is away she felt it was her Good Samaritan
duty to make sure I didn't overwork myself, was not
comforting!   How did she even know my wife was away?
I certainly didn't tell her.   I didn't want to be
rude, so I indulged her in the impromptu picnics, but
her presence was more of a hindrance than a help.

Her flirtatious overtures, the sitting close, leg
touching, deep staring into my eyes, make me so
uneasy.   How awful that I had to hide the fact that I
was going back into the office on Saturday. I
couldn't tell her because I was afraid she would
insist on coming too.

How many times did she call me on Saturday???-
"to check up on [me] and make sure [I] am surviving
without my wife" and "to let [me] know that if [I]
want her to meet [me] at work she is more than
available" and "to just see what [I] am doing for
dinner because it would be no problem to cancel [her]

date." I did feel a little bad not returning any of her calls. Of course, this morning, the first thing she asks me is if I had gotten any of her calls. Thank goodness I was able to quickly make up a lie about my phone being off and not receiving her calls until it was too late to call. She looked so disappointed but placated. I don't want to hurt her feelings, but I don't want to lead her on either.

I can't believe with all of the available men in town and how beautiful Maggie is that she hasn't made a connection yet. I do feel sorry for her. She does seem rather lonely. But gosh, how much more of her over-the-top flirting can I handle?! Maybe I should suggest that she spread out her workload and help other architects in the office, so she can get a more rounded experience. I'll see what I can do. I don't want to make her feel worse.

Why didn't I tell Susan about Maggie? There is nothing going on. I don't like this feeling.

CHAPTER 12

Susan barely makes it into Eggsactly on Tuesday. She is still so tired from the weekend. Then last night, Jess got her period for the first time and Susan was up consoling her until 1:00 a.m. Jess didn't want "to become a woman!" Jess didn't want "to wear a big disgusting pad of cotton in [her] underwear every month!" "How embarrassing!" Maybe she would "just stay home until it went away." No, that's not going to happen. All women get them and go about their daily lives. Jess will just have to get used to it. Pout, pout! Sob, sob!! So exhausting! Thank goodness she won't have to go through this again. She just has the crazy antics of two teenage boys to look forward to. But at least that's not for another 5 years!

Maybe She will be here today and I can get my weekly home-town soap opera fix. Sure enough, She comes. She sits right next to Susan. Thank goodness, I won't have to strain to see what she is writing.

She looks tired too. I wonder what she did over the weekend to make her look so exhausted. Maybe she had another one of her crazy dates.

Settles in. Pen out. Stationary out. Orders breakfast. Poached eggs. Cinnamon roll. Cappuccino. Begins writing.

Dear Molly,

How was your weekend? How was the home-town parade? Did the kids enjoy being on the float?

I know I said I wasn't dating anymore, but this time I mean it. I'm joining a convent and becoming a nun!

I let one of the architects at work talk me into going out with his nephew. The date itself wasn't as bad as the others, but I think I may have a stalker on my hands.

Latte arrives. Pen down. Big sip. Burns tongue. Pen up.

So, Mike, my blind date, knocks on my door. When I open it, I say, "Hello" and he just stares at me and doesn't say anything. I finally ask, "Are you Mike?" More silence. I ask, "Can I help you?" More silence. Finally he stammers out, "Oh, I am so sorry. I just didn't realize you were going to be so beautiful. I'm embarrassed. You're way out of my league." If I thought he was just being charming, it would have been cute, but he was serious.

He wasn't even that bad. Just really average, maybe even a bit better. Brown hair. Brown eyes. Average height- maybe about 5' 10". Average weight. Nice facial features. Nice black button down shirt. Regular jeans. There wasn't any need for him to be so insecure.

Anyway, he escorts me to his clean well-kept Honda, opens my door then waits for me to get in before he gently shuts the door. Extremely polite. He says he is going to take me to a little Italian restaurant that he knows of nearby, but it's not that fancy and maybe I would rather go somewhere else. I assure him that it is fine. He apologizes again for not being better looking or planning a better date for someone as stunning as me. Flattering, but wimpy.

48

Food arrives. Pen down. Eats heartily. Pen up.

This is how it went all night long. Every other sentence he was apologizing "for not being someone more up to my caliber," "not having a better car," "not having a better job" "not being more exciting." I assured him that his Honda was fine, that being a research assistant at UCLA was a perfectly good job, that he was nice looking, that I was fine with going to a local Italian restaurant. It was really tiring.

He tried really hard to please me- he even offered to cut my chicken parmigiana for me. If he wasn't so self-deprecating and apologetic, he wouldn't have been so bad.

He didn't talk about himself at all. He asked me tons of questions and seemed really interested in everything I had to say. When I asked him something about himself he would just quickly answer and then go back to me.

More bites.

When we got back to my apartment he walked me to my door. The conversation went something like this-

"Don't worry I won't try to kiss you or anything. I know I am not your type. I am just not good enough for you, but I just want to walk you to your door to make sure you are safe."

"Thank you.   Don't put yourself down so much, Mike. You are a really nice guy. Don't be so hard on yourself. You have a lot to offer someone."

"Really? Thank you. That means so much coming from someone like you. Anyway, I know we can't be boyfriend and girlfriend, but if you ever

49

need anything, please feel free to call me. I know you are sort of new to town and probably don't know a lot of people yet, so I'd be happy to help you in any way I can."

"Thank you. That is very sweet."

"Seriously, if you ever need anything, call me. I can go grocery shopping for you, fix any of your appliances, take you to the airport if you ever go anywhere, wash your car, anything."

"Thank you! Well, good night. I had a nice time."

"No, thank you! Going out with you was like going out with a supermodel. I feel very privileged even to have met you. I mean this was the best date I have ever had. I know for you it probably wasn't much fun, but for someone like me, it was awesome. Just getting to sit at the same table with you was a treat. Not only are you beautiful, but you are so smart and nice and funny. Wow."

"I'm really not all that, Mike, but thank you. You take care."

"You take care, too. Don't forget I will always be your friend."

"Okay. Thank you! Good night."

"Good night."

Finishes breakfast.

So Sunday he leaves me 3 voice messages–

1) 11:30 a.m. – "Hi Maggie. This is Mike. The guy you went out with last night. Hope you remember me, even though it probably wasn't very memorable. Anyway, just wanted to say thank you again for an awesome time. If you ever need anything give me a call [leaves number]. Hope to hear from you sometime. I'll totally understand if I don't though. Anyway,

hope you are having a good day.   My number again is [leaves number].
Hope the ringing of the phone didn't wake you. You are probably out doing
something really fun. Anyway hope to hear from you.   You know just as
friends. I know I am not your type. Well, I'll call you later."

2) 3:30 p.m. – "Hi Maggie. This is Mike again– the guy from last night.
Hope you are having a good day. I called you earlier and left my number,
but in case there was too much static and you couldn't understand it– here
it is again [leaves number].   Hope to hear from you.   Your friend, Mike."

3) 7:30 p.m. – "Hi Maggie. This is Mike again– the guy from last night.
Sorry to bother you. Just wanted to check in and make sure you didn't need
anything.   Hope you got your beauty sleep– not that you need it because you
are so beautiful.   Well, give me a call sometime [leaves number].   Talk to
you soon hopefully.   Oh yeah, by the way, I had a great time last night.
Have a great day at work tomorrow. Miss you."

More sips of latte. Orders cinnamon roll.

Monday morning, 7:13 a.m., I receive a text message from him,
"Good morning, beautiful. Your friend, Mike."

Monday night, 9:47 p.m., another text message– "Sleep well. Call me
sometime, please. Mike, the guy from the other night."

Loud buzzing. Takes cell phone out. Reads
message.

Oh my god, I just got another text message from him– "Hey, what's
up? Haven't heard from you in a while. Miss you. Call me. Mike."

Are there any normal guys out there?

Muffin arrives. Takes bite.

However, on the side of good news, I am totally getting closer to Mr. Married Boss Guy. On Thursday, I overheard his secretary say that Mr. Married Boss Guy's wife and kids were going to be out of town to visit some sick relative over the weekend. So, we totally spent Thursday and Friday night together. Sure, it was at work. But that's a start. I knew he was staying late, so I offered to stay with him. He was so cool. He tried to get me to leave saying that I shouldn't be staying so late, but I knew deep down he wanted me to stay, so I did. Both nights, we ordered take-out. I set up a picnic for us on the conference room floor. Luckily, I still had some tea-lights in my car from when I bought them last week, so I put them out to make it more romantic. I could tell by the look on his face that he really liked it.   We sat really close to each other, and I could tell when I touched him, he felt sparks.   He was definitely giving me signals.

Eats more muffin.

He didn't kiss me or anything, but I know we are getting to that point.

I called him a few times on Saturday, but unfortunately, he had accidentally turned his phone off, and by the time he got my messages it was too late to call me back.   He explained that to me first thing when I saw him Monday morning.   It was obvious that he felt bad about not getting to return my calls.   Such a bummer!   I would have without hesitation cancelled my date Saturday night and hung out with Mr. Married Boss Guy.

You don't think I am terrible, do you? How could you- Jerry was married when you first met him and now look at how happy the two of you are.

Oh my god, it's so late I have to get to work. I'll call you later, unless of course, I am making mad passionate love with Mr. Married Boss Guy!

Xo, M

Gathers things. Wraps half eaten muffin in napkin. Stuffs in bag. Pays bill. Leaves.

Susan is even more exhausted after sneakily reading Her letter. What a life! Thank God I am not dating! I still need to ask Jack if he knows this girl.

Susan is finishing her cold breakfast when Cherise comes in.

Cherise screams, "I got a part. I got a part. I am going to be a day player on this Mexican Soap Opera!"

"Congrats, Cherise. I didn't even know you speak Spanish." Big hug.

"Yeah, I am fluent. My dad is from Argentina."

Rose, Bobby and Nico join Susan in a toast to Cherise with big glasses of orange juice.

CHAPTER 13

Susan decides to throw Cherise a
"Congratulations" party.   Luckily, she is excellent
at throwing parties together at the last minute.
Cherise is very touched as she doesn't have that many
friends here in town.   On Thursday, Susan gets a list
from Cherise of the friends she does have, who she
wants to invite.   Of course Eddie, Drew, Marion,
Rose, Bobby and Nico are invited.   Susan tells Eddie
to bring Tyler because her kids will be there too, and
he can play with Sammy.   She thinks of inviting The
Letter Writer too, but unfortunately she does not come
into Eggsactly on Thursday, so Susan has no way of
getting into contact with Her.

Susan calls all of the guests on Thursday
afternoon to invite them because she doesn't have
enough time to send out invitations, as the party is
only two days away.   Fifty people are invited in
total, including some of Susan's and Jack's friends, a
friend for each of their kids, Susan's family, the
Eggsactly regulars and employees and Cherise's list of
friends.

The party is Mexican themed in honor of the soap
opera.   They have a taco bar, margaritas (virgin ones
for the kids), a Mariachi band, a Mexican hat dance
contest and a pinata filled with soap related items
i.e., bath salts, scented soaps, small bottles of
detergent, dryer sheets, bubbles, wash clothes.

Everyone who was invited shows up, including Drew
and Marion. Susan wasn't sure they would come, being
as they are so much older, but they have a good time

54

too. They actually win the hat dance contest.

Rose brings her husband Saul. Bobby and Nico come together. Bobby is quite smitten with Sophie. Susan has to watch them closely because Sophie seems to be taken with Bobby, too. Bobby is only four years older than Sophie, just like Susan and Jack, but when the four years are between sixteen and twenty it seems like a huge gap.   Bobby is a good guy though.

Susan had thought that Bobby had a crush on Cherise, but when she corners him at the taco bar and asks him, he tells her "Yay, Cherise is hot and all, but I am not into the whole acting thing. I like smart girls. Cherise is more like a sister."   Well, if he likes smart girls, Sophie is definitely the one for him.

Tonight, Nico is Mr. Social Butterfly, making the rounds with all of the available women, mostly Cherise's friends, dancing up a storm and teaching the party-goers how to do the Tarantella.

The party should have been titled "Love Connection, Mexican Style."   The party is a big success.

The biggest success is the chemistry flowing between Eddie and Cherise.   They seem to never leave each other's side all night long.   Cherise teaches Eddie how to salsa dance. Eddie surprisingly picks it up very quickly.   Apparently, neither Cherise nor Eddie think Cherise is too young for Eddie.

Cherise and Tyler hit it off as well.   After Cherise teaches Eddie to salsa dance, Tyler wants to learn, too.   So, Cherise teaches all of the kids. Tyler and Sammy do quite well, but poor Myles just has

two left feet. He doesn't mind though. He has a lot
of fun trying and turns it into a one-man comedy
routine.

The last guest doesn't leave until after 2 a.m.
Cherise is very thankful! Eddie too! Chuck Woolery
would be proud.

CHAPTER 14

A month later, Susan is at Eggsactly talking to Bobby about Sophie when She walks in. Bobby and Sophie have been out quite a bit since the Mexican fiesta. Susan and Jack aren't sure if they should let it go on, but know that if they try to stop it, Sophie will just rebel and sneak out to see him, so they both think it is better to just have it out in the open and keep tabs on it. Besides, both Susan and Jack really like Bobby and know he is a good guy.

Susan realizes she hasn't seen the Letter Writer in quite a while and wonders where She has been. Susan notices that She doesn't look quite as happy as She did the first time She came into Eggsactly.   In fact, She looks kind of sad and what is it… lonely, yes, that's it. Lonely. Susan feels sorry for her. Apparently nothing much has changed in the last month as to her routine.

Pen out. Stationary out. Orders hearty breakfast. The Saul Special Omelette. Canadian bacon. Extra potatoes. Cinnamon roll. Latte. Begins writing.

(Luckily for Susan She sits only two stools down, making it easy to sneak peeks at her letter.)

Hey Molly,

Sorry it's been so long since I last wrote.   This last month has been crazy.   Work is really busy, which is good, because it keeps me busy and my mind off of my loneliness.

Boy did I peg her right, Susan smiles to herself.

I had such high hopes when I first got here, but being in this big city without any real friends or family or boyfriend really makes a girl lonely.

I've been interviewing for roommates. Oh my god, it's just as bad as dating. I had one girl apply who is a self-proclaimed chronic smoker with five cats and ADHD. She told me that if she moves in, everything has to be in a particular place and I wouldn't be able to move it or she would freak out. Thanks, but no thanks!

`Latte arrives.  Sips.`

I interviewed this scraggly, long-haired, Birkenstock wearing masseur whose eyes never left my chest. He said if I would lower the rent he would throw in weekly massages with "happy endings." No thank you!

I met with a lesbian couple who seemed nice at first, but then promised me that within one month they would convert me and we would be a happy trio. Again, thanks, but no thanks.

`Food arrives.  Eats.`

I thought I finally found the perfect roommate- this sweet looking- non-smoking- animal free-sane-heterosexual (not that I am against lesbians, I just don't want the pressure) girl in her early twenties. Everything was fine until I did a background check and found out she is wanted in three states for larceny, burglary and assault. After doing a quick check of my house, I discovered my diamond studs were missing (you know- the ones Vince gave me on our one year anniversary. At least it was those, the small ones, and not the big ones, mom and dad gave me for my 25th birthday.), a charm bracelet I had just bought, and hadn't even worn yet, and that four leaf clover necklace you gave me as a going away present- sorry! I made a police report, but the officer basically told me I'd better put it out of mind because it was very unlikely that she would be found. The officer said, even if she is found, she probably would have already disposed of my jewelry. So sad!!

So I am still roommate free. I better find someone fast because my savings, which is supplementing my rent, is about run out.

Speaking of Vince - have you seen him lately? Heard anything about him? Maybe I should have just married him! To think we were together for three years and I just didn't feel it. He was nice and all, but I just want something more. You know - butterflies. He just didn't do it for me. I still feel bad about breaking up with him right before I left. I hope he finds someone soon. He deserves to be happy. I deserve to be happy, too.

Eats more.

Maybe I expect too much. I want romance, passion, excitement. I don't want hum-drum. Did I ever tell you that Vince had to make-love in the same way, every time or he "would lose [my] rhythm and not be able to function properly"? It was like having sex by connect-the-dots. One time, I bought some furry handcuffs, and he ran from the bedroom and hid himself in the bathroom. I had to promise him to throw them away before he would come out. Then he refused to have sex with me that night because he said I ruined the moment. I still have those handcuffs somewhere. Where is my man that will cuff me to the bedpost, ravish me, and then tell me how much he loves me and can't live without me????

Big slurps of frozen drink.

Susan gets lost in thought reminiscing about the

time she and Jack played dominatrix- handcuffs, whip,
leather and all. Maybe if I can get all of the kids
out of the house this weekend I will unpack the adult
toys. Jack and I could use a night of fun!

Speaking of bedposts and handcuffs, boy do I want Mr. Married Boss
Guy to ravish me! I bet he's the type. He's conservative at work, but I
know with the right woman he would be an animal in the bedroom! The
way he looks at me just makes me shiver with excitement. I know he fancies
me (that sounds so English, doesn't it? - I watched Bridget Jones's Diary for
about the tenth time this weekend). I can just sense it. I want him so
badly. And not just sexually. He is a really good guy. His wife is very
lucky. He is so tender.

Eats more. Drinks more.

The way I feel about him is like nothing I have ever felt before. He is
just perfect. I know the feelings aren't one-sided. He's constantly brushing
up against me at work. When he talks to me he looks me right in the eye.
He is always asking about my dating life. I know it's because he's jealous.
Not only would he make a great husband, but a great father too.

You should have seen how tender he was with his son. A few weeks
ago, we were on a job site when he got a call from his son's teacher that his
son had fallen off the jungle gym and broke his arm. We rushed to the
school and Mr. Married Boss Guy ran to the nurse's office where he so
tenderly scooped up his son and wiped away his tears. I went with them to
the emergency hospital. I don't even think his son knew I was in the car.
He was so hysterical. Mr. Married Boss Guy was so caring and loving and

gentle. What an awesome father!   I don't know where his wife was. I was hoping she would come to the hospital, and I would get to meet her, but Mr. Married Boss Guy got me a cab to take me back to work because "[he] didn't want to impose on me." I said it was no problem, but he was just so considerate. He was still thinking of me, even though his son was in emergency.

Now this is a real coincidence! Myles broke his arm two weeks ago and Jack went to get him. I was at a luncheon honoring Barbara for her work in the pediatric unit. When I got there Jack didn't mention bringing an intern. In fact, Jack hasn't mentioned an intern at all. I really must ask him. Hmmm, isn't this interesting?! Does this woman I have been sitting next to for months have a huge crush on my husband? Does my husband have feelings for her, too?

Gosh I am so lonely here. What if Vince was the one I should have married? All of my friends back there at home are married. What if I missed my chance? I can't believe at 28 I already feel like an old spinster. I want Mr. Married Boss Guy!

Have you seen mom and dad lately? They said they are going to visit soon. When are you going to come? I am excited about coming home next month for Katie's bridal shower. She is the last of my group of high school friends to get married. Then it's just me. I hope it happens soon. We just need to get Mr. Married Boss Guy's wife out of the way! ☺

Sip. Sip. Sip.

I'll call you this weekend!

Love you, M

She's lost in thought. Susan's mind is running a mile a minute, too! After a few more minutes, both of them pack up and leave at the same time. She walks out just in front of Susan.

Susan almost forgets to say "good-bye" to everyone at Eggsactly. Almost.

"Bye, Rose, Nico. Bobby see you Friday night. Sophie is looking forward to your date!"

CHAPTER 15

That night, the Martinelli household is uncharacteristically chaotic. Myles is in a particularly grouchy mood, which is rare for him. His arm is itching and he is tired of the cast. The novelty of it has worn off.

That afternoon, Sammy had gotten into a fight with a kid on the playground who had been making fun of "Sammy's little brother, the klutzy one." Sammy spent the afternoon in the principal's office. Even though, Susan and Jack secretly are actually quite proud that Sammy stood up for his baby brother, they hide their feelings, so as not to encourage fighting. They take away Sammy's television privileges for the night.

Jessica is having her second period and is still not taking it well. Unfortunately, she also has cramps.

Sophie is upset because she wanted to visit Bobby that night and Susan and Jack said "no." It is a school night, and although they both like Bobby they want things to go slowly, if at all. Sophie, as she is known to do, pouts all night long in between texting Bobby about her "dictator parents."

Jack is exhausted! It is the first night he has been home before 9:00 p.m. in weeks. He has been working on plans for a very sophisticated new office building with demanding clients.

With all the chaos, Susan almost forgets about the Letter Writer again.

As Susan and Jack are finishing cleaning the

kitchen after dinner, Susan asks Jack if anything is new at work, to which he replies "No, just the usual- too much work, too little time, unrealistic deadlines, demanding clients."

"Maybe you should get some help- an intern or something?"   I'm so clever, thinks Susan.

"We have some interns. But, they can't help with the difficult stuff. It's all on me."

"How many interns do you have now?"

"I don't know exactly. They are always coming and going.   How was your day?"

Why don't I just ask him straight out if he has a beautiful, buxom intern who has a crush on him? Why am I hesitating? Maybe I don't want to know. Maybe I want to keep spying on her letters.

Jack leaves the kitchen rather abruptly to go watch television with the kids before they go to bed, well of course, except for Sammy who is sulking in his room. Why didn't I mention Maggie?   Why haven't I told Susan about her? I always tell her about the people at work.   It's not as if anything is going between us. In fact, I wish she would be assigned to someone else. She won't leave me alone. She's stayed late with me every night at work these past few weeks, even though, I have insisted she leave. She's ordered dinner for us each night as if we are on a date.   There is just something not right about her. She stands too close. Looks at me too longingly. Tries to hand-feed me.

Oh my God, and that day Myles broke his arm, I practically had to force her in a cab. She would just not leave.   I didn't want her to be there when Susan got there. Again, I don't know why. Everything is perfectly innocent. I just know how women are. Susan would see this beautiful girl and start asking me all of these questions. Last thing I want is for Susan to feel insecure. Susan is my life!

Susan comes to join everyone in the family room. She snuggles up to Jack on the sofa. This is how life is supposed to be. Jack really loves me. I can feel it in the way he holds me. If the Letter Writer is his intern, I know the feelings she has are purely one-sided!

I wonder if she will be there on Thursday.

CHAPTER 16

The next week Susan shows up at Jack's office to surprise him for lunch. As Susan is going up the elevator, Maggie is coming down. Maggie left early for the day because she has a doctor's appointment.

Susan slips into Jack's office, covers his eyes with her hands and nibbles on his ear.

"I sure do hope this is my wife or else I am in big trouble."

"Hey sexy man, want to have lunch with a sex-craved forty-something married woman with four kids?"

"Most definitely. But maybe we should satisfy your craving before we satisfy your hunger. Please don't tell my wife."

"Okay as long as you don't tell my husband!"

Susan and Jack leave hand in hand. They do as planned- first satisfy Susan's sex craving in the back seat of Jack's car, and then have a quick bite to eat at a local Mexican restaurant. Jack doesn't get back to the office for three hours.

Jack is still totally mine! Any worries I had are completely gone!

What a great surprise from Susan! Thank goodness Maggie wasn't here. I just have a feeling she would have spoiled the mood.

CHAPTER 17

A month later, Susan is relishing her breakfast at Eggsactly while contemplating the end of the school year. Susan is excited the kids will be out of school in a couple of weeks for summer, but sad that her weekly routine will be somewhat disrupted with them off.

Well, at least I was able to have a girls' spa-weekend with Debbie before the summer chaos starts. This last weekend was great. Debbie and I always have so much fun. Bacara Resort was beautiful as always! I love that hotel. My massage was exquisite. Karaoke-ing downtown Santa Barbara was a blast. I can't believe those college boys tried to pick up on us. What an ego boost! If I weren't married, who knows, maybe I would have gone for it. That Harley guy was sure a hottie! Who cares that he is 18 years younger than me. I bet I could still give him a run for his money. What a great weekend! I am still in shock that Debbie and I just chucked all of our responsibilities and stayed over an extra night until Monday. Debbie really needed it.

I am so sorry for Debbie that things aren't going so great between her and Larry right now. How awful that she hasn't gotten pregnant. I can't believe they have been trying ever since they got married 2 years ago. It happened so quickly for me and Jack. I guess we were a lot younger. I was so excited for Debbie when she finally met Larry, only excited for Debbie though, not myself, because I never really could stand the guy. By the time she met Larry at 38 years old, poor Debbie had given up all hope of getting married. But within a year of meeting, they were married. I guess she was afraid of losing him.

Hopefully for Debbie this is just a bump in the road because I know how much she loves him. For me, personally I wouldn't mind if she found someone new. I still can't figure out what she sees in Larry. He always looks at me like he would like to take a bite out of me. It's creepy. And he is always flirting with any girl that passes. I hate that. Gosh I am so lucky that Jack doesn't have a roving eye.

How sweet was Jack when I got home last night! And what a trooper, he didn't mind me staying over an extra night. I know it was just more work for him with the kids. I loved that he had ordered in my favorite Chinese take-out and had it all set up so romantically outside by the pool with the tea-lights and fresh cut flowers. He was quite lovey-dovey last night. What a homecoming! How nice he still misses me when I am gone for the weekend! Making love to him was the perfect way to end a beautiful weekend. It was just what we needed.

Oh my gosh, come to think of it, we haven't made love since I surprised him at work. That was over a month ago. In the past few weeks, I have hardly seen Jack. He has been working so furiously against that deadline. He hasn't been home before midnight in weeks. Well, he certainly made up for lost time last night. He could show Hottie Harley a thing or two!

While Susan is lost in thought about her weekend and Jack, She walks in.

She looks exceptionally beautiful and happy. She

has a glow about her. You know the kind women have when they are in love. She is wearing a cream colored silk button-downed blouse, perfectly tailored to her buxom frame. It is tight around her breasts, but not too tight so as to have the buttons pop open, and fitted just right at her waist. She has it tucked into a pair of cream colored silky suit pants. Her high-heeled cream colored sandals match perfectly. The long gold chain with a four-leaf clover charm is situated precisely at the top of her chest. It gives the classy outfit a bit of sexiness. She sits down right next to Susan.

She just sits there for a few moments with this look of satisfaction on her face before She orders.

Just tea and toast.

Quite a difference from her usual hearty meal.

Pen out. Stationary out. Begins writing.

Dear Molly,

It finally happened! Oh, I'm skipping ahead. I just gave away the ending- well, not the ending- I am hoping just the beginning.   Let me start from a few weeks back.   Actually let me start with "how are you and yours?" ☺

Okay, so for the past few weeks Mr. Married Boss Guy and I have been working really hard to finish these plans for a new "Green" hotel- you know all that eco-friendly stuff. We have been staying really late at work to get it finished.   Every night, we ordered food and had dinner together in the office.   I stopped trying to make things happen and just started talking to him like a friend. I told him about all of my terrible dates here and about

Vince and about our family and about my search for a roommate.   He is a

really good listener.   I made him laugh with all of my outrageous stories.

Tea arrives. Sips slowly.

He talked about his wife and his kids and his childhood. We really

bonded. It was great. Even though I wanted to give up on the idea of us

together, it was still there in the back of mind. It felt good, like we were

really forming a friendship.   Although I wanted to hear him say something

negative about his wife, he didn't. She sounds like a saint! But even so, it

was nice that he was sharing his life with me.   We got really comfortable

with each other.

So last week, I overheard that his wife was going to be out of town-

some spa weekend thing with her college roommate or something.

Small gasp from Susan. She looks over.
Continues writing.

So I thought- wouldn't it be nice to hang out not on work-time.   I

didn't just want to straight out ask him because I thought he might take it

wrong. So as we were leaving on Friday night, late again, I asked him if he

would follow me home and check out my apartment because I was really

scared of Stalker Date- It was mostly true. Remember a while back I went

out with that stalker guy, Mike? - well, he started calling and texting me

again.   And I swear I think I have seen him sitting in his car outside of my

apartment a few times.   He really does freak me out!   So it was partly

true and partly a little bit of an excuse to get Mr. Married Boss Guy to come

over.

Toast arrives. Nibbles.

70

He agreed to follow me, although a bit reluctantly. When we got to my place, you could tell he was totally nervous. He quickly scanned my apartment and then was about to leave when I offered him a glass of wine. He said he had to get home, but then I reminded him that he told me that his wife was off for the weekend and all of his kids had sleepovers. Caught in a lie, he agreed to a quick glass of wine. Thank goodness I don't have much furniture yet because it forced us to both to sit on the sofa. I tried to get the conversation flowing, but he was sweating bullets. He looked so uncomfortable, I almost felt sorry for him. But then I started thinking that if he was truly not interested in me, he wouldn't be acting all guilty.

Susan has been holding her breath while reading- hoping that something would let her know that this isn't Jack.

More nibbles of toast.

I turned on the television, and we watched Letterman. He seemed to finally start to relax. Next thing I knew, I looked over, and he was sound asleep. I guess all this working late caught up with him. While he was sleeping I went to get ready for bed or whatever else might happen! ☺ I must admit, I put on my sexiest lingerie- my sheer black lace teddy with the big bow on the low back with the matching panties. When I got back he was still passed out, but was now curled up like a baby on the couch. I quietly laid down next to him, so that he was spooning me. I threw a blanket over us. We stayed like that for over an hour before he started stirring. He was still kind of groggy when I turned around. That's when we finally started kissing. He was a bit hesitant at first, kind of disoriented *maybe, but then he really got into it.   Mr. Married Boss Guy/Jack is an awesome kisser.*

Loud gasp from Susan. Susan knocks over her glass of water as she flings her hand up to cover her mouth. She looks over, but doesn't really pay attention. She is much too interested in writing her letter.

"You okay Susan?" Nico calls from the back.

"Yeah, yeah, fine. I'm fine. Sorry about the water glass, Rose."

"No problem, baby. You sure you're okay? You look awfully pale."

"No, I'm fine. I'm sure. I am just distracted thinking about all I have to do before the kids are out of school. Thank you."

Oh my God, it can't be Jack. It can't be my Jack. Jack is a very common name. Maybe it is another Jack who just happens to be an architect who has been working long hours for the past few weeks and whose wife was out of town this weekend for a spa get-away with her college roommate and whose kids all had sleepovers on Friday night!   Please be another Jack!!!

We kissed and kissed and kissed. It seemed like forever before we undressed each other. We made love right there on my couch like two hungry teenagers. It was awesome! It was absolutely the best sex I have ever had. That is really saying something given that usually the first time is so awkward. But it wasn't. It just flowed naturally. Don't worry, big sister, we used protection. When it was over, we laid there for a long while

72

just holding each other.

      `Tears stream down Susan's face.`

      `Sips more tea.`

Then all of sudden he pushed me off the couch- literally! I fell on the floor- and said he had to go. It happened so quickly. One minute we are both relishing in our love-making and then the next he acts like I have the plague. It was so weird. But then I had to remind myself that he was probably just feeling guilty. Especially because of the way he was so passionate with me.

I know it's crazy, but I can really feel a connection with him, and I know he feels it too. I just have to be patient.

      `More tears.`

      `Finishes toast.`

I didn't hear from him the rest of the weekend which I kind of expected. With his wife gone, he had all of the responsibility of the kids, plus he was probably trying to figure out what to do. Even though I didn't expect to hear from him, I was bummed. I didn't call him either. I wanted to give him some time- not be a stalker chick. I know he'll come around.

He didn't come into work yesterday either. So I haven't seen him since Friday night. We'll see what happens when I get to work today. I hope it's not all awkward, and he doesn't make up excuses about what happened. I know he wanted it to happen as much as I did.

I am excited about coming home this weekend for Katie's wedding. I wish I could bring Jack as my date. I think I have crossed over the Mr. Married Boss Guy crush line into something more. Now he's Jack! Jack and Maggie- doesn't that sound perfect!   I wish you could meet him. You would love him.   Jerry would really love him- Jack is an avid golfer. Maybe one day we all will be brunching at the country club and then the boys will take off to hit the greens! ☺

I'll call you tonight to let you know what happens.   I guess I'll have to re-tell all this to you on the phone. LOL!   I hope you are saving all of my letters. They'll memorialize my and Jack's love affair. Our grandchildren can read all about how it started! ☺ Hopefully, you'll get this letter before I see you this weekend.

Miss you!

Love,   Maggie

P.S. OMG- I forgot to thank you for sending me another four leaf clover charm to replace the one that was stolen. Maybe that's what's responsible for my luck changing!!! So, thank you, thank you, thank you!!!! I love it!!!

Susan watches as She, the woman who has just wrecked her world, folds her letter, stuffs it into the envelope and licks the seal.   Boy would I love to just rip that tongue out!

She gathers her belongings and leaves with a happy skip to her step.

Susan sits there with more tears just pouring down her face.   She can't move. It's as if she is chained to the stool.

"Oh my god, baby, what's wrong?" Rose's big loving arms come and embrace Susan as she sits there and just sobs uncontrollably.   Susan can't speak.

74

Nico comes out from the kitchen and rubs Susan's back. Bobby is off for the day.

The three of them stay like that for a long time. Finally Susan finds her voice. She doesn't want to tell them what happened, but needs to tell someone, so she blurts out everything. She makes them promise not to tell anyone, especially Bobby as he is still dating Sophie, until she decides what to do.

Rose makes her promise that she won't do anything foolish and that she won't confront Jack just yet. They make a plan that they won't discuss this for a week, so Susan can absorb it, and then they will get together next week to talk about what Susan should do. Susan is in a state of shock but feels better that she was able confide in someone, two people actually, Rose and Nico.

Susan leaves Eggsactly in a daze. She forgets to pick up Myles. She pulls into her driveway before she realizes that Myles isn't with her and has to turn around to go back and get him from school.

This is not Eggsactly as Susan planned!

CHAPTER 18

While Maggie is writing about her and Jack's one night tryst and Susan is reading it, Jack is sobbing uncontrollably at his desk. As soon as he gets to work that morning he locks himself in his office and tells his secretary that he is not to be disturbed.

He goes to his desk. Puts his head in his hands and just starts crying. He can't stop.

What the hell was I thinking? I knew she had a crush on me! Why did I go with her to her apartment? I don't even know how it happened. One minute we are watching Letterman, then the next I am coming out of some groggy state realizing I just had sex with my intern! How did it happen?

And I thought things had finally gotten to a place where we really could be friends. I told her all about Susan and the kids. I thought she understood how happily married I am. I was even going to introduce the two and see if Susan knew of anyone to fix Maggie up with or be roommates with.

What am I going to do? I will die if I lose Susan!!! Okay, Jack, relax! Pull yourself together. Susan doesn't know. It will **never** happen again! No good will come out of telling Susan.

And to top it off, how I am going to face Maggie. She will probably come in here today expecting me to pledge my undying love for her and all I want to do is tell her to go back to where she came from- to where she was before she ruined my life. Okay your life is not ruined… yet. You just need to settle down and think.

First, I am going to have Maggie transferred to
Cliff. He has been complaining for weeks how he needs
help. He's single. Maybe the two of them will hit it
off.

Oh my god, what if she files a sexual harassment
suit against me?!?! Calm down, Jack. You are getting
ahead of yourself. Maggie is not a psycho. She just
has a crush on you! Sure she "just" has a crush on
me. That's how it always starts in the movies.
Didn't I see Fatal Attraction? The Hand that Rocks the
Cradle?

What if she goes after Susan? What if she won't
leave me alone?

And God help me, but why did I have to enjoy it?
I know I was groggy and I can barely remember it, but
I still know that it was good sex! Why couldn't it
have been like putting my penis into a jar of cacti?
Why did it have to feel all warm and soft and gooey
like a Koozie full of hot fudge? Oh and those lips-
why did they have to be so plump and succulent and
soft like a ripe peach? Why couldn't kissing her have
felt like kissing a thin piece of hard sand paper? No
doubt about it, Maggie's body and lips are made for
sex! God save me!

Not that making love with Susan has ever been
anything other than amazing, but Maggie was just so
new and tantalizing and perfectly shaped for
scrumptious sex!

This can't be happening! I have always been so
faithful! What did I do to deserve this? I can
hear Phil now saying "yeah buddy, what a hardship-
having a gorgeous young girl lusting after you- it

must be hard!"   It is hard!   I don't want a
gorgeous young girl lusting after me!   I only want
Susan!

Breathe.

Picks up phone. Dials Cliff's extension.

"Cliff, you lucked out- you got the help you
need.   I am transferring Maggie to you today. Please
clear a space for her right away. I will send her to
you as soon as she gets in."

"Thanks, Jack! That's awesome. Is Maggie that
hot intern?"

"That's the one."

"Are you sure you don't want to keep her?"

"More than! She is all yours!"

"Thanks, man!"

Step one- out of the way! Step two- resume life
as it was pre-Maggie!

CHAPTER 19

After Susan picks Myles up from school, they go to the nearby park, so Myles can play and Susan can think. Susan is in quite a daze. Even Myles notices. "Mommy are you okay? Your face looks sad and confused?"

"Yes, baby. I'm fine. Everything is just fine. I just heard some bad news today about a friend of mine, so I am sad. But, it will be okay. I will make sure that it is okay."

"Okay, mommy. I love you!" Myles gives her a quick hug before he takes off for the jungle gym.

Tears pour down Susan's face. Luckily Myles becomes so absorbed in playing with the other kids that he doesn't notice.

I can't believe this. I need to talk to someone. But who? Definitely not Barbara. She is very cut and dry. She would just offer to come over and help me throw all of Jack's things to the curb. She has no tolerance for infidelity. If Carl ever cheated on her, the marriage would be over before Carl even knew what happened. I love my sister, but she and I are very different. I am more forgiving. Is that wrong? Am I a fool? Should I just confront Jack and tell him it's over?

That is not what I want to do! I love Jack. I always have. I have never wanted anyone else. I can't imagine living my life without him. And the kids. They would be devastated.

But can I live with the knowledge that he has been with someone else? And what if he doesn't tell me? Will I ever be able to trust him again?

Maybe I should talk to Debbie. No, she is going through her own problems with Larry. I feel so alone.

What about mom? Should I talk to her? No, I don't want her to worry about me or ever think anything bad about Jack. She loves Jack as much as she loves me, Barbara and Michael. Jack is like one of her own. Often she calls to just talk to Jack.

You are not alone, Susan. You have Rose and Nico. You have a plan. You will sleep on this for a week. Then next week you, Rose and Nico will come up with a plan.

"Mommy, can we go home now? I'm hungry!"

"Sure, baby. How about we stop and get a big banana split?"

"Yes, yes, yes, yes, yes!" Myles jumps with joy!

Who could be sad while eating a banana split with an adorable 5 year old who loves you dearly?! That's my plan for now!

CHAPTER 20

Susan doesn't know how she is going to face Jack that evening and act as if nothing has changed. But she does. Surprisingly, all of the Martinellis are home that evening. Usually at least one of the kids is at a friend's house or Jack is working late, but not tonight. Jack actually gets home early and suggests having a barbecue. While Jack prepares the meat, Susan prepares the salad, corn and baked beans.

"It's nice to have you home early, Jack."

Jack. Why is she calling me Jack? She never calls me Jack. Unless she is mad at me. Oh my God, could she possibly know about Maggie? No, there is no way.

"It's great to be home early, LG. Nothing better than a barbecue with my family. Maybe we should all take a dip in the pool first. It's a beautiful night."

"It's always a beautiful night here in sunny California."

Wow, where did that sarcasm come from? Does she know?

"You okay, baby. You seem a little tense."

"No, I'm fine. Sorry. Just still tired, I guess, from the weekend. It was exhausting, you know having to fight off all of those college guys!" Half-hearted smile. Relax Susan. If you don't want to give anything away, you need to start acing normally.

"I guess I just won't be able to let you out of my sight again with all that competition coming after you!"

Hmph, won't that put a crimp in your sleeping with your intern?   Stop Susan! You have to stop thinking about it for now.   Let it go for now. Just enjoy the evening.

"Those boys are no competition for you.   You are my main squeeze and always have been.   A dip in the pool before dinner will be nice."   That's better. That's the Susan Jack knows and loves. I hope he still loves me. God please don't let him leave me for that, that, that woman!

"Kids, put on your bathing suits. We are all going for a swim before dinner. Hurry up. It's a Martinelli pool party."

Myles and Sammy squeal with delight and are downstairs and in the pool before the girls have even begun to change clothes.

Okay Jack, make this a good evening.   Get the whole Maggie incident out of your head. Forget about how she left your office today in tears.   It's over and done with.   Move on. It was one mistake. It doesn't need to ruin your life and your family's life! Get your trunks on and make the evening a splash!

Despite the unspoken turmoil, the evening turns out nicely. The Martinellis have a girls against boys pool volleyball contest. Girls win.   Since everyone is home, the conversation is never ending with the kids all talking at once about everything from schoolwork to the bullies in the boys' classes to the snobs in the girls' classes to Sophie gushing about Bobby to teasing Sammy about his new "girlfriend," Rebecca, to the plans for the family vacation to Hawaii in July.   Jack and Susan get so caught up in the family that they are each actually able to put Jack's infidelity out of their minds for a little while.

However, the tension comes back when Jack and Susan get into bed that night. The tension is thicker than ever, but neither acknowledge it.

Jack kisses Susan "good night" with overflowing passion and holds her as tight as he can. Maybe if I can just get that one evening with Maggie out of mind we can just go on as if nothing ever happened. I love this woman beside me more than life itself! What if she finds out and leaves me. I wouldn't survive without her and the kids. I have to make it up to her. But I can't tell her. It would destroy her and it wouldn't do any good. I have to just go on with this secret for Susan's sake. Stop thinking, Jack. Just hold your wife. Go to sleep.

Susan goes with the moment. Maybe if I just don't say anything, it will be like nothing ever happened. We can go on with our lives and be the perfect happy family we have always been. No one is perfect. Jack just made a mistake. I am not going to throw away all we have for one mistake. Maybe I am a fool. What if it was just the beginning of something and he is just being so affectionate because he feels so guilty. Oh my god, what if he's kissing me now but thinking of her. What if he is wishing She were in this bed with him right now instead of me. She is so much younger than me. She is so beautiful. Those lips, that figure, that hair, that skin- if I were a guy, I'd want to sleep with her, too. Maybe she is more fun than me. Stop Susan. Jack is

holding you. He wants you! You have a life together.
You have four awesome children.   Stop thinking. Go
to sleep.

They sleep holding each other all night long.
Both needing to hold on to something they do not want
to lose.

CHAPTER 21

Susan contemplates not going to Eggsactly on Thursday. She is so afraid that She is going to be there. She also doesn't want to talk about the situation with Rose and Nico yet. They had agreed to wait a week before discussing it and that is what she wants to do. But no matter how much she feared going to Eggsactly, her car just drives her there. It is like it is on auto-pilot.

Susan enters the diner looking as if she is entering a doctor's office. She quickly looks around and is quite relieved to see that She isn't there; although, in the past, She has never arrived before Susan. Susan takes her usual spot and smiles at Rose and Nico. Then she notices Bobby and says "hi" to him. She gives a nod to Rose and Nico indicating she does not want to talk about the incident today. They both understand the signal and go on as if nothing happened.

Fifteen minutes later, She walks in. Her face is streaked with dry tears. Her hair is a mess. Her clothes look like she has slept in them, all wrinkled and spotted with food stains.

Susan holds her breath as She sits down right next to her. The place is full, except for the one seat.

She orders. Coffee. Black. Hot. Nothing to eat.

She takes her time getting her writing materials out. It's as if she is in a fog, moving in slow motion.

Coffee arrives. Sips. Burns tongue. Drinks water furiously.

Serves you right, smiles Susan.

Dear Molly,

Sorry I was so short with you on the phone this morning. I am still so upset about what happened with Jack. I didn't even go to work yesterday. I stayed in bed all day and cried. I didn't even shower, you know I must be feeling awful then.

So here's what happened.~

I got to work on Tuesday afternoon after not seeing him since our love-making on Friday night.

Deep breath intake from Susan.

I walk into his office expecting him to greet me with delight and possibly/hopefully a secret kiss when he formally tells me I am being given a new assignment and transferred to someone else in the office- some guy named Cliff. He doesn't even have me sit down. He just tells me to get my stuff and go check in with "my new assignment." I couldn't believe the harshness and coldness. I just stood there.

Once I regained my composure, I shut his door and asked him to explain. He said, "No explanation. Cliff needs help. I can manage on my own. You'll get a more rounded experience."

Me- "You know what I mean, Jack. What about Friday night? Didn't it mean anything to you?"

Him- "Maggie, you know it was a mistake. Honestly, I don't even know how it happened. I am sorry. But you know that I am a happily, very happily married man."

Me- "Jack, you know it was more than sex. It has been leading up to that for months. Don't brush me off as if it was nothing."

Him- "Sorry, Maggie, but it was nothing. I had no intention of going there with you. Like I said, I don't even know how it happened. Please let's just put it behind us. It will be easier for both of us if you work with someone else. "

Me- "I don't want to work with someone else. I want to work with you. And I want to keep seeing you."

Him- "We are not seeing each other- never have been. Please don't make this harder than it has to be."

Me- "Is this the way you treat all of your interns, Jack?"

Him- "This has never happened before. And it won't happen again. "

Me-   "Why are you being so cruel?"

Him- "Sorry if you think it is cruel. It's the best way to handle things. Please go."

I left with tears pouring down my face. He didn't even offer me a hug.

Breaks. Gulps cooled-down coffee.
I knew it was a one-time thing for Jack. He must have just been really vulnerable with me gone, all the late nights working. Okay Susan, it's not that bad. You can forgive a one-time mistake. It just can't happen again!

I know he is just fooling himself.   He totally was into it. I don't know what I am going to do. He is everything I have ever wanted in a man.

I am not giving up!!!

Then to top it off, I go to "my new assignment" and this Cliff guy looks at me like he just won a prize. He salivated every time he looked my way. I know I should probably be flattered, but I don't want Cliff, I want Jack. What should I do? I know his wife can't compare to me! Who can? Not to be conceited or anything, but I am a catch- beautiful, smart, fun, great in bed! Who could resist me?! My God he's been with his wife for so long, isn't he bored with her yet?! He must be or else he wouldn't have so easily made love to me.

Deep grimace from Susan.

Thank God I am coming home tomorrow. It will be great to see you, Bob, the kids, mom and dad and to hang with all of my old friends. I hope I am not too depressed at Katie's wedding. We will just have to come up with a plan of action. You can remind me how you got Jerry to finally leave his ex for you.

Miss you! Looking forward to seeing you!

Love,

Maggie

Finishes cold coffee.

Forget about any plan you have, Missy, Jack is mine and always will be!!! Why don't you go home and stay home!!! Get out of town and don't come back.

Maggie nurses her cold coffee a bit longer then leaves.

Susan feels a bit better. Susan leaves, too.

"See you all on Tuesday! Have a great weekend!"

"Have a great weekend, too, Susan," choruses Rose, Nico and Bobby. Rose and Nico know Tuesday is the day they will deal with Susan's problem.

"See you Sunday, Susan!" Adds Bobby. Bobby and his parents are coming over for dinner, so the families can meet.

CHAPTER 22

Just as Susan is falling back to sleep for about
the fourth time that night, the shrill sound of the
house phone ringing wakes her up.   Getting out of bed
and running to answer it before it wakes the rest of
the family she trips over a pile of Jack's sneakers.
Ouch! The whole family is sleeping in today before
they begin their Memorial Day celebration- a family
day at the Beach Club.   With a skinned bloody knee,
she breathlessly answers the phone.   The caller is
crying so uncontrollably that Susan can't make out who
it is at first, but soon realizes it is Debbie, from
the snippets of words she can decipher in between
Debbie's sobbing- Larry, affair, going on for
months, asshole, credit card bill charges, room
service for two, asshole, secretary, asshole, ruined
life, asshole, over-the-hill, old spinster, asshole,
die alone, asshole!

Susan sneaks out of the bedroom and goes outside
on the deck to listen to Debbie.

Apparently last night while the Martinell's were
having a BBQ with Bobby's family, Debbie discovered
Larry's six month on-going affair with his secretary.
All of Larry's out of town work weekends and late
nights were just a sham for his secret rendezvous'.
Larry met the 22 year old Russian girl on the
internet. He personally paid for her to come to the
states and set her up with a job and an apartment-
their love nest as Debbie described it.

After fighting for four hours straight, Debbie
told Larry to get whatever he needed and get the hell

90

out! It was over! There was no turning back. "Go drink Stolichnaya and eat caviar with your young Russian mail order girlfriend!" Debbie tells Susan were her parting words to Larry.

Debbie is distraught. She sobs hysterically into the phone, "What if I never find someone now? I'm too old. No one will ever want me again. I know Larry wasn't perfect, but at least, he was mine. It took me 38 years to find a husband and now what. And I am childless! We all aren't as lucky as you, Susan."

Oh yeah, I'm lucky alright- my husband cheated on me, too! I'm certainly not going to share that with Debbie right now. She would tell me to kick him to the curb. It's just different with Jack. It was a one-time thing. And the girl was the instigator. I just know it. I know it will never happen again. Jack and Larry are not the same. I can't bear to hear Debbie tell me that all men are losers and I should stand up for myself. Our situations are completely different. I know she just wouldn't understand right now and think that I am a fool for going on as if nothing happened.

"Debbie, are you sure you want to end it? You sure you don't want to try and work things out? "

"What, Susan? Are you mad? Yes, I want to end it. My husband has been lying to me and cheating on me for months. It wasn't just a one-time thing, Susan."

"Oh, so if it was a one-time thing you would forgive him?"

"I have no idea, but it wasn't. He spent our money to fly his little whore over here from borscht country! And has been shacking up with her while I am desperately trying to get pregnant with his child! He is a royal asshole! I don't know what I saw in him in the first place. That's what desperation will get you!"

"I am really sorry, Debbie! Is there anything I can do for you?"

"Yes, give me Jack! He is the only perfect man I know!"

He's not perfect either, Debbie.

"Sorry can't do, Debbie. Anything else?"

"Make this pain go away!"

"I wish I could, baby. Want me to come over and we can burn some of Larry's things?"

"Great idea! And bring gallons of ice cream! Who cares if I'm fat now!"

"I'll be there in 20 minutes with ice cream and matches."

That's exactly what Susan does. She leaves Jack a note saying she'll meet him and the kids at the Club. She goes to Debbie's bearing 2 gallons of ice cream- mint chocolate chip and coffee mocha chip and a new box of matches.

They char one corner of one of Larry's favorite shirts before stopping and admitting that it is childish and really not going to do any good. But for a moment, the vengeance does make Debbie feel better.

By the time Susan leaves, Debbie has calmed down. She knows Larry wasn't really a catch, but doesn't want to start all over again looking for someone new. The dating world is just not fun for someone over 30.

As Susan drives to the Beach Club, her own situation comes rushing back to her thoughts. Oh please let Jack's dalliance be a one-time thing. Please don't let him do it again. I just couldn't take it.   Larry was never good enough for Debbie. Jack isn't like that.

Right before Susan gets to the Beach Club to meet her family she pulls over on PCH and cries. It is really hard trying to keep it together for everyone. She just has to let it go.   Luckily, tomorrow she can talk to Rose and Nico about her situation. How funny that out of all her close friends and family those two are going to be her confidants in this matter.

She reapplies suntan lotion to cover up the tear marks on her cheeks, turns her car over to the valet, takes a deep breath and enters the Club. She will have a cheerful-everything's-completely-normal Martinelli family beach day.   Please let me get through this!

CHAPTER 23

Tuesday morning, Susan cautiously walks into
Eggsactly fearing that She would be here.   Oh that's
right, she went back home for her friend's wedding.
Whew! Rose and Nico are hard at work when Susan sits
in her usual spot.   Bobby is there, too.   How are we
going to discuss my situation with Bobby around?   I
don't want him to know because he'll tell Sophie.   I
guess we'll just have to wait for him to get off.   Oh
that's right, Sunday night he said he was getting off
early today because he had to start studying for
finals.   So, at least, he should be gone soon.

Both, Rose and Nico, smile at Susan as she sits
down and give her a conspiratory nod. Bobby leaves at
about 11:00 a.m.   Luckily by then, the place has
cleared out. Only customer left is a twenty-something
guy finishing up his latte sitting at one of the
outside tables.

"So, how you doing, sweetie?"

"I don't know, Rose."   Tears emerge.

Nico joins, gives Susan a big bear hug and then
starts rubbing her back in a brotherly fashion.

"Donna malefica!   Donna malefica!"

"What Nico?"

"That woman.   She is evil!"

"You can say that again.   She looks evil.
What am I going to do? Should I confront Jack? Let
it pass.   See if it happens again? Why can't life be
easy?"

"Aw, honey, I don't know what to tell you.   We
know this- you love Jack."   Rose sounds like the voice

of reason.

"More than anything!"

"Well, this is how I see it- if you confront him and he wasn't planning on doing it again, you'll never know for sure if that is truly what he was feeling or if he just resisted because of guilt- you don't want a husband who is with you out of guilt, right?"

"Right. I guess so. I don't know. Maybe I don't care why he is with me as long as he is with me."

"Don't be silly! You know that one of the reasons you love Jack so much is because he loves you so much and makes you feel that way."

"Used to make me feel that way."

"Well, to be certain that he still feels that way, you have to make sure that he chooses on his own to not continue with that little hussy- the Donna Malefica, did I say that right Nico?"

"Yes, perfect- Donna Malefica."

"What I suggest is, you keep this under wraps and just keep on reading her letters. Jack already transferred her. That shows he doesn't want her around."

"Maybe he just doesn't want to be tempted at work."

"Well, maybe. But I don't think so. I think that woman had her sights on him from the beginning and put everything into motion. Men are weak, honey."

"Yes, we men are weak!" Nico agrees.

"Look we can all keep an eye on her. If you read anything compromising, Nico and I can help thwart her advances."

"How?"

"We'll figure out something."

"Do you think I am a fool for not just confronting him and kicking him out right away?"

"Not at all, sweetheart. We all have to do what is right for us. Don't let what others would do influence you. Nobody knows what is best for someone else. Nobody wears the same exact same pair of shoes as anyone else, and so no one can truly feel or know what someone else is feeling."

"Thanks, Rose. My life has always been so blessed, and I don't want to give it up."

"You won't have to. I know it. Nico and I have your back- isn't that what you young kids say now-a-days?"

Susan laughs. "Yes, that's what we young kids say!"

Right then, Drew and Marion walk in.

"What is this little tete-a-tete all about?" Drew asks in his boisterous voice.

"Hey Drew. Hey Marion." Chorus Rose, Nico and Susan.

"Susan, are you crying?" Marion instantly is next to Susan and holding her hand.

"What, oh no, oh I'm okay."

"Hey, everyone!" Eddie and Cherise call out as they enter Eggsactly. Cherise is home for the week from shooting on location in Mexico, and so Eddie has taken the day off to spend with her.

"Why does everyone look so serious? You all okay?" Eddie asks.

"We are all fine, Eddie. How are you? How are

you, Cherise? How is the TV show coming along?"
Susan tries to play off the serious tone.

"Don't try to fool us, Susan. I'm too old for
you to pull the wool over my eyes. What is wrong?
Are your kids okay? Jack? Are you sick?"

"No, we are all fine, Marion. Thank you!"
Another burst of tears.

"Oh who cares if you all know- Jack slept with
another woman!"

"What? Where is he? I'll give that man a good
whipping until he comes to his senses." Drew takes
a fighting stance with his fists in the air.

Susan stares at Drew and then bursts into
giggles- a much needed release. One by one, the rest
of the group begins to laugh. Drew just looks so
ridiculous! Sweet, charming, caring, but ridiculous!

A few moments later, the laughter dies and Susan
can't get the story out fast enough.

"He doesn't know I know. His little Jezebel
comes in here for breakfast and she has been writing
letters to her sister and telling her about her crush
on her boss, an architect named Jack and I kind have
been reading the letters over her shoulders. The
weekend I was away, she asked Jack to escort her home
because of some "stalker" or something and she lured
him into her apartment where she seduced him. She
knew I wasn't home because she overheard someone at
the office say so. She doesn't know of course that I
have been reading her letters or that I am Jack's
wife. It's just awful. Rose, Nico and I were just
discussing what I should do."

"Well, I'll be. Now isn't that movie of the week

material." Marion comments.

"It does sound like a soap opera, but unfortunately it is my life."

"I'm sorry, Susan. I know how it feels to find out your spouse cheated on you. But remember, you read for yourself that she did the pursuing. And as far as you know, it only happened once. With me it was different. My wife was cheating on me with my best friend for months." Eddie looks as if he could feel Susan's pain.

"Sorry, Susan." Cherise doesn't know what else to say. She has never experienced anything like this.

"So what's the plan?" Marion asks with true concern.

I can't believe I am revealing all of this to everyone here, but it feels so good to be able to talk about it. Maybe Drew and Marion will have some words of wisdom for me. They have been together for almost sixty years. I know Eddie and Cherise will offer support.

"Right now the plan is to just wait and see what happens. I love Jack more than words can express. I love my life. I don't want things to change."

"If you don't mind me putting in my two cents, I think that is a great idea. Like they say- you don't throw out the whole carton because of one rotten egg. Is that what they say? Heck, I don't know. But that's what I say. Listen honey I am going to share a little story with you about me and my beloved here, Drew. Drew hates this story."

Drew is visibly cringing. He knows what story is coming.

"It was 1959. Drew and I had been married 9 1/2 years. Our eldest, Cathy, was five. Our middle girl, Becky, was three. And I was 7 months pregnant with our youngest, Patti. Things were going great but chaotic. Drew's career was really booming. It was the year he won his academy award. Actually what happened, happened on the night of the Academy Awards, April 6, 1959. I was so excited to be going to the Awards show again. We had gone one time before in 1953, the first year the Awards were televised. That time was so much fun. They were held at the Pantages Theatre and Bob Hope was the emcee. God wasn't he a charmer! "The Greatest Show on Earth" won for best picture. I wish I still had my dress from that night. It was a form fitting white spaghetti strap number with beading along the bodice. Absolutely stunning! I'm pretty sure Cathy was conceived that night!

In '59 the awards were again held at the Pantages Theatre and Bob Hope was again the emcee along with Jerry Lewis, David Niven, Sir Lawrence Olivier, Tony Randall and Mort Sahl. What a funny and debonair group- great actors. "Gigi" won for best picture. Wasn't that a great movie! " Marion gets lost in thought for a moment.

"Anyway… I was so excited to be going to the awards show again. We got all dressed up and rented a limousine. I wore a royal blue satin gown with black beading. Even though I was pregnant, I still looked stunning. Didn't I Drew?"

"You were the prettiest girl there!" Drew agrees.

Without skipping a beat, Marion continues, "It

was really magical. Drew was beaming. He bought a
tuxedo just for that night, and he wore a royal blue
bow tie that matched my dress perfectly. We looked
like the prom King and Queen. Didn't we?"

"Yes, we did, honey."

Again continuing without much time for Drew to
interject, "I was so happy for him! All of the cast
and crew were there. After the show we went to a
couple of parties. It was a night to remember. But
Drew wasn't ready for it to end. He wanted to go to a
few more parties, but I was just too tired. So I
told him to go on without me. I was pregnant and
taking care of two young ones. In those days husbands
didn't help out much with childcare. Sorry, Drew,
but you know it's true."

"Yes, Dear."

"The girls and the housework were all up to me.
I was just exhausted. Drew didn't want to continue on
to the other parties without me, but I insisted. This
was his moment. I wanted him to enjoy it to the
fullest. I was really happy for him and felt bad that
I couldn't celebrate all night long, but I was just
pooped. Anyway, I had the limo driver take me home
and Drew went with guys from the show. Drew didn't
get home until after noon the next day. I was a bit
worried, but just figured he passed out on one of the
other guy's couches. But the minute I saw his face I
knew. I knew. He didn't have to say a word. And he
didn't for quite a while. He just started sobbing."

Marion's storytelling gets a bit more somber.
"He had spent the night with the costume designer's
assistant. Talk about a hussy! She wore a Harlot

100

red dress with sky high heels and no pantyhose! Such a slut!

Needless to say Drew was drunk!   Very drunk! After crying for some time he confessed that he slept with that girl. He apologized over and over again. I was sick to my stomach. Here I was, the mother of two little girls with one on the way.   I couldn't speak. I told him to just leave me alone for a while.

Drew stayed with the girls, and I went for a walk at the beach. I walked for hours. There was no doubt in my mind that Drew loved me and was truly sorry about what had happened. I knew in my heart it was a one time mistake. So I decided to let it go and forgive him. I thought to myself, I could get mad, we could argue and then eventually make up, but what was the point if I didn't want to leave him anyway. So I just forgave without a fight.

I went home and told him that, of course, I was hurt, but that it wasn't going to ruin our lives and we would never talk about it again AND he would NEVER do it again!

That's what we did. We have never talked about it until now. Our girls don't even know. We went on as if nothing ever happened. And I truly think that was the best decision we ever made. We have had close to 60 years of a happy marriage with 3 great children and grandchildren and great grandchildren.   I am glad we did not throw it away because of a one night mistake.

Please don't think it was easy because it wasn't. There were times when I wondered if it would happen again on the next movie set, but I had to trust. Drew didn't let me down. After that night he was more devoted than ever. He always came home when he said he would and would call if he was going to be late. He never went to a party without me again.

Susan, you have to do what's right for you, but don't let one night of sex ruin a lifetime of love."

Tears stream down Susan's face. Drew doesn't move. He sits as still as a statue. Rose, Nico, Eddie, Cherise stand silently by Susan.

"Thank you for sharing that with me, Marion. I am going to forgive, too, silently. I am not going to confront him right now. But I am going to be on the lookout."

"We all will. That little tramp won't get her hands on your Jack again. Or else she will have to face all of us!" Declares Nico taking the same fighting stance as Drew had! More laughter erupts!

My posse- Rose, Nico, Drew, Marion, Eddie, Cherise! I am a lucky girl! That little Miss Homewrecker won't wreck my home!!!! Keep your hands off, girl! Or else you will have us to deal with! Susan smiles as she looks around at her support group- the diner owner, the young Italian Stallion, the 80 year old Old Hollywood couple, the P.E. teacher and the actress.

CHAPTER 24

Susan doesn't see Her again until a month later-
the week after the Martinelli's return home from their
annual Klein summer family Hawaii vacation.   Kauai
was awesome.   It was just like it had always been.
Family, laughter, fun and sun!   Every year Susan,
Jack, the kids, Susan's sister, Barbara and her
family, Susan's brother, Michael and his family and
Susan's parents spend a week in Hawaii at the
beginning of the summer vacation.   The Martinellis
then take another week vacation at the end of the
summer right before school starts up again.

Susan remarkably was able to let go of the one-
night stand and enjoy herself in Hawaii.   There was no
sign of turmoil at all.   None of Susan's family seemed
to detect anything.   Like Drew after his one-night
stand, Jack seemed even more devoted now.   He was
totally attentive to Susan.   He didn't even golf as
much as he normally did so he could spend more time
just sunbathing with Susan.   Barbara even commented
about how Jack was extra lovey-dovey that week.
Whatever the reason, Susan just enjoyed it.

Susan is sitting in her usual spot telling Rose,
Nico and Bobby about Hawaii and showing them pictures
when She walks in.   Bobby has already heard most of
the details from Sophie, as she called him the moment
she got home from the airport.   She didn't even unpack
before she went over to see him.   Sophie had missed
Bobby desperately and didn't know if she could live if
she didn't see him right away, so she yelled as she
scrambled out the front door.   Oh, the melodrama of

teenage girls!   Jack and Susan were coming off a
blissful high from the family vacation so didn't put
up much of a fight about Sophie going out the moment
she got home. Let her have fun. She's just a
teenager once. Jack and Susan agreed.

She sits two stools down. Immediately She begins
her usual routine.

Pen out. Stationary out. Orders breakfast- just a
cinnamon roll and coffee.

She does not look good. She has lost too much
weight, making her look emaciated. Her hair is dirty
and stringy. Her jeans and t-shirt are wrinkled, as
if she had just taken them out of the hamper, and
because of all of the weight she has lost, they just
hang on her.

Susan, Rose, Nico and Bobby stop talking. Rose
and Nico get back to work. Bobby doesn't know why the
conversation has ended so abruptly but figures it's
just because the hot woman customer just arrived.
Rose asks Bobby to go make a quick run to farmer's
market down the street as they just ran out of lemons.
"Be back quickly, Rose. See ya' Susan."
"See ya' later, Bobby."
Susan picks up the family photos lying on the counter.

Dear Molly,

I am a mess!!!   I rarely wash my hair. I wear dirty clothes. I have

no desire to do anything. You know this is not like me. I am usually the best

dressed, best groomed woman in the room. And I love to socialize. You

should see me today. I look like a bum! I just can't get over Jack!

Maybe I should have just stayed back there when I came home last month. Maybe I should just move back now. I am miserable at work. My new boss, Cliff, is a lech. He always is making these sexual comments to me, staring at me and accidentally on purpose brushing up against me. He creeps me out! I don't know what to do! I know working here is a great opportunity, but I am miserable. I just want to go back to working for and being with Jack.

Maybe I should fan these family photos right out here on the counter right under her nose. Won't she be surprised to see a picture of her Mr. Married Boss Guy aka My Husband Jack tanning with me beside him. That would really knock her off of her stool! Susan smiles to herself. No, I think I will keep this a secret a bit longer. Rose and Nico look over at Susan as she is playing with the family photos. They hold their breaths waiting to see what Susan is going to do. Susan puts them back into her tote bag. Rose and Nico exhale deeply!

Muffin and coffee arrive. She just looks at them. Doesn't touch them.

What am I going to do? I have never been this miserable over a guy before. Well truth be told no one has ever rejected me before. I am always the rejector. This is new territory for me, and I don't like it!!! Worst part is, I know he wants to be with me too! How could he not?! I am sure he just feels an obligation to that wife of his. They do have children together. But who cares- he has a right to be happy too! Maybe I should write him a letter telling him that I still want to be with him, that he hasn't lost his chance with me and that we could be awesome together. We have so much in common- we both come from Chicago, we both are architects (well, I am not technically one yet, but I will be), we are both beautiful ☺ But most of all, there is that undeniable attraction between us- we just have chemistry- the kind you can't manufacture in a lab!

That's what I am going to do- I am going to write him a letter- Okay, gotta go!
Hope all is well with you and the fam!

Talk to you this weekend. Oh, I almost forgot it's 4th of July weekend... that's perfect! I'll ask him to meet me to watch fireworks!   That will be so romantic! Are you going down to the high school to watch fireworks like always? Have a big juicy dog with lots of mustard and kraut for me!

Love you, Maggie

Folds stationary.   Stuffs into matching envelope. Bites cold muffin. Sips cold coffee.

Don't get out your red, white and blue outfit yet, honey! My husband will be with me on the 4th of July.

Fresh stationary out.

Dearest Jack,

I just wanted to tell you how much I miss you! I miss our late night dinners! I miss working with you! I miss your laugh! I miss talking to you! I miss the way you look at me so lovingly! I miss the way you wipe chili off of my face! I miss you protecting me from stalker dates. I miss the way you touched me so softly and gently the night we made love!

Loud throat clearing from Susan.

I just MISS YOU!   I want us back!   I know you must miss me too! Please don't think I won't take you back. I am still here.   I still want to be with you. Please don't throw your life away because you feel some sort of obligation to your wife.

More throat clearing from Susan. Rose and Nico look over at Susan with raised eyebrows. Susan snarls her lip in Her direction.

She looks up. Susan, Rose and Nico put their heads down and go back to sipping tea, cleaning counter and cooking, respectively.

Another bite of cold muffin. Another sip of cold coffee. Pen back to paper.

I know we would be so happy together.   I totally understand if you want to keep things the way they are at work, but please don't shut me out of your life. I can be discreet. We can take things slowly. I am not even asking you to leave your wife right now. No demands. I just want to be with you!

This weekend is 4th of July. I would love to watch fireworks with you. We can recreate our own fireworks like we did the night we spent at my apartment.   I'm going to make us a picnic dinner, and we can go watch fireworks at the beach. I will wait for you at my apartment.   The door will be open – just come on in.   Please come, Jack! I will wait for you!

Looking forward to being with you again!

xoxoxoxoxoxoxoxoxox, Maggie

Folds stationary in thirds. Places it on the counter. She thinks for a moment then takes out her deep sensuous red lipstick, applies it carefully then

unfolds the letter and kisses the bottom leaving a big
red lipstick mark.

Satisfied, refolds the letter. Stuffs it into a
matching envelope. Takes out perfume. Spritzes
envelope with perfume.

Big loud sneeze from Susan.

"Sorry! God bless you!"

"No problem. Thank you."

No, God Bless You, You Wanna Be Homewrecker,
because you are going to need it if you keep messing
with my husband!   You'd better pack a picnic for one
because there is no way my husband is joining you!
You red-lipped tramp!!!!

Packs up. Pays. Leaves.

"So, what did little Miss Thing have to write
today?"   Rose asks as soon as the door closes behind
Her.

"That little tramp wrote a letter to Jack asking
him to meet her for 4th of July fireworks. She said
she was going to wait for him with a picnic. I think
Jack and I and the kids are due for a little impromptu
get-away!"

"Good for you, honey. Get out of town.   Let
that little hussy eat alone!"

"I can show her some fireworks, if you want,
Susan."

"Thanks, Nico. But I don't want you to get
burned. She's explosive! I better get going. Seems
that I have a weekend get-away to plan!"

"Happy 4th, Susan!"

"You, too, Rose, Nico!"

CHAPTER 25

The answering machine light blinks furiously as Jack walks into the office on Tuesday morning after the three day weekend. Oh God, why I am afraid to listen to my voice messages. I just pray it's not more messages from Maggie. The 11 messages she left on my cell phone over the weekend were enough. I couldn't even bring myself to listen to them until I was in the car on my way to work this morning. They really creeped me out.

MESSAGE 1- Friday, JULY 4TH, 2014, 5:45 P.M

Hey, baby. It's me, Maggie. Just wondering what time you are going to get here. Fireworks start at 9:00 p.m. Can't wait to see you. I've really missed you. Picnic is all ready.

MESSAGE 2- Friday, JULY 4TH, 2014, 6:15 P.M.

Hi, sweetie. Just checking in again. Hope you are on your way. Can't wait for you to see me in my Independence Day outfit. I think you'll really like it. (Cackles) I've got the red, white and blue covered. Well the white and blue are in the open but you'll have to go looking for the red. (Insane laughter)

MESSAGE 3- Friday, JULY 4TH, 2014, 8:47 P.M.

Hey. Fireworks start soon.   I haven't eaten. I'm still waiting for you. You'll love my Brownies.   Be careful driving. Hope you are okay. See you soon.

MESSAGE 4- Friday, JULY 4TH, 2014, 11:59 P.M.

Well, 4th of July is over in one minute. I guess we aren't spending it together. I wish you could have come. You know what, if you are still planning on coming, it's okay, still come. Even if I am sleeping, I'll just get up. I miss you! Hope you are okay.

MESSAGE 5- Saturday, JULY 5TH, 2014, 9:14 A.M.

Aren't you up yet? I just wanted to say sorry you weren't able to come last night. But don't worry, I'm not mad. I just want to see you. I understand if something got in the way. Call me please!

MESSAGE 6- Saturday, JULY 5TH, 2014, 5: 41 P.M.

Where are you, Jack? I really need to talk to you. Please call me.

MESSAGE 7- Sunday, JULY 6th, 2014, 7:52 A.M.

Jack, please call me. I HAVE to talk to you.

MESSAGE 8- Sunday, JULY 6th, 2:34 P.M.

Is your phone broken???? Why aren't you calling me back?

MESSAGE 9- Monday, JULY 7TH, 2014, 6:13 A.M.

Hey, I was hoping to catch you on your way to work. I need to talk to you. Please call me.

MESSAGE 10- Monday, JULY 7TH, 2014 7:02 A.M.

Jack, call me! Please!

MESSAGE 11- Monday, JULY 7TH, 2014, 8:00 A.M.

Hey. You are not there yet? Alright, I'll just see you when I get there. I need to talk to you. Hope you are okay.

Don't you get it, Maggie? I don't want to talk to you! That's why I didn't pick up or return your calls. Get it, Maggie! Leave me alone.

Catalina would have been perfect if I hadn't seen Maggie's caller ID number on my cell phone every twenty minutes. She is really beginning to freak me out. Visions of Glenn Close pop into my head now every time I think of Maggie. It was so sweet of Susan to plan the impromptu weekend get-away. The kids loved it. The fireworks were amazing. Why did Maggie have to infringe on my good time.

Did she really think I was going to show up at her apartment to spend the 4th with her? She must be nuts. I have not given her any indication that I want to be with her since that one night mistake. Even that night I didn't come on to her.   To this day it is still foggy as to what happened. I certainly never had any intention of sleeping with her. What is wrong with her?

Okay Jack, brave it, listen to your messages, just do it.

Closes office door. Locks it. Pushes playback. Automated woman's voice announces:

You have 13 messages:

Message 1- Friday, July 4th, 2014, 5:55 p.m.

Hi Jack. It's me Maggie. I'm here at my apartment waiting for you. It's 6:00 p.m. I left you a message on your cell phone, but you didn't answer, obviously. Anyway I thought you might be at work.   The fireworks start at 9:00 p.m.   I made us a great picnic. Brownies. I know you love those. I hope you get here soon.

Message 2- Friday, July 4th, 2014, 6:27 p.m.

Hi Jack. It's me Maggie again.   I was hoping you'd be there. Okay, I'm here.   Picnic is ready. I'm all decked out in red, white and blue. Although you'll have to look for the red. You can't see it at first glance. You'll have to dig deep if you get my meaning. (Crazy laughter) Looking forward to watching fireworks with you and doing whatever else that pops up! (More crazy laughter)

Message 3- Friday, July 4th, 2014, 9:00 p.m.

Well, I guess we are going to miss the fireworks. But that's okay, you are probably just held up with family obligations. Still come. We can still eat brownies and you can still look for the red! (Insane chuckle) Can't wait to see you!

Message 4- Friday, July 4th, 2014, 10:30 p.m.

I'm still up. Please come over! I want to see you so badly. Even if it is for just a little while.

Message 5- Saturday, July 5th, 2014, 8:59 a.m.

I thought I might catch you at work this morning. I know sometimes you go in for a little while on the weekends. I was really disappointed you weren't able to make it last night. I hope you are okay. Please call me. I'll be around all day. You do still have my cell number, right? Well, just in case, it's (310) 555-5678. Hope you are having a good morning!

Message 6- Sunday, July 6th, 2014, 11:47 a.m.

I guess you didn't make it in to work this morning either. Just wanted to say "hi," so my voice is the first thing you hear when you get to work. I really miss you, Jack!

Knock knock. Ouch. Jack bangs his knee as he jumps off of his chair. The chair goes toppling.

"Hey, Jack, it's me Cliff. You in there? Your door is locked."

Jack opens door rubbing knee.

"Hey. Sorry I must have accidentally locked the door. What's up?"

"Is Maggie in here?"

"No! Why would Maggie be in here? She doesn't work for me anymore. She works for you. Why would you think she is in here?"

"Relax dude. Man you're jumpy! I just thought I heard her voice."

"Well, she is not in here. I was just listening to my voice messages and maybe you heard Ms. Katz' message. Her voice sounds a little like Maggie's. But Maggie is not in here. Haven't seen her in a long time. She never comes by anymore now that she works for you."

"Okay. Got it. She is not in here. Anyway, just wanted to know if you had a copy of the drafts you did for the condominium complex you did in New Mexico last year. I might want to copy some of your designs."

"Sure. No problem. Ask Betty. She does the filing. She should know where a copy is. Speaking of Maggie. I thought you were hot for her. Anything happening there?"

"No, nothing. She is definitely not interested in me. Not that I won't keep trying. But she seems to be hung up on someone else."

"Did she say that? Did she tell you who she is hung up on?"

"No. I can just tell. Maybe it's you, dude. The whole office knows what a crush she had on you!"

"It's not me. Don't be ridiculous. I don't even talk to her anymore, let alone see her. It must be someone else. What do you mean the whole office knows she had a crush on me. She never said anything to me. That's absurd."

"I was just kidding. Relax. Hard weekend? You seem really on edge! Nice tan by the way."

"Sorry, dude. Thanks. We went to Catalina for the weekend. It was a last minute thing Susan planned. It was great, but I guess I am not back into work mode yet. Anyway, ask Betty for those drafts."

"Cool. Catch you later."

"Later."

Jack, you are so lame. What is wrong with you! Calm down, man! You are going to get everyone talking if you keep acting like this. Deep breath.

Resumes listening to messages.

Message 7- Sunday, July 6th, 2014, 4:37 p.m.

Please call when you get this.

Message 8- Sunday, July 6th, 2014, 8:32 p.m.

I thought maybe you came in late to catch up on some work since we didn't work on Friday. This 3 day weekend has been so lonely without you. I am already in bed. Wish you were here with me!

Message 9- Monday, July 7th, 2014, 6:43 a.m.

I was hoping you were at work early and I could come in and see you. Please call me right when you get this. I really need to talk to you.

Message 10- Monday, July 7th, 2014, 7:15 a.m.

You're still not there. I guess you had a long weekend, huh?!

Message 11- Monday, July 7th, 2014, 7:52 a.m.

What the heck, Jack?! Why aren't you calling me back?   Let's meet for lunch today before I have to be at the office. Please!

Message 12- Monday, July 7th, 2014, 8:16 a.m.

Are you even coming in to work today?   You never come in this late. Are you trying to avoid me?

Message 13- Monday, July 7th, 2014, 8:51 a.m.

Well, I guess I'll just see you when I get to work.   Don't be afraid about talking to me. I am not mad that you didn't show up Friday night. I understand you have certain obligations. We can make this work, Jack. Trust me. We'll talk when I get there.   Hope you are having a good morning.   See you in a bit.   Kisses!

DELETE ALL!

"Betty, I will be out of the office the rest of the day. Call me if you need me."

"Will do, Jack. Oh and um, I have all of your travel arrangements made for this weekend for your conference in Arizona."

"Awesome. You're the best. See you tomorrow."

Jack, you can't keep avoiding Maggie. You can't leave the office just because you are afraid of running into that psycho!   I know. Just today. One more day. Tomorrow I will figure out what do about her.

CHAPTER 26

"Good morning, Susan. How was the weekend?"

"Hey, Rose. Nico. Bobby. It was great! The weather was great. The fireworks display was amazing. It was wonderful!"

"That's what Bobby said, too. That was very nice of you to let him go along. If things keep going so well between Bobby and Sophie, we may be family someday!"

"Sophie is too young to be thinking that far in advance. But, you never know. We love Bobby. Don't we, Bobby?"

"Huh, did you say something, Susan?"

"Don't worry, Bobby. I was just saying how we all really love you!"

"Aww, thanks! Thanks again for the weekend. I had a blast."

"No worries. We were glad you could come. What did you do, Rose? And anyway we are already like family!"

"So true. You are like the daughter I always wanted."

"Thank you! And you are like a second mom to me."

"Thank you! Anyway… Saul and I went over to my sister's house and we played canasta and ate hot dogs."

"Sounds fun. What about you, Nico?"

"I don't remember. I think it involved girls and beer. My cousin and I woke up on the beach in our boxers. I'm sure I had a good time!"

"Oh, to be young and reckless!"

Rose leans in closer and whispers, "Any updates on the other situation?"

"Not really. Jack seemed very happy all weekend. His cell phone was ringing off the hook though. Finally he just turned it off.   Poor Little Miss Thing had to spend the 4th all by herself.   Boo-hoo!" Rose and Susan share a laugh!

"And then he came home early from work yesterday. He said he just needed one more day to rest. He didn't get much rest though. All the kids were out for the day. We made our own fireworks." Wink, wink. Susan blushes.

"I wonder if She'll come in today!"

"She's probably at home licking her wounds!" More shared laughter.

She doesn't come.

Unfortunately for Susan, She is elsewhere planning her next attack.

CHAPTER 27

Susan is not in a good mood when she walks into
Eggsactly the following Tuesday morning. Jack came
home from his weekend conference in a foul mood. He
was uncharacteristically snapping at everyone. He
said he was just tired, but Susan sensed it was
something more. He didn't snap out of it on Monday
either. However, his mood did change from grumpy to
forlorn. When he got home from work he went straight
to bed. Didn't even come down for dinner. Susan knew
something was wrong, but was afraid to probe too much
given the secret she already knew.

When She walks into the diner just moments after
Susan, Susan knows it is just about to get worse. She
sits down on the stool right next to Susan.

She smiles from diamond studded ear to diamond
studded ear. Her hair is back to looking like the
finest, shiniest, black, long flowing silk. Her eyes
sparkle like never before. Her cream colored fitted
shirtdress snugs her curvaceous figure in all the
right spots and her caramel colored strappy heels make
her legs look like works of art.

"Good morning! Beautiful day, isn't it? May I
please have the Eggs Benedict with a side of pancakes
and home fries and a big glass of fresh orange juice.
Thank you!"

Her cheeriness makes Susan want to vomit! The
scent of Her perfume pierces the air, overpowering the
smell of bacon frying in pig fat. It really pisses
Susan off. Susan sneezes loudly!

"God bless you, ma'am! Hope you are not catching

a cold!"

"Thanks!" How dare she call me ma'am! All of the sudden she cares about my health?! We have been sitting next to each other for months and she never so much has blinked in my direction and now she wishes me good health. Well, screw her! Oh my god, what's wrong with me. I never talk like that. Well, I guess at least I didn't say it out loud, but I don't even usually think like that. Relax, Susan. There could be many reasons why she is all of the sudden in such a good mood. She could have a new boyfriend. She could have won the lottery. She could have rekindled her romance with the guy from back home. It doesn't necessarily have anything to do with Jack. But then why do I have this sinking feeling that it does?!

Stationary out. Pen out.

Dear Molly,

What a great weekend! I am on the road to recovery! Don't ever count me out! Thank goodness, because after the 4th of July weekend I thought I might be out of the game. Alright, so remember I told you that I had asked Jack to meet me to watch fireworks on the 4th and he never showed up? I was really bummed, but then Cliff (my boss) told me in passing conversation that Jack's wife had planned a surprise weekend for their family and they spent the whole weekend in Catalina. (I haven't been there yet, but I hear it's a really quaint little island that's just a short boat ride over from here. Maybe when you come out next month we can go and check it out. It would be a great day trip! I am sure the kids would love it!)

Orange juice arrives. Slurps through a straw.

So, I began thinking that it wasn't that Jack didn't want to be with me on the 4th, but he had no choice. His pathetic wife just swept him away.

Susan loudly clears her throat. Rose and Nico look over. She rolls her eyes in Maggie's direction.

"Would you like a cough drop, ma'am? I think I have some in my purse."

"No. Thank you." Again with the ma'am. Isn't she chatty Cathy today?! And soooo helpful!

I think the woman sitting next to me has a cold. I want to move seats, but I don't want to be rude. I'll just turn my back to her.

Shoot. I can't see her letter. Her back is blocking it.

"OH NOOOO! I am so sorry, Rose. I don't know I how I just spilled my water glass. Luckily I caught it before it fell to the floor and broke, but this seat is soaking. I'll just move down a couple of seats. Oh, I'm sorry, ma'am, did I get you wet? Did your letter get wet?" Ma'am right back at you, you Little Miss Cheery!

"No, I'm fine. The letter is fine. I can move down though."

"Oh no, I don't want to trouble you. I will just move to the seat on your other side. Luckily it's open. Sometimes this place is packed shoulder to shoulder."

"Don't worry, Susan. I'll take care of this."

"Thanks, Rose. Sorry."

She can't turn her back to me now or else her precious little letter will get wet! Take that ma'am!

Now the woman with a cold just spilled a whole glass of water all over the place. What a klutz! Luckily she didn't get my shoes wet! They're brand new- Jimmy Choos! I know you're thinking I shouldn't be spending all that money on shoes, but what the heck, I am going to marry me a rich architect soon!   So, I splurged a little!

```
    Breakfast arrives.  Pours half the bottle of
syrup on the pancakes.  Eats.  Eats. Eats.
```

Okay, so anyway back to Jack~ So, since I realized that Jack hadn't intentionally stood me up, I decided to forgive him. I figured he didn't call me because he was too afraid that I was going to be mad at him for being a no-show. I wanted to let him know that I forgave him, but I didn't see him all week. I didn't see him on the Monday after the weekend because he apparently decided to leave early and work from home. Then I was out of the office on both Tuesday and Wednesday because I had to go with Cliff to check out some new site. We were gone all day, both days. That guy really gets on my nerves by the way. He is so needy. Don't you hate that in a guy?! He just fawns all over me- yuck!   Then on Thursday Jack was in meetings all day, so I didn't get to see him again.   But my opportunity to make my next move arose!

```
    Eats more.  Drinks more.
```

I went to Jack's office to finally talk to him, but he wasn't there. Like I said, he was in a meeting. I asked his secretary when she thought he would be done. She told me she thought the meeting would last all day because they had a lot of things to finalize on Jack's new project before he left on Friday for his conference in Arizona for the weekend.   Being the sly devil that I am- I engaged Miss Betty- that's his secretary, in conversation about where Jack would be staying. I explained that I had been there many times and just wanted to know if he was staying at a nice hotel because even though some of the hotels sound prestigious they are really below standard. I assured her that the hotel she booked, Four Seasons Scottsdale, was up to standards.   She was so thankful for my expertise on this matter because she "would hate to send Jack to some dumpy hotel!"

I must stop shaking and sweating. This is bad. I can feel that this story is not going to get better! Maybe I should have some more tea. Maybe that will calm my nerves.

"Rose, may I please have some more hot water?"

"Sure, honey." Susan and Rose's eyes meet. Rose can see how uncomfortable Susan has become. Oh my, what is that girl writing. I do hope for Susan's sake that it's not more bad news!

I went right back to my desk and booked a plane ticket to Scottsdale for Saturday afternoon. I knew Jack would be in the conference all day, so there was no point to lose beauty sleep to get on an earlier flight. I wanted to go Friday, but being so wise with my money ☺ I figured I shouldn't take Friday off of work. And it's cheaper to fly on Saturdays. Did you know that?

You will not believe how easy it was to get a key to Jack's room. I simply explained to the front desk agent that I was Jack's wife and had come to surprise him.   He took one look at me and handed the key right over. I really must say- I looked hot. I am sure he was thinking he wished he had a hot wife like me! Just like that song- Don't Cha Wish Your Girlfriend Was

Hot Like Me!

She begins humming and twerking in her seat.

If she doesn't stop humming and twerking, I am going to throw her down any minute!!! Oh my! Who am I?!?! Deep breaths, Susan, deep breaths! In and out. In and out.

She finishes her own private concert and resumes writing.

So, I went right into Jack's room. I called down to room service and ordered the honeymoon special- champagne, chocolate covered strawberries and roses sprinkled all over the bed in a heart shape. I took a shower, shaved everywhere (I know TMI), sprayed myself with perfume, applied lipstick and put on a sexy little black teddy. By the time I got out of the bathroom, the room was ready. The room service attendant had come and placed the roses on the bed in the heart shape while I was in the shower. (Luckily I didn't walk out naked- that would have been some tip for the room service guy!) The champagne and strawberries were chilling. I dimmed the lights and waited.

Orders another orange juice.

Jack got back to the room a little after ten. I had set out a glass of champagne for him with a note to enjoy himself, signed Love, Your Wife. Okay, so it was a little deceitful, but I didn't want him to get all paranoid and righteous and freak out before he saw me. I waited for a little while in the bathroom until he had a chance to drink the champagne and anticipate my entrance- well, technically his wife's entrance, but I figured he would be all the more happy to see me. After about a few minutes, I appeared in the bathroom doorway in my teddy and heels (Yes, I bought new heels, too- don't kill me- it was worth it!).   I must have looked really hot standing there with only candlelight illuminating me.   I took his breath away- really- I actually heard him gasp!

He pretended to be shocked.   He even tried to tell me to get out. But I could tell he didn't mean it.   How could he?   I guess he did yell at me to leave him alone for a good while, so it wasn't exactly the start I wanted, but it got better.   After about ten minutes, I could tell he was losing resistance.

He slowly started to undress and then just plopped down on the rose covered bed. I got behind him and started to rub his shoulders and back. He tried to push me off, just for show I think, because he really wasn't pushing that hard. I mean if he really wanted me out he totally could have gotten me out. He is so much bigger and stronger than me. I know he was just putting up a fight for appearances; although, of course, no one else was in the room. Whatever- he probably just wanted to have an excuse in case his wife found out- like to say "I was the victim- this beautiful girl got into my bed and I tried to resist, but she just wouldn't leave- what was I to do?"

Deep breath. Deep breath. Calm down Susan. Be strong. You've got to find out the rest now. Don't stop reading!

So we started kissing. Truth be told, I started kissing him, but I know he enjoyed it. He wasn't quite as responsive as I wanted, but given the circumstances, I thought it was to be expected.   After much fondling, I realized he just wasn't "up" for it- if you know what I mean. So we just cuddled all night long. It was really nice. I have never enjoyed spooning as much as I did with him. It felt so real- so right. I just want that for the rest of my life.

> Okay, so he didn't have sex with the slut again. That's a relief. But he did sleep with her all night long. That is almost worse. That is almost more intimate. What am I going to do? Now I can't just chalk it up to a forgivable one-night stand. Stop hyperventilating, Susan. You are going to draw attention to yourself or pass out. Be calm.

Unfortunately, I had an early flight and had to leave before he woke up. I had hoped to have breakfast in bed with him, but he was just so out of it. I left him a note telling him how much I enjoyed being with him and couldn't wait to do it again! All in all, I was happy with the way things turned out. Of course, I would have liked to have made love to him again. But, I am sure it will happen again soon.

I actually haven't seen him since Sunday morning, and he was asleep then, so not sure that actually counts. But, I just know when I see him today everything is going to be back to the way it was between us. Actually better. For some reason, our paths didn't cross at work yesterday, but I know today we'll talk and work everything out. I don't expect him to leave his wife right away, but eventually. I know he has children, so we need to be sensitive to them.

I am so excited about being back with Jack. Can't wait for you to meet him! I just know things are going to work out.

Whew! My hand hurts from writing so much!

How are you? Anything exciting happening over there?

Can't wait to see you here next month. It will be so much fun- you and Jerry and the kids and me and Jack- all hanging out!

I'll call you tonight to let you know how everything goes; although, I am sure it will be great!

Love,

Your Very Happy Sister

Smiles big! Folds stationary. Stuffs envelope. Orders a bowl of bananas and cream.

Can't she leave! I am going to explode if I can't talk to Rose and Nico soon. Go home Home-Wrecker, go!

She relishes her bowl of fruit while Susan seethes and manages to keep the tears in check.

Finally She pays her bill and leaves.

Susan bursts out crying.

"Oh, I knew it was bad! I just knew it! What did She do now?"

"Rose, it happened again! That psycho followed him to his conference in Arizona, pretended to be his wife so the staff would let her into his room, then she seduced him again! They spent all night together!" Buckets of tears pour down Susan's face.

"What a little stinker! Remember, Susan, Jack is not doing the pursuing!"

"Does it really matter now. Now it happened twice. I can't just chalk it up to a one-time mistake. I am going to have to confront him. I hate her!"

"Baby, I am so sorry. Want me to poison her

coffee next time she comes in?"

"Would you, please?"   Little smile.

Nico rubs Susan's back.

"I've got a couple of Sicilian cousins who could break her kneecaps!"

"Good to know, Nico. I will keep that in mind!"

Talking to Rose and Nico really helps. Thank goodness Bobby was off today, so I don't have to worry about him finding out.   I've got to go home and just think before the kids get home. Luckily, the boys are in day camp all day and the girls are out shopping with their friends.

"Thanks Rose, Nico, for listening. I've gotta go sort this out."

"Okay sweetie. Remember we are here if you need us. Everything will be okay. We'll make it okay."

"Thanks! See you Thursday!"

"Let me know if I should call my cousins."

"Thanks, Nico!"

CHAPTER 28

How could I have gotten lost coming home from Eggsactly?! I must really be out of it. I guess the blurry vision from all of these tears didn't help. What am I going to do? I have to confront Jack. This really sucks! How could he do this to me? If he didn't want to be with her he could have called security to have her removed if he didn't want to manhandle her himself. He must have wanted to be with her. What did I do wrong? Am I just not pretty enough for him anymore? Am I too old? Am I too stupid? Oh God help me, but I don't want to lose him! But I **am** super pissed right now. No wonder that jerk has been so grumpy since he has been home- he probably just wanted to continue "spooning" with Her and not come home to his pathetic wife and kids. We probably bore him now that he has Her! He probably feels trapped. Is that my head ringing now? Oh, it's my phone.

Oh no, it's him. I don't want to talk to him right now. Answer it, Susan. Don't be such a baby! You can't just avoid him for Pete's Sakes.

"Hello."

"Hi, LG. How's your day going?"

"Fine! What's up?"

"What's up? Wow! Don't you want to talk to me? How come so cold?"

"That's a funny thing to say after the way you have been since you've been back from your vacation."

"Vacation? It wasn't a vacation. It was a work conference."

"Okay, whatever. What do you want?"

"Ouch! You're right. I have been a bit of a jerk since I've been back. Sorry. Just overwhelmed with work, I guess! Speaking of work, that's why I am calling. I just wanted to let you know that I am going to be late tonight."

"That's great. You weren't home all weekend then you've been a jerk since you got back and now you are going to be late. Terrific. Hope you get your work done."

"My, you're pissed. Are you okay? You are usually so understanding about my work."

"Just fine."

"You don't sound fine. Sorry, Susan. Look, after tonight everything will be back to normal. I'll make it up to you this weekend on our date night. Think about where you want to go. I'll go/do wherever you want!"

"Fine. Gotta go, my other line is beeping. It might be one of the kids."

"Okay. Love you! Be home as soon as I can!"

"Sure. Have fun with work!"

He is going to meet Her tonight. I just know it. What if he comes home and tells me he wants a divorce. Oh my God, I can't handle this! Maybe I should just surprise him at work. No, that will just prolong the inevitable. I guess I will just have to confront him on "date night." That way it'll just be the two of us and we can spare the kids. How did this happen to me? Toughen up, Susan. Whatever happens, you can handle it! You are a strong woman. No, I'm not! I need Jack! I need things to go back

to the way they were before that slithering-letter-
writing-hussy came into our lives!

Deep breaths! Deep breaths!

CHAPTER 29

If I didn't know better, I'd think Susan knew about what happened this weekend with Maggie. But that's impossible. There is no way she could know. But then why was she so hostile to me right now. She is never so un-understanding about my work. I do feel badly about lying to her about working late tonight, but in a way it is work related. I know Maggie from work.

I just have to get this Maggie situation under control. When Maggie meets me tonight, I am just going to lay it all out on the line. Either she stops stalking me or, not only is she going to be fired, but I am going to go to the police and get a restraining order. Sneaking into my room in another state- that was way too far! This girl is nuts!

How could a girl as beautiful as her be so whack-o and desperate? This bizarre behavior is going to end tonight.

What even happened this weekend? I guess the Martinis at dinner and the glass of champagne in the room really hit me. It is all such a fog. One minute I am standing in the room looking at the beautiful heart shaped rose arrangement covering the bed, sipping champagne and expecting Susan to come out of hiding and then the next moment there is Maggie standing in the bathroom doorway looking like this crazy seductress. I know I told her to leave, but then it gets so blurry. All of the sudden, I just felt dizzy and hazy. Next thing I know, it's morning and I am all alone. At first I thought I must have just dreamt that Maggie was there, but then I saw her note *"Thanks for a wonderful evening, sleepyhead! Sorry I had to leave so early. We'll make it up! Xoxoxoxo, Maggie"*

I'm almost 100% sure we didn't have sex! Okay maybe 95%! Alright maybe 80%! Maybe it's more like 60%! Shoot, I hope we didn't have sex!

It is going to end tonight! I will make it up to Susan this weekend on "date night!"

CHAPTER 30

Please don't let Her be here today! The past two days have been so hard- trying to be cordial to Jack without blowing up. When he came home on Tuesday night, it was all I could do to not scratch his eyes out! He came home acting all satisfied as if everything was all right with the world. Doesn't he realize he is breaking my heart? How can he be living such a lie? I guess only two more days until everything is out in the open. Oh and his constant talking about "date night" and making the past week up to me- give me a break! Does he really think taking me to a fancy restaurant will make up for his illicit affair? Why did he have to be so weak?!!

Darn! There She is! What a difference a couple of days make. She looks like shit! Excuse my language.   Are those tear streaks I see on her cheek? Yep! Good!   She better not sit right next to me or else I might have to push her fat ass off of her stool. Excuse my language again! To be honest, not fat, but it is big! Sure enough, right next to me.

"Just coffee."   What, no please today, Little Miss So Happy!

Stationary out. Pen out.

Molly,

Sorry I haven't returned your calls. Things did not turn out the way I had expected- to say the least.   I am devastated! When I got to work on Tuesday I finally saw Jack for the first time since our wonderful night together in Arizona.   He asked me to meet him after work for a cup of coffee. I was so excited. I knew he was finally going to profess his undying love for me!

I knew he was meeting her that night! Working
late, my ass!

Coffee arrives. Ignores it.

Boy was I wrong. I left work early to go get a mani/pedi and arrived at the coffee shop 10 minutes early. I had butterflies in my stomach from the excitement of the anticipation.

He got there right on time, which I saw as a good sign, except that he looked all somber and serious- not the look of one who is bursting with love and excited to see their lover. He immediately tore into me- telling me that I have to stop "stalking" him. Stalking? I am not a stalker. I may initiate things, but stalker- please! He told me that in no uncertain terms- he was not interested in me and he was going to fire me and get a restraining order if I did not leave him alone. Can you imagine a man wanting a restraining order against me? What is he gay? I was in shock! I couldn't believe he was saying all of these things after the nights we spent together. If he really didn't have feelings for me, he never would have made mad passionate love to me the first time or spent the night with me that second time in Arizona. Why is he being such a pussy! (Sorry I know you don't like that word!)

I tried to convince him that he was just feeling guilty and that he shouldn't throw away what we had out of some sort of obligation to his wife. He actually laughed in my face. He said we didn't have anything and he wasn't with his wife out of obligation but out of love. Barf! Give me a break!

I know he feels something for me.   How do I get him to come to his senses?

I thought things were going so perfectly.   Of course I had hoped that we would have made love in Arizona, but I guess that really was my fault. I shouldn't have doubled the amount of "roofies" I slipped into his champagne.

Loud gasp!

All eyes turn to Susan.

"Are you okay, ma'am?"

"Yes, just fine. Thank you!" Said through clenched teeth. Rose and Nico look over. Susan nods indicating she will tell them what's going on later. Oh my god, this woman drugged my husband. Thank you, God! But, this is bad! This is really bad! But at least it wasn't Jack's fault. Whew!

Oh, did I forget to mention that I kind of, maybe a little, sort of slipped Jack a little itty bitty "roofie"?   Yeees, I did it the first time, too, if you are wondering.   Don't be mad— you're married. In this day and age, a girl has to do what a girl has to do! I guess I gave him too much the second time.   The first time it worked like a charm.

Anyway, I just figured that once he got a taste of me he wouldn't be able to resist. I never expected him to take his vows so seriously!

How am I going to get him to come back to me?   I am not giving up! I hope he doesn't think for one moment that the threat of being fired or a court ordered restraining order is going to make me give up on us. What we have is too special!   He will see that! I just know it. But for now, I just need to shower.

I wish you were here!

Miss you!

Love, Your Very Depressed Sister

Doesn't touch coffee. Pays bill. Folds stationary. Stuffs into envelope. Addresses envelope. Leaves.

"Hurry, Rose, give me a piece of paper and a pencil."

"Sure, honey. Here you go. Are you okay?"

"Much better."

"What are you writing?"

"Her address. Aren't letters with return addresses the bomb!"

"What are you going to do? Go to her house?"

"Not today. But you never know when it may come in handy."

"What did she write that has made you so happy?"

"She drugged my husband! She put 'roofies' in his drink." Susan yells with delight.

"Oh my God! And that makes you happy?"

"Very! Now I can't blame Jack! He had no control."

"And what is a 'roofie' by the way?"

"I think it is also called 'the date rape' drug. I don't know much about it. But it is all over the news now-a-days. I think it is some sort of drug with sedative, hypnotic and amnesiac effects. People, usually men, slip them into drinks at bars and then the women are easier to get into bed. The women are less resistive and can't remember what happened. I saw a story about it on the news a few months ago."

"What are you going to do? Are you going to go to the police?"

"Oh, no! This nice girl will take care of this herself. You know you can only push us nice girls around for so long until we break. The police will just make a big mess of this. And Jack doesn't need this kind of publicity. I will make her pay my way."

"You are scaring me!"

"Me, too!" Nico joins the conversation.

"What's your plan?"

"I don't know yet. But it'll be good. Let me tell you about the one other time some little hussy tried to steal my man.   It was the eighth grade."

"You had hussies in the eighth grade?"

"Oh yes. Amanda Burns. The original hussy. Amanda was my arch enemy. We were both popular but were in different cliques. She was daddy's little princess and was used to always getting her way. She always had the perfect hair and the most expensive designer clothes.   She was such a snob. If you didn't live in a mansion, have a maid and a chauffeur she wouldn't have anything to do with you.   I am not saying that I didn't grow up well-to-do, but I didn't rub it in people's faces. I still had chores and limits to what I could spend.   I didn't judge people based on how much their daddy made.

Anyway, it was right before the spring dance. I was infatuated with Peter Norse. I loved him since the sixth grade when he moved up here from Newport Beach.   He was the typical surfer boy- blonde hair, blue eyes, always wore OP shirts and shorts and flip-flops.   He was so cool! Well, he finally asked me

out- to the spring dance. I was so excited. My mom
bought me this awesome pink strapless dress and
matching pink shoes. My sister, Barbara, said I
looked like an Easter Peep, but I didn't care. I've
always loved Peeps. What's there not to love?
Marshmallows and colored sugar in cute bunny and chick
shapes. Yum!

Anyway, I was so looking forward to the dance.
Then all of the sudden, my world came crashing down.
Thursday, two days before the dance, Peter calls me
and tells me he doesn't want to go with me anymore.
He tells me that he decided to go with Amanda. And,
oh sorry, hope there are no hard feelings.

Well there were hard feelings. I couldn't
believe it! Not only was I being dumped by the love of
my life, but for my rival Amanda. It was more than I
could bear.

My mom let me stay home on Friday because I was
so upset, but my best friend, Kelly, called me when
she got home from school to give me the scoop. She
told me she heard from Jan who heard it from Sandra
who was Tony's sister who was Peter's best friend that
Amanda had told Peter that I was going to dump him at
the dance for this new guy at our school, Charlie, and
since she felt so sorry for him she would go with him
to the dance to show me. I was so mad, but there was
no way I was going to let that little princess put one
over on me.

So, I called Peter. I figured Peter was too
stupid to be mad at and anyway he was duped too. I
told him I had no intention of dumping him for
Charlie. I didn't even know Charlie and I had really

wanted to go with him. He apologized for being so stupid and said he should have just asked me before he called off our date, but if I was still willing, he really wanted to go with me too. I agreed and convinced him to not tell Amanda.

Boy was she mad when Peter never showed to pick her up for the dance. There she was in her custom made designer dress with nowhere to go! Serves her right!"

"Sounds like she got what she deserved!"

"Oh yes, she did. But it didn't end there. I didn't think being stood up was quite enough for what she did to me. So for the next week I made it my mission to get back at that tramp! It started with putting a tuna fish sandwich in the back of her locker. Every day she would come to school with a gourmet homemade lunch packaged in a pretty painted gift bag secured with a frilly bow from her mom. It was as if she were getting a present for lunch every day. Anyway on Monday, I saw her toss her gift bag in the trash can and I picked it out.

On Friday, the last day of school before Spring Break, I enlisted Peter to help me. Amanda had just opened up her locker when Peter called her over to speak to her. She left her locker wide open and went over to speak with Peter. Luckily for me, the girl was not only a snob but a slob too. I guess since she didn't have a maid at school, there wasn't anyone to straighten out her locker for her. It looked like a dump site. Anyway, I walked by and threw her lunch bag with the tuna fish sandwich I made with lots of mayonnaise, into the back, so it was hidden.

I didn't plan on the maggots, but they were just an added bonus. When we got back from Spring Break, Little Miss Amanda opened her locker to a reeking odor and hundreds of maggots crawling all over. Rumor had it that her daddy paid the janitor to clean and disinfect the locker, but that wasn't good enough for Amanda. She had to be given her own personal locker in the teacher's lounge. Amanda never knew I was behind the sandwich escapade. She just figured she had forgotten about that lunch and had left it in there."

"Remind me to never make you mad at me!"

"I could never be mad at you, Nico! But that wasn't the only revenge I got. I didn't even plan the next thing. It just fell into my lap as it were.

Amanda and I were in the same American History class. That same Friday before Spring Break started, our history report was due. We had been working on this assignment all year. We were all given a date in history and a state and we had to write a story as if we were someone living at that time and place and describe what was going on. I had 1843 in Massachusetts. I got a B. It was actually a really fun assignment.

Anyway, we had to pass our reports up to the front of the class. Amanda sat in back. When the pile of reports got to me, I saw Amanda's sticking out. That's when I got the idea. My book bag was opened at my feet. I leaned down as if I was getting my report out of my bag and just slipped Amanda's report into my bag. I threw it away on my way home from school in a dumpster behind this grocery store.

Apparently, Mr. Johnson, our teacher, called Amanda's parents at home on Saturday and told them Amanda had not turned in her report and if she didn't have the report on his desk first thing on Monday morning after Spring Break he would have to fail her. Word had it, Amanda cried and insisted she turned in her report and yelled someone must have stolen it. Unfortunately for Amanda, she was known to lie, so no one believed her. For once her parents couldn't get special treatment for their daughter. So, Amanda had to recreate her report during the Spring Break. You know we didn't use computers back then and apparently Amanda had thrown away all of her research materials and rough drafts, so she had to start all over from scratch. The best part was she had been bragging all year long about how she was going to Paris over Spring Break with her cousin. Well, she had to cancel!

When we got back from Spring Break, she accused me of stealing her report, to which I, of course, played ignorant and acted as if I had no idea what she was talking about.   She never found out."

"Wow, I never would have thought you had that in you, Susan."

"Like I said, you can only push nice girls so far!"

"What's the plan for your revenge here?"

"I don't know yet. But believe me it will be good. Oh, I gotta go. I need to go shopping for something extra special to wear on 'date night.'   See you all later!"

"Bye, Susan!"

"Ciao, Susan!"

CHAPTER 31

"How was "date night?" Nico yells from the
kitchen as Susan walks into Eggsactly on Tuesday
morning.

"Great. Well, mostly great." Okay, don't see
Bobby or Her here, so I can talk freely.

"Jack was waiting for me in the living room when
I entered in my new 'date night' outfit. He
definitely liked it. I must say I did look pretty
sexy for a forty-something woman. I bought this
awesome turquoise wrap-around dress and a pair of
white strappy high-heeled sandals. I wore them with
my big sapphire hoop earrings."

"I'm sure you looked sexy for a twenty-something
woman!"

"Thanks, Nico. Anyway, we toyed with the idea of
staying in, but I didn't want to waste my new outfit,
so we drove up to Geoffrey's. You know that
restaurant in Malibu overlooking the ocean."

"I've heard of that restaurant and have been
asking Saul to take me there for years, but of course
he hasn't. He said maybe on our fiftieth wedding
anniversary. I don't think I want to wait another 15
years. Who knows if we will still be together then!
Maybe I will find me some young stud to take me there
before then. Maybe Nico here and I will hook up.
Hook up- that's what you young kids say, right?"

"Yes, that's what we young kids say!" Susan
laughs. "Although Nico would be lucky to have you,
I'm sure you and Saul will still be together. You are
too perfectly matched, Rose!"

"A girl can dream though!"

"Saul is a dream!"

"Yes he is. He's my dream. Anyway back to your 'date night.'"

"Okay, so as we are leaving the house, I notice this silver Jetta parked down the street. And it looks like someone is sitting in the car, but I couldn't see that well. For some reason it gave me this uneasy feeling. Anyway, Jack and I put the top down on our Mercedes and drive up the coast. It was a beautiful night, all warm and seductive.

Everything is going great at the restaurant. Jack is back to his normal self. We are flirting like we always do, when all of the sudden I notice Her sitting at the bar staring at us!"

"Her? You mean, Maggie? The letter writer? The hussy? The homewrecker? The seductress?"

"The one and only! We were sitting kind of far away, so I don't think she recognized me. I looked so different than when I come in here. I was all dressed up and in here I'm all sloppy.   But to be sure she didn't see me, I moved my chair so my back was facing her. I got so nervous, but I didn't want to tell Jack, or else I'd have to explain the whole thing and I didn't want to get into it. The night was going so well.

Jack did notice though that I was all of the sudden so uncomfortable because he commented on it. I just blew it off as if I was antsy to get back home to continue our 'date night' in the privacy of our own home. That seemed to satisfy him. But, I think he also may have seen her because all of the sudden he started getting weird. So there we are both seeing her and both pretending that nothing's going on. Luckily we were already eating dessert when we saw her, so she didn't ruin our entire dinner. We both kind of rushed through the dessert on the pretense that we couldn't wait to be alone.

On our way home, both of us were slyly looking in the rearview mirror, and there she was in that silver Jetta that I had seen parked in front of our place when we first left. I didn't know if I should say something or not because now she was kind of scaring me. Anyway, I didn't say anything and neither did Jack. At one point, I noticed she wasn't behind us anymore. When we got home, she was already parked on our street. She must have sped around us. I was actually afraid she was going to confront us and do something, like maybe pull a gun on us or threaten us or something. Luckily, Jack parked the car in our garage and closed it. She stayed there for at least an hour because I looked out the window right after I turned off all the lights for bed and she was still sitting there. That woman is crazy!

Nice girl revenge is now on in full force!"

"My goodness, Susan. Maybe it's time for you to report her to the police!"

"I don't know, Rose. The police are just going to take so long and I want this girl stopped now AND to learn a lesson!"

"I know, honey, but she could hurt you or Jack or the kids."

"I know, but I think I can take care of her. I have some ideas. Nico, I need your help though."

"Whatever you need!   You want me to call in my cousins now?"

"Not yet, but maybe soon."

Nico and Susan plan their first act of revenge.

CHAPTER 32

How am I going to fire Maggie? She doesn't even work for me anymore. Everyone will suspect something if I fire her. What am I going to do? I can't believe Maggie is actually stalking me now. Thank goodness Susan didn't notice anything on 'date night.' The night started out so perfectly, too. Susan looked amazing, so sexy.

Even after all of these years, I still love flirting with Susan. If it hadn't been for Susan's new outfit, we wouldn't have made it out of the house. There I was thinking about what a lucky man I am and about how I wanted to make it up to Susan for the way I had been behaving the past week when she came into the living room in that eye popping dress and those F*** me sandals.

Our little repartees are always so charming!

"WOW! Maybe we should just stay in, LG! I've got some ideas of how we could spend the evening!"

"What and waste this beautiful new dress? I don't think so. You are going to show me a spectacular night on the town, CB. And then maybe, if you are lucky, we can try out some of your ideas when we get home."

"Your wish is my command, lovely lady! I will be on my best behavior to make sure I get lucky later on!"

"Well, don't be on too good behavior- that wouldn't be any fun!"

"Whatever you say!" Aaaaah, and the kiss we shared- so passionate!

"I'd better stop or else we will never get out of here. But you sure do taste yummy! Where are we headed, Miss?"

"The beach!"

"The beach it is!"

I could not believe it when we pulled out onto the street and I saw the Jetta. I knew Maggie drove one, but I just didn't want to believe it was her on my street.

I knew it was definitely her when I handed my car keys to the valet and again saw that silver Jetta two cars behind us in the valet line. Even though the driver was wearing a baseball cap, I just knew it was her. I told myself to shake that dreadful feeling, that it couldn't be her. But sure enough, it was. Thank God we got through dinner before I noticed her at the bar. What a psycho! What was she thinking?

I was actually afraid that she might try to drive us off the road on the way home. Boy was I thankful when we lost her. But then there she was, back on our street. She must have driven like Danica Patrick to get there before us.

I am such a wuss! I didn't do anything. Luckily, Maggie just watched and didn't take any action. How I was able to remain calm and make love to Susan knowing Maggie the Stalker was outside is beyond me. I guess I am just good- excellent, according to Susan! God I love her so much. Please let this Maggie thing pass!

Okay, Jack, be a man! Stop making threats to Maggie and DO something! But what?! How am I going to resolve this situation without getting Susan

involved? She doesn't need to be hurt or scared by
this.   Breathe, Jack! Breathe! Think and act!

CHAPTER 33

Susan sits smugly in her Eggsactly spot the following week hoping for Her arrival. She does not disappoint.

She enters and heads straight for the last seat at the counter, three seats down from Susan. Her head is down and her hoodie is up.

Sits and removes the hoodie.

Oh My Gosh!!! She looks like Cruella de Vil in a blender!

Orders black coffee. Oatmeal. No cinnamon roll. Stationary out. Pen out. Writes.

Dear Molly,

You are not going to believe what happened! I think I am cursed! It was the most bizarre weekend.

Friday night I am home alone (unfortunately!) drowning in my depression when I hear knocking on the front door. I answer it, and it is a Domino's Pizza delivery guy delivering my pizza – only thing is, I didn't order a pizza. He says "Aren't you Maggie Papadopoulos?" (Of course, he doesn't pronounce it correctly. He makes it sound more like a board game than the beautiful Greek last name that it is!) Anyway, obviously, I reply yes, but I explain I didn't order the pizza. He gets pissed thinking I just changed my mind and leaves in a huff. I'm thinking that's weird – how did he know my name and address.

Coffee arrives. Sips.

So about a half hour later there's another knock on the door. I go to get it and it is a Chinese food delivery guy with enough food for a party of eight. He also says he has a delivery for Maggie Papadopoulos (you can only imagine the way the Chinese guy tried to pronounce our last name– it sounded like a fatal disease). Again I didn't place an order. This guy was more than pissed! He started yelling at me that I would have to pay for it or he was going to call the police. At least I think that is what he was yelling. His accent was so thick and part of it was in Chinese. He was so loud that some neighbors came out to see what all the fuss was.   He finally left after about 15 minutes of yelling at me and calling me names in both broken English and Chinese.

Oatmeal arrives. Adds brown sugar, raisins and milk. Eats.

15 minutes later I get another delivery from another pizza restaurant.   30 minutes after that another delivery from a different Chinese restaurant.   1 hour later another pizza delivery.   All of the delivery guys knew my name.   I didn't order any of them or had never ordered from them before. Clearly, someone was playing a joke on me, but I can't imagine who.   Maybe some neighborhood kids have seen me and got my name from my mailbox? I don't know. Anyway, it was irritating and embarrassing.

Then yesterday morning I am taking a shower and washing my hair when I start smelling something that does not smell like my regular shampoo. My head is all lathered up.   The smell was seriously overwhelming! At first, I couldn't figure out what the smell was but then I realized it smelled like bleach. My eyes starting watering. I quickly rinsed out my hair but apparently not quick enough.   Chunks of my hair started falling out. And I do mean chunks.   As if that wasn't bad enough, the hair

150

that remained on my head was streaked with white - I looked/look like a messed up raccoon. Of course, I started freaking out. I called the customer service number on the back of the shampoo bottle, but, of course, they denied any wrongdoing. The woman on the phone accused me of using the shampoo bottle for some cleaning purpose and then forgetting about it and putting it on my head. As if I am that stupid!

Eats more.

I immediately called my hairdresser to see if she could fix it and luckily she said she had an opening right then, but I had to hurry down to the salon. I threw on some sweats and called work to tell them I was going to be late. I rushed out to my car and backed up to pull out of the space - the car in front of me and the car behind me had boxed me in, so I started to work my way out. But I didn't get that far. (By the way it is all parallel parking here. I never had to parallel park back at home. I hate it!!!) Anyway, I backed up and then heard the sound of a popping tire and felt my car slowly leaning to the right. I went to check it out and sure enough someone had left a broken Dr. Pepper bottle behind my back passenger tire - who even drinks Dr. Pepper anymore?!!

I couldn't drive, so I had to cancel my hair appointment. She didn't have another one for another week. I know I could go to someone else but you know how fussy I am about my hair. When I find someone I like I am afraid to trust anyone else. So for the next week I am walking around looking like Pepe' Le Pew on a bad hair day.

Then I had to wait for the AAA guy to come. As my luck would have it, my tire warranty just expired last month, so I had to pay for a new tire out of pocket. Actually two tires because the guy selling me the tires said

that it would put my car out of alignment if I only got one tire. It cost me

over $300.00. Just what I need when I am already struggling financially. I

still haven't found a suitable roommate. And I know my hair is going to

probably cost at least a couple of hundred to fix. Since everything took so

long, I didn't make it into work. I am not looking forward to all the jokes

about my hair today.

Drinks more. Eats more.

For once I don't want to see Jack at work today. I look so horrible. If

he didn't want me before, he certainly won't want me now.

Last week I so wished you were here. I kind of, sort of, just a little

stalked Jack. It was a week ago Saturday. I first parked on his street and

watched his house. Remember how we used to do that back in high school

when you liked Derek? So don't get all hoity-toity on me. I know I am

supposed to be more mature now, but whatever...

Anyway I sat there for about a half hour when he and his wife came

out. As usual he was looking hot in his black short sleeved button down shirt,

jeans and loafers. His wife looked pretty, too, I guess, if you like the Barbie

doll type. They got into their Mercedes and put the top down. (That is so

the life I want!) Anyway I don't know what possessed me, but I followed

them. They went to this celebrity filled restaurant in Malibu overlooking the

ocean. I even followed them into the restaurant. I sat at the bar and just

watched them. It really made me sick to see them together. They looked

like this perfect couple without a care in the world. Little does his wife know

that her husband isn't all that faithful. I just wanted to tell her right then and there, but I stopped myself.   The place was filled with all these rich Malibu types, including a bunch of celebrities- Pamela Anderson, Courtney Cox, John Stamos- boy is he still hot! And he is Greek, too.   I should have just flirted with him when his wife stepped away from the table. I'm sure I could have gotten him to ditch his wife.   Anyway, I just didn't have it in me. I was just too focused on my Jack! Since I didn't want to make a scene, I just sat there and watched Jack and his wife.

Jack may have seen me, but he didn't say or do anything. When they left I followed them- well half way- half way home, well to Jack's home, I sped around them and went and parked back on their street. I didn't have a plan at that point. I guess I just wanted to watch them a bit more. They looked all lovey-dovey! It really pissed me off.   I thought again about confronting him in front of her, but talked myself out of it. I still want Jack, and I didn't think that would get me any closer to getting him.   I am still trying to figure out what to do next. I am not giving up!

Finishes cold oatmeal and coffee.

So, anything exciting happening with you? ☺ Only two more weeks until you come- Yay!!!   Can't wait. Hope Jack and I are back together by then. If not, you can help me figure out how to snag him! ☺

Tell everyone I said "hi."

Miss you,

Your Frazzled Salt and Pepper haired Sister

Stuffs envelope. Pays. Leaves.

Even though She sat too far away for me to read her letter today, I didn't need to. I know all about the weekend, Susan smiles.

"Thanks, Nico!"

Nico winks and raises his bottle of Dr. Pepper in a gesture of cheers.

"Please tell your friend I said thank you, too!"

Nico comes closer and whispers conspiratorially, "Will do, Susan. Wasn't that a stroke of luck that Benny does the maintenance at Her building. He enjoyed helping out. He said it was no problem getting into her place and filling her shampoo bottle with bleach. He just wished he had the kind that didn't smell. Are you done with her?"

"Not yet. Just the beginning! War's on!"

CHAPTER 34

Phone rings incessantly Thursday morning as Susan is making sandwiches for all the kids who are over for the impromptu pool day.   By the time she answers it, the caller has hung up. The caller ID reads "private number."   This happens six more times in the next two hours. Susan almost doesn't answer the phone the seventh time, but can't resist.

"WHAT?"

"Susan, is that you? Are you okay?"

"Debbie is that you? Oh my God, I am so sorry. The phone has been ringing off the hook all morning, but by the time I answer it, the caller hangs up. It's not you, is it?"

"No, it's not me. This is the first time I've called today. Sounds like you have a stalker or maybe Jack is having an affair and it's his mistress calling, but hangs up when you answer. You know that old joke- hang up if a man answers!"

"It is NOT a stalker and Jack is NOT having an affair. Just because Larry had an affair, don't go assuming all men are having an affair! What did you want?"

"Whoa, relax, Susan, I was joking. Sorry. Hit a nerve, huh?"

"Sorry, Deb. I have 10 kids swimming here. I guess I just am a bit frazzled. Sorry. What's new?"

Get a grip, Susan. Hopefully Debbie bought that lame excuse about being frazzled because of the pack of kids.

"No worries. I was just thinking that it's been

two months since Larry and I split and it is time for
me to have some fun. Want to go out this weekend?"

"Sure. Sounds great. I have an awesome idea.
How about you, me, Jack and Dave- remember Jack's
cousin- go out. Dave and his girlfriend just split up
and I think he could use some cheering up too. We
could go dancing like we used to when we were in
college."

"Sounds perfect. Gosh, why didn't Dave and I
ever hook up?"

"I don't know because I know he had a crush on
you for a long time."

"Really? I had a crush on him, too. But I think
he had a girlfriend at the time."

"Maybe just bad timing. Maybe the time will be
right now."

"Don't get ahead of yourself. It's just dancing
with old friends."

"Whatever you say. Want to go buy something new
to wear tomorrow?"

"Okay. Can't hurt to look sexy for my first
night out since my failed marriage."

"That-a-girl! Century City tomorrow? We can do
lunch first."

"Perfect. How about 12:30 p.m.?"

"Great. The kids all have other plans. I'm
totally free. Maybe I'll get something new, too.
Can't let you out-sexy me."

"Never! See you tomorrow."

"Looking forward to it. Kisses!"

Whew, Debbie bought it. I just know the caller
is Jack's little stalker. Okay, Missy, bleached

156

hair, a flat tire and multiple deliveries clearly weren't enough.   Now I am going to get serious!

Susan calls Cherise and Drew.

CHAPTER 35

Susan sits in her usual spot Tuesday morning. It
is exceptionally busy today. Rose and Nico are too
busy to talk. Summer tourism always brings business
to the diner. Bobby is off for the day. He and
Sophie are at the beach together.

Susan smiles as she relives the weekend.

Saturday night was so much fun with Debbie and
Dave. There may be a love connection sprouting.
Finally, after all of these years. Debbie did look
sexy in her new LBD. Dave seemed to think so, too.
The Paradise Beach Cove was so much fun. Jack and I
need to go there more often. It's so romantic and
fun.

It would be so awesome if Dave and Debbie became
a couple. How perfect would that be? They are both
such good people. They deserve to be with someone
equally good. I am so glad Debbie is finally rid of
Larry. It seemed she is already over it too. And
Dave's last girlfriend- Mata- was pretty much a
nightmare, too. Beautiful, but what a prima donna.
They way she used to boss Dave around made me sick.
Debbie would be so good for him. Too bad they didn't
get together when we were all in college together. Oh
well, better late than never.

I wonder how Little Miss Telephone Stalker's
weekend was. I hope it went as planned. Hopefully
She'll come into Eggsactly today, so I can read her
take on it.

In She walks.

Boy, She looks like hell.

```
Rose, Nico and Susan all eye each other with a
secret smirk.
     She sits right next to Susan. Unpacks. Orders
coffee. Cinnamon roll.  Pen out. Stationary out.
Writes.
```

Dear Molly,

I think I may be going mad. Someone is definitely messing with me. You almost got a call from your sister this weekend from jail. Yes, you read that right- JAIL! I have never been so scared in my entire life. I am still so shaken up, I can't even talk about it. That's why I haven't called you. But hopefully I will be able to get it down on paper.

So Sunday night I am sitting outside of Jack's house- yes I am still 'stalking' him!- get over it. I hadn't seen him all week since I was avoiding him because of my hair situation.   So I was definitely jonesing on seeing him. Anyway, it's about ten o'clock and I've been there for about an hour, nothing much going on. I saw him walk by the front window a few times, but nothing else really. I called the house line a few times and hung up (alright maybe more like five times, but who's counting?).

```
     Coffee and cinnamon roll arrive.  Eats and
drinks.
```

Anyway, I decide to call it a night but first call him one more time. So as I am pulling away from the curb and dialing his number, I see flashing red lights in my rearview mirror.   I start thinking that maybe someone in the neighborhood had a problem and called the police- maybe a domestic fight or something- not that one would expect a domestic fight in the type of neighborhood, but you never know.

159

So I drive down the street and the red flashing lights are following me- ME! Then I hear a voice over a bull horn ordering me to pull over. I was so confused. I hadn't done anything. I had just started to pull away. So I pull over and this huge- I mean huge- 6'7'' at least, guessing 300 pounds- cop who is as dark as the night, comes over to my window and asks for my license and registration.

I ask him what the problem is and he just grunts and repeats that he needs to see my license and registration. Of course, I give it to him, but was utterly confused as to what I had done. He goes back to his patrol car and gets on his walkie-talkie, apparently he radios in my information and then comes back and orders me out of my car.

I ask him again what I did, and he still won't give me a straight answer. Just orders me out again. I hesitated a bit, I guess, so then he asks if I want to add resisting arrest to my charges. I get out, he reads me my rights and then does a pat-down search of my enitre body. I was so scared especially when his hands lingered for quite a long time on my butt. I still didn't know what I did. Then he puts me in handcuffs and puts me in the back of his car. He then locks up my car and gets into the patrol car with me. By this time I am hysterically crying and screaming at him to tell me what I did.

Finally, he tells me that he has had several calls reporting that I was trespassing in the area and causing a nuisance. Moreover he says he saw me talking on my cell phone while driving. I explain to him it was a public street and I was just sitting in my car not causing anyone any harm and I had just pulled away from the curb when I started to use my phone. He

tells me, the calls were from several residents in the neighborhood who felt I

was a threat, and moreover, the laws had just changed, so that talking on a

cell phone while driving- no matter how short the distance- was not only a

citable offense but a jailable offense.

Breaks. Inhales deeply. Shakes out wrist.
Resumes writing.

He then drives around for about ½ hour before we get to some bizarre

looking police station on the lot of Fox Studios- you know the movie studio.

The police station is this flimsy looking small grey building in the middle of

what looks like a street from an old Western movie. Anyway, I ask him why

we are at the movie studio and he gives me some lame excuse that because

the crime occurred on a residential street in the middle of the night this was

the only police station available to book me. Huh? I didn't get it, but Mr.

Big Bad Policeman was in no mood to explain further. So we go into the

building and there is this one lone weasly looking policeman behind the front

desk. He's like 5''2', 110 pounds, stringy brown hair, a long pointy nose,

receding chin and beady brown eyes.

Mr. Big and Bad and Mr. Weasly leave me handcuffed in the front

and go into the back to have some private tete-a-tete. When they come

out Mr. Weasly tells me that they will need to strip search me! That's right-

STRIP SEARCH! I freaked out! This was way too much. I start screaming

and asking for the captain or sergeant or whoever is in charge. Mr. Big and

Bad and Mr. Weasly tell me no one else is in the station and push me into

the one and only cell in the back. I notice that there are no other prisoners.

They order me to get undressed and wait for them in the cell. I didn't know

what to do. I was so scared! So I got undressed, afraid of what they would

do to me if I didn't follow orders. I am sitting buck naked on what looks

like a bug infested cot for what seemed like an hour just waiting. Finally Mr.

Weasly comes to tell me "It's your lucky day, lady. We have another more

pressing and dire incident to take care of, so we are going to have to let you

go. Get dressed!" But then before I could get dressed he snaps a photo of

me - naked! He mumbles as he walks out, "Booking photo." Whoever

heard of a naked booking photo! Anyway, then I got dressed as fast as I

could.

Then Mr. Big and Bad comes to get me and tells me because of the

other emergency he and Police Officer Weasly (not the name he used!) had to

leave and so they couldn't wait around for someone to pick me up. He said

they would drop me off on the way to the other emergency. But, they

couldn't take me all the way to my car because it was out of the way, so he

would leave me off about ½ way and then I could call a ride. I reminded him

that he had confiscated my cell phone when he arrested me. To which he

says that because of the circumstances he is going to give me back my phone,

but that I should take this as a warning and he better not find me

trespassing, stalking, being a general nuisance or talking on my cell phone

while driving ever again. In fact, he continued, he was going to post my

booking photo on the police department's in-house web-site to advise other

officers to be on alert.

Then all three of us piled into the patrol car and they ordered me to get out somewhere near Westwood and Santa Monica Boulevard.   I know

you don't know the area, but it's a fairly large intersection in Westwood.

There was a gas station, so I waited there for an UBER which took about an

hour. Apparently it was a busy night and right around the time the bars

closed.

When I got back to my car, I quickly got in and started to drive

home. Don't think this nightmare is over yet!   About three blocks down the

road, my car starts sputtering and then finally just dies.   I call AAA and

wait! - Another hour! Apparently they were having a busy night, too. AAA

guy tells me I am out of gas which is really weird since I just filled it up that

morning.   Then all of the sudden I remembered- as I got back into my car

after the UBER dropped me off, I did smell something odd, but I was so

focused on getting home and ending the night I didn't check it out.   The

AAA guy brought a couple of gallons of gas with him, so he was able to start

up my car.   I went back to check out the area where my car was parked

and sure enough there was a puddle of what looked like and smelled like gas.

After getting some more gas, I finally drove home where I stayed in bed until

this morning. I called in sick yesterday.

Sighs deeply. Rests hand. Eats. Drinks. Resumes writing.

This morning I woke up early to have my car checked out and go file

a complaint with the police department for the way I was treated. The guy

at the auto shop told me nothing was wrong with my gas tank and that

someone just must have siphoned my gas out. Why would anyone do that to

me?!!! It just doesn't make any sense.

Then I went back to Fox Studios to file the complaint at their on-site police station where I was taken. The security guard wouldn't let me in and told me that they don't have an on-site police station. I kept insisting that they did and told him about how I was held in a cell there on Sunday night. He just laughed at me and wouldn't let me pass.

I called several other police stations to ask if they had a station at Fox Studios, and they told me no. I gave them both Mr. Big and Bad's and Mr. Weasly's names and ID numbers which I got off of their badges, and they said no such people worked for the police station and there were no such ID numbers.

I am in such a fog. It was so unreal. And now I feel like I am going crazy, not being able to even find the police station where I was held captive. I keep waiting for Aston Kutcher to jump out and tell me I've been Punk'd.

Pen down. Shakes hand. Eats. Drinks. Ponders.

I am really freaked out. So many bizarre things are happening to me. What did I do to deserve this? I just wish I could cry on Jack's shoulder. How long will it take for him to realize I am the one for him?!!! Speaking of Jack, I better go. I'm already late for work. I'll call you tonight.

Love, Your Almost Convict Sister

One last sip of coffee. Pays bill. Packs up quickly. Leaves.

As soon as the door closes behind Her, Rose and Nico pounce on Susan. Drew, Marion and Cherise also come out of hiding from the corner table where they have been sitting since about 15 minutes after She walked in.

"So did it work?" Cherise is the first to speak.

"It certainly seems so. Little Missy is apparently very freaked out. Although 'she just doesn't understand how this could happen to her.'" Susan mimics in a poor-me voice.

"Thank you all so much!"

"Glad to be able to help. I guess working for the studios all those years has its fringe benefits. Luckily, they hadn't dismantled the police station set before we needed it. I talked to my friend, Rusty, the set designer, yesterday. He said they tore it down first thing Monday morning.   Hopefully she won't see the new Hugh Jackman movie or she just might recognize the police station and jail cell." Drew laughs.

"Oh wouldn't that be hilarious. I can just see her in a movie theatre on a date watching the Jackman film when the police station comes on screen and she freaks out. I would have loved to have been there when she was explaining to the security guard how she was locked up at the police station on the lot by 'Mr. Big and Bad' and 'Mr. Weasly.'" Susan squeals.

"Awww, she called my friends 'Mr. Big and Bad' and 'Mr. Weasly'? Toby and Raymond will be so hurt!" Cherise giggles.   "I actually spoke to both of them this morning and they said to say 'thanks.' They had a blast and love their memento. They're going to tack her picture up on their refrigerator door to remind them why they are gay!   Neither of them have had any good acting gigs lately, so they loved it."

"Please tell them all I said 'thank you!'"

"Any more plots in the making?"

"Not yet, Nico. But I will let you all know if I

need any more assistance. Thank you!"

"Cool. Oh and my cousin told me to tell you 'thank you.' He was just out of gas that night, so Little Missy's gas came in real handy for him, especially with gas prices these days!"

"Please tell him he is more than welcome, Nico. Anytime!" They all burst out laughing!

CHAPTER 36

Hello Cruella De Vil! That Maggie sure looked like a mess! I almost felt sorry for her. But then that psycho stalker personality came out and any sympathy I felt for her went right out the window. What was she thinking? Coming in here all sad-like and miserable telling me about all her problems- the multiple food deliveries, the tampered shampoo bottle, the flat tire, the bizarre non-existent police episode, the empty gas tank! Maybe she is on drugs and just making these things up. There is no way that whole police story could be true.

Anyway here I am just listening to her, being a nice guy, lending her my shoulder to cry on, when all of the sudden she just grabs my face and kisses me, full-on on the mouth. Why does she not get it? I am not interested in her!!!! Thank god Philip came in and scared her off! But the way Philip looked at me as if Maggie and I were having some sort of illicit affair, oh no! I explained to him that she was just telling me her problems and gave me a thank-you kiss. Thank-you kiss, right! Philip did not buy it for one moment. His conspiratorial wink said it all.   Why can't she just find some single guy to latch onto?

CHAPTER 37

Susan settles in at her usual spot at Eggsactly feeling like the world is back in alignment.   I can just feel we are done with Little Miss Homewrecker and things can get back to normal.   Maybe she will finally pack up and move back home. She must be feeling doomed right about now. No one could handle all the "bizarre" events she has been through lately without feeling the effects. To celebrate I will order something really decadent- maybe Rose's famous Stuffed French Toast! YUM!

You've got to be kidding me. What is She doing here?!!! And why is she looking so hot?!!! Perfectly snug form fitting jeans that show off her perfectly round butt so perfectly. Starched white buttoned-down man's shirt, unbuttoned down to her firm perfectly rounded breasts, revealing just a hint of a white lacy bra that just makes her look sexy not manly at all.   High heeled royal blue sandals that show off her newly painted red toenails.   Freshly washed and perfectly dyed hair flowing down her back with soft sexy curls!

What is up?   This cannot be the same girl that was here two days ago!   What is she a Super Human Bionic Robotic Creature? Unbreakable? Indestructible? Invincible?   How dare She sit down right next to me!! Can't She feel my venomous stare?   How can She be so oblivious? Maybe I will just end this all and stab Her with my fork until she bleeds to death!!!   No, better yet, maybe I will push Her face in Rose's waffle iron until she is permanently scarred.   No.

Wouldn't want to ruin Rose's mother's waffle iron that has been in the family for fifty years. Okay, get a grip, Susan. Maybe she is just over everything and moving on. Who knows maybe she met someone new, uhm, yeah, like yesterday! Right! Okay just breathe!

Smiles. All smiles. Pen out. Paper out.

"Good morning! Hope you are having as wonderful a day as I am! May I please have an order of wheat toast and some coffee. No, scratch that. I'm starving. How about an order of your famous wonderful Stuffed French Toast with a side of crisp bacon and a hot chocolate with lots of whipped cream. Thank you!"

Rose looks at Susan with a "what is this all about" look.

That bitch! She took my Stuffed French Toast. Calm down, Susan. There is enough Stuffed French Toast for everyone. I'm not going to eat what she is eating. I'm not even hungry anymore. I'll just get my usual. Whatever!

Dear Beautiful Sister,

Life is grand! Okay I had a few speed bumps, but now the road is smooth and bump free. Remember how I wasn't feeling all that great on Tuesday? Well, after I wrote you, I went into work. First person I see is Jack, my beloved! I guess I wasn't looking so hot. Anyway, you should have seen the concern in his eyes. It was so sweet!

Food arrives. Dives in. Makes humming noises. Eats half of it ravenously.

So we go into his office and I pour my heart out to him. I tell him about all of the things that have been happening to me from the odd food deliveries, to the tampered shampoo bottle, to the flat tire, to the police escapade, to the gas leak. (Of course, I didn't tell him I was pulled over outside of his house! Full disclosure is completely overrated! ☺) He was so awesome! I could just feel the concern and care. After listening to me so intently, we kissed. It was just like I hoped it to be- so full of love and passion and care. And I didn't even have to drug him! Unfortunately Phil, one of the partners, barged in and interrupted us. I just know the kiss would have led to a behind closed doors office love-making. Oh well, no hurry. It'll happen. Everything I've gone through these past few weeks will be of no importance if Jack and I end up together- which we will- I'm confident!

Loud guttural sound from Susan.

Only one more week until you are here! Yippee! Anything you want to do in particular? I'll have to ask Jack about places we should see. Hopefully he'll be able to join us. We'll definitely have to hit Venice beach- it's like going back in time to the 60's- with all of these sidewalk performers, street vendors and weirdos. And The Grove- this awesome shopping center in between Beverly Hills and West Hollywood. It has a dancing waterfall, restaurants, movie theatre and shops. It's really cool. Lots of celebrities go there. We should probably do Disneyland for the kids. Oh, we'll figure it out. There is so much to do and so little time. I wish you could stay longer than a week!

Can't wait to see you!

Love, Your Rising to the Top again Sister

P.S. I finally had my hair done yesterday, and it looks better than ever. I am back to the stunning beauty I have always been. Mwah-Mwah!!!

Finishes breakfast. All of it! Packs up. Pays. Leaves. Practically skips out. Whistling.

"SHE KISSED HIM AGAIN!!!"

"Susan, honey, shh, voice down. You don't want everyone to hear you!"

"I don't care anymore, Rose. She is CRAZY! Apparently she and Jack kissed again. She told him all about what's been happening and he kissed her!"

"He kissed her?"

"Well, they kissed. I don't know who kissed who first. It doesn't matter. Jack didn't push her away!"

"How do you know, Susan? You are only reading half the story and we know she is crazy and manipulative. She probably threw herself on Jack when he wasn't looking. She's evil!"

"Whatever! It doesn't matter. Now I am going to get serious! I need a plan to put a stop to this for good!"

"You're scaring me, Susan!"

"Don't be scared! It will be good. I just have to think." Susan taps her fingers to her scalp in a Lucy Ricardo thinking manner.

"Rose, Tuesday morning, let's get everyone here-Drew, Marion, Cherise, Eddie, Nico, you and me, and we will devise "Operation Get-the-Bitch-Out-of-Dodge" plan!"

"I'm in!"

CHAPTER 38

Okay, this has gone on way too long now. Why isn't Jack saying anything to me about his Stalker Girlfriend? If it's nothing serious, why doesn't he just tell me? Whatever, I will just deal with it. I know he loves me. He probably just wants to save me from the drama. Just focus, Susan. Debbie and Dave are coming for dinner and swimming. It'll be fun. The kids are all out. It'll be a strictly adult evening.

What's that ringing? Oh, the doorbell. Gosh, you are out of it, Susan! Get a grip on yourself.

"Hey Deb! You look Fab-U-Lous! Oh, hi Dave. I didn't know you two were coming together."

"Yes. We decided to be Green and save gas! Besides Debbie is only 5, 10 okay maybe 20 miles out of my way!" Big Dave smile. Big Debbie blush.

"Jaaaaack- Debbie and Dave are here. Togeeeether! Come on down."

"Don't need to make a big deal about it Suz!" Debbie says in a whisper.

"Hey, guys. You came together, huh?!"

"Hey, Jack. Yes, we came together. Now that everyone is on the same page- Dave and I came together- can we eat? I'm starved."

"Sure, appetizers are on the patio. What can I get you two to drink? Oh Debbie, is that a new outfit?"

"Yes. It's a new outfit! Okay I bought it for tonight. I wanted to impress Dave. Are you impressed Dave? Hope so. Let's go ahead and get this out of

the way too- I am also wearing new underwear!
Everyone satisfied?"

Silence!

"Uhm, gosh, uhm, maybe we should just skip dinner
and swimming and move on to the underwear portion of
tonight's activities, Deb! I'm game! I've been game
since college."

"Shut up, Dave. Let's eat. Underwear's for
later." Wink, wink. Debbie and Dave walk arm in arm
to the patio.

Well, that seems like it is off to a nice start!

"Baby did you buy new underwear, too? Because we
can move to the underwear portion of this program,
too." Charming Jack!

"Sorry, honey, same old married woman's panties.
But they come off easily!" Susan's hand glides down
Jack's chest as she saunters off towards the patio.
See Susan, he still wants you! Stop being paranoid.
It's just that Girl's imagination!

CHAPTER 39

And to think I almost cancelled tomorrow's
meeting of "Operation Get-the-Bitch-Out-of-Dodge!"
That Girl has some nerve. She better not show her face
at Eggsactly tomorrow. How dare she send flowers to
Jack. At Our Home!!! I couldn't believe it when I
went out to get the paper and saw those beautiful
tulips. Of course I thought they were for me from
Jack. After the wonderful weekend we had I thought he
was just topping it off with flowers. What a
disappointment to read the card- *"I'll miss you this week. Would
love for you to meet my family. If you get a break from work and family
obligations please join us! Xo, Maggie"*

Family Obligations!!! Jack is not obligated!
Jack wants to be with his family! That chick is
crazy! How dare She try to cause problems for us!

Well at least it gave me a chance to finally ask
Jack about Her. Boy was he sweating when I handed
him the flowers and card. He did look pissed though.
"She's just an intern who has a crush on me. No big
deal."

What does he mean "no big deal." She's seduced
him, drugged him, stalked him, followed him, sent him
flowers. What does he mean "no big deal."?!!? Well,
it won't be a big deal soon. Because she will be
gone! Gone! As God as my witness I will drive that
Girl out of town!

And to think I woke up in such a good mood after
this glorious weekend. Saturday night's dinner and
swimming with Deb and Dave was awesome. So much fun.

Dang, Dave is looking mighty good. Who would have thought he would fill out a mankini so well! Deb should enjoy that, especially after being with flabby, teeny weiny Larry all those years. I've got a good feeling about those two. No doubt Dave got a chance to see Deb's new undies when they left here. Jack also got to see how easily my married woman's panties came off. Thank goodness the kids didn't surprise us and come home early and catch us having our own little skinny dipping pool party after D and D left.

I imagine we looked like a hot romance movie scene. Both of us naked in all our glory looking hot, if I do say so myself, Jack with his ripped abs, golden skin, dark hair and penetrating eyes and me in my tight little yoga body, golden blonde hair and adorable smile, in the moonlight at opposites ends of the pool diving in to meet each other in the middle for some wet wonderful pool love-making. The ripples we made in the water were like a love song. Whew! I'm getting hot just thinking about it!

Sunday was equally enjoyable with our Klein family BBQ. It was great to see all my family. It's been a while since we all got together. I loved the new song Justin and Dustin wrote. It's sure to go Platinum! I can't believe Patrick is off to Harvard in a few weeks. And my little Sophie is a senior- off to college next year. How time flies!

Speaking of time flying- how will I get that Little Miss Stalker to fly right out of town. Hope the Eggsactly gang will have some good ideas tomorrow.

CHAPTER 40

Flowers to my house!   This girl has got to go. No more Mr. Nice Guy. And I am not waiting until she gets back from her vacation. Too bad I am going to interrupt her time with her visiting family. I've got to put a stop to this immediately! It has gone on for too long! I'm calling her right now!

"Hey Maggie. It's Jack. Sorry to bother you…"

"Hey Jack. So great to hear from you! Did you get my flowers? Can you join us? Hope so. My sister would love to meet you. You'll love my brother--in-law. And my niece and nephew are adorable. We're going to Disneyland today. Can you come?"

"That's exactly why I called Maggie. You can't…"

"Great! I knew you'd re-arrange your schedule to join us! When can you be here? We'll wait for you."

"No, Maggie, I can't come. You've got to stop…"

"Today's not good for you. Okay tomorrow then? We're going to the Farmer's Market and The Grove. Want us to pick you up?"

"No Maggie! Not today. Not tomorrow. You have to stop this…"

"The next day then. Whenever is good for you. We'll be hanging out all week. All right then, you have a good day. Don't work too hard! Toodles!"

Click.

She hung up on me!

Oh no! I am not letting this go. I'll just call her back and just say it.

"Maggie, please don't hang up. We need to talk. The flowers…"

"Oh, how sweet! You called back to thank me for the flowers. Molly, he called back to thank me for the flowers. How sweet. My sister says she can't wait to meet you! But I really have to go. The kids are anxious to get going. Kisses!"

Click.

She hung up on me again!

"Maggie.   Don't hang up on me. You cannot send flowers…"

"Hello. Hello. Hello. Is someone there?"

"Maggie. It's me, Jack. Don't hang up!"

"Can't hear you. It must be a bad connection. Oh well. Bye."

"Maggie. Maggie."

Nothing.

She hung on me again!

I'll just call again and get straight to the point.

"Maggie, You're fired!"

"I'm pregnant!"

Silence. Shock.

"Excuse me."

"I'm sorry, Jack. I didn't want to tell you this way. I wanted to surprise you with dinner and candle lights and flowers.   Oh well, the cat's out of the bag. I'm so excited. I hope he looks just like you. We can celebrate next week when my family leaves. Love you baby!"

Click.

"Maggie, are you there? What do you mean you're pregnant? How could that happen? Maggie? Maggie?"

Silence.

Oh my god! This is not possible! Breathe, Jack!
Breathe!   Please God, don't tell me I had sex with
her in Arizona. I was almost certain we did not. At
least 50% sure! Maybe it was more like 40% sure!
WTF! Damn, I have no idea if we had sex or not. That
night is a complete fog! Get a grip, Jack! She is
probably just making this up! That girl is crazy!

CHAPTER 41

Drew and Marion are already at Eggsactly when Susan arrives. Eddie and Cherise arrive just moments later. Luckily the breakfast rush is over, so Nico and Rose are able to sit down with the gang and discuss Susan's problem. Susan brings everyone up-to-date with the latest developments, including Jack's odd behavior the night before.

"Jack acted so oddly last night. When he got home from work he looked defeated- like he had just lost his best friend, his job, his family and his dog. I asked him if it was work related. He just grunted. He wouldn't talk to me. He skipped dinner and went straight to bed. I know he didn't fall asleep though. He was tossing and turning all night. I guess the flowers must have really disturbed him. That girl is ruining our lives. Okay, so any suggestions on how to get rid of Her and get Jack's and my life back on track?"

Nico- "I could have my cousin Guido take out her kneecaps."

"Too messy!"

Rose- "I could poison Her breakfast waffles."

"Too risky!

Marion- "You could ask Her kindly to stay away."

"Too wimpy!

Cherise- "We could find someone to offer Her a job in another state."

"Too difficult!

Eddie- "We could report Her to the police."

"Too complicated!

Drew- "You could offer her a threesome- you, Jack and Her."

"Too gross!"

Marion- "Drew, you're eighty three! Get your mind out of the gutter, dirty-old-man!"

Drew- "You know what they say- if you can't beat 'em, join 'em!"

Apparently the gang is just not creative enough (except for Drew) or devious enough to come up with a plan. Luckily for me I am creative and devious enough. Oh, I've got the perfect plan. And what luck that everyone here either knows someone or has some sort of connection that can help me execute the plan. Watches synchronized. Plan "Operation Get-the-Bitch-Out-of-Dodge"- On your mark. Get Ready! Get Set! Go!

CHAPTER 42

Monday morning! All week I've been dreading this
day. The day Maggie comes back to work. The day I
need to talk to her about, about, about … I can't even
think it, let alone say it. I need to talk to her
about…uhm… her situation. The situation. Our
situation. Oh my god, there had better not be an "our
situation." I've been such a wreck all week. And
Susan has been bouncing off the walls, singing,
dancing, whistling. What is with that? Did she win
the lottery and forget to tell me? I have been such an
ass to her this week. If she did win the lottery, I'd
be lucky if gave me enough money to buy a stick of
gum!

After I speak with Maggie today, everything will
be resolved. She'll tell me that I heard her wrong.
She didn't say pregnant. She said uhm…uhm… what sounds
like pregnant, uhm… uhm… president. Yes, that's it.
She must be the president of a new club.   No, that's
stupid. Okay, maybe she said pregnant, but she didn't
say it was mine. She just said she hopes he looks
like me. It could be anybody's. Who wouldn't want
their son to look like me? I'm a stud! So what if
she said "we'll" celebrate.   She could just mean
"we'll" celebrate her good fortune with some other
man.   Stop fooling yourself, Jack, you know that's
not the case. Stop thinking. You will just have to
confront her. She should be here any minute. She'll
definitely see the note you left her, first thing when
she gets in. You posted it right on her computer.
She can't miss it.

Knock. Knock.

Oh my god. She's here.

"Jack, it's me, Maggie. Can I come in?"

"Yes, please come in. Please close the door
behind you."

"Oh baby. I'm so excited! Aren't you?" Kiss.
Kiss. Hug. Hug. "I know it's not what we planned, but
we'll work it out.   I don't expect you to leave your
family right away. We can work out the logistics
later. Look how big I am already!" Pulls up blouse.
Reveals a perfectly flat tummy!

"Maggie. Stop! Are you sure you are pregnant?"

"Of course!   I missed my period. I am always on
time. Plus, I haven't been feeling well in the
mornings, and my stomach is huge."

"First of all, your stomach is not huge! Second
of all, okay there isn't a second of all. How late
are you?"

"I don't know. I don't keep track."

"Okay, you just said that you are always on time.
How do you know you are late if you don't keep track?
Have you seen a doctor yet?"

"Oh my god, stop being so technical and such a
detective. No, I haven't been to a doctor yet.   I
thought we'd go together the first time. We are
having a baby and that's all that matters."

"Please keep your voice down. I don't want the
whole office to hear."

"I don't care. I want to yell it from the
rooftops. I AM HAVING JACK'S BABY!"

"Shhhhhh! Maggie! How did this happen?"

"You don't know, Jack? And I thought you were so

182

worldly!"   Giggles.

"Maggie, you know what I mean! Are you sure this baby is mine? I don't even remember having sex with you!"

"That hurts, Jack! That really hurts! Of course it is yours. I haven't been with anyone else since we've been together. I wouldn't do that to you. I love you way too much! And to say you don't remember the mad passionate love-making we had in Arizona, that really stings! It wasn't sex, Jack, it was making love. It was one of the best nights of my life. And you don't remember? Wow! Shot right to my heart!" Crocodile tears pour out of Maggie's eyes!

"Maggie, stop right now! We need to figure this out. I will take you to the doctor as soon as possible. When can you get an appointment?"

"I don't know. I don't even have a doctor here. I don't need a doctor to tell me I'm pregnant. I know I am. And I know it's going to be a boy. You are going to have another son! Aren't you excited?"

"No. Maggie. I am not excited. And yes, we do need to go to a doctor. Right away. If you don't have one, I'll look one up on-line."

"I don't want to go to some backwoods on-line doctor. I'll find one myself."

"Fine. Find one. And make an appointment right away. Like tomorrow."

"I can't go tomorrow. I am going with Cliff to a site inspection."

"You'll need to cancel on Cliff. Besides I already told you, you're fired!"

"Fired? You are firing the mother of your child?

This is certainly not the reception I had hoped for when I told you we'd be bringing another child into this world. How can you be so cruel?"

"Maggie, I am not being cruel. I don't know how this got so far out of hand, but it is going to end. Now. If you are pregnant, we'll deal with it. But as far as work goes, you are out of here."

"You sure about that, Jack? I thought you didn't want anyone to know about us."

"Are you threatening me?"

"I wouldn't call it a threat, Jack. But how will it look if I tell people you fired me. I don't even work for you. And then I turn up pregnant. It won't take Einstein to put two and two together. Everyone can feel the chemistry between us."

"Chemistry! What chemistry? You stalking me and making my life a living hell is not chemistry! It's a chemical- a chemical in-balance in you!!!"

"That is no way to talk to the mother of your child, Jack!"

"Fine, Maggie. You can keep working here until we figure something out. But make a doctor's appointment for this week. I'll go with you! Let me know when it is."

"Sure. Now that's more like it. You taking an interest in my well-being and wanting to be with me every step of the way." Light peck on the cheek.

"Please go, Maggie. I need to re-group."

Maggie sashays out, clearly pleased with herself.

Okay. That was painful! Should I tell Susan right away or wait until after Maggie sees a doctor? This is awful! I'll wait. Who knows maybe she isn't even pregnant. God willing!

CHAPTER 43

She walks in just as Rose and Susan are
estimating how long the Plan will take to get Her out
of town.

"Definitely by Christmas!"

Plops down right next to Susan. Fast and
furiously takes out pen and stationary.

"Just coffee, thanks."

Dear Molly,

I may get caught this time. Jack and I talked yesterday. We
discussed my "pregnancy." I don't think he fully believes me. He wants to
go with me to see a doctor. I know you told me when you were here last
week that I may have gone a bit too far- don't want to admit it, but I think
you may be right. I'm bummed you didn't get to meet Jack then you would
see why I am so desperate to keep him. He really is awesome!

What am I going to do? Jack can't go with me to a doctor, then he'll
know I'm not pregnant. I told you I thought I could just buy myself a couple
of months of being "pregnant" and then when Jack was so into me and the
baby, I could just unfortunately have a "miscarriage" or maybe by then I
would actually be pregnant.   I don't know what to do! Do you know
anyone who could send me some phony pregnancy test results?

"Unbelievable!!!" Susan can't help saying it out
loud.

"Excuse me, ma'am, did you say something to me?"

"Oh no, I was just, uhm, talking to myself.
Sorry."

Sips coffee.

What am I going to do? When I see Jack today I know he is going to expect I have a doctor's appointment scheduled. Help!

By the way, I loved you being here last week. It was so much fun! You should move here. I know the kids would love it. I can't believe how much they have grown since I saw them last and it was only a few months ago.

Any ideas on what I should do, please let me know asap!

Xo, Your "Pregnant" Sister ☺

Throws down a couple of dollars. Packs up. Leaves.

"Oh my god, Rose. She has Jack believing she is pregnant with his baby. Poor Jack!"

"But that can't be. You told me they didn't even have sex when she snuck into his hotel room in Arizona."

"I know. But apparently Jack doesn't know. That drug must have really messed him up. She wants to get a fake pregnancy test result. She really is evil. Well, she has met her match. I think we are going to have to tweak our plan a bit and put it into gear sooner than anticipated! I'm going to call Cherise right now and see if she was able to make the arrangements."

"Sounds like a good idea. Let me know how it goes."

CHAPTER 44

I cannot believe it! How could I have gotten Maggie pregnant?! I still don't believe her, even though, she swore to me she took three home pregnancy tests. Until we see a doctor or I see the results of some home test myself, I refuse to believe she is pregnant. This nightmare has to end. I have been such a jerk to Susan and the kids all week. I can't even help myself. I can't imagine what Susan must be thinking. Maybe I should just tell her. Oh I so don't want to do that. Let me just wait a bit longer.

How ironic that today is Sunday- a day to repent. Boy am I repenting. I need to do penance for my behavior this week. What shall I do? I know. I'll take the whole family on a shopping trip. I'll let the girls get some new swanky outfits for school, the boys a new game and Susan a piece of jewelry. I'll be as sweet and patient as a saint. And maybe if I exhibit divine behavior I will be rewarded and Maggie won't be pregnant.

CHAPTER 45

"Poor Jack! Rose, he was such a nightmare last week. I think living with the idea that That Girl is pregnant is too much for him to handle. He was so awful. He yelled at Myles for spilling his drink on the kitchen floor. He never does that. He got mad at Sophie for coming home 10 minutes late. He wouldn't toss a baseball with Sammy. He screamed at Jess for singing too loudly in the shower. He wouldn't even talk or look at me, except to tear into me about having a going away party for my nephew, Patrick, who is off to Harvard next week. He did finally mellow out on Sunday when he took the whole family shopping. Look at my new bracelet by the way. Isn't it beautiful? I've been wanting a pink sapphire piece for so long. I guess some good things are coming out of this nightmare That Girl has caused!"

"Oh my God, that bracelet is beautiful. Too bad I can't get Saul to think that he accidentally got some girl pregnant too. I need a pink sapphire piece, too!"

"Rose, you are too funny! I thought you didn't like to wear bracelets. You said they get in your way."

"Okay, well it doesn't have to be a bracelet, but a nice pair of earrings would do just fine. I think I'll just have to keep dreaming though because I don't think Saul has been with any hottie lately."

"You're the only hottie Saul wants!"

"So true! Anyway, that's too bad Jack has to suffer, but it will be worth it in the long run when

She gets what's coming to her. Were you and Cherise able to get the plan into action?"

"Yes. It's working out perfectly. Plan should be in effect this weekend. Speaking of this weekend, I hope Jack is still not sulking on Saturday during Patrick's going away party."

"I thought you said Jack yelled at you for having the party."

"He did. Do you think a little yelling is going to stop me from throwing a party for my brainiac nephew? I don't think so. You know how I love any reason to throw a party. You and Saul should come by."

"Thanks sweetie, but we can't. That's our bowling team's annual awards night. You'll have to tell me all the details next week."

"You know I will."

"Well, it looks like She's not coming in today."

"Maybe she's at a fake doctor's appointment. Maybe she's having twins! Oh, speaking of which, I gotta go and take the kids to the dentist. See you next week. Have fun at your bowling thing."

"Thanks honey. You have a good weekend too. Can't wait to hear about the party and the "plan.""

"Tell Saul I said 'hi.'"

"Will do. Now get out of here before your kids' teeth fall out!"

CHAPTER 46

Susan strolls into Eggsactly the following
Tuesday as if she is on cloud nine.

"Good morning, everyone!"

"Buon giorno, Bella."

"Nico, you're looking as sexy as ever!"

"Grazie! Now if I could just find a woman as
lovely as you for myself!"

"Hey, Susan. Great party Saturday. Thank you!
That was a lot of fun!"

"Thank you, Bobby! You did great at Trivial
Pursuit, but no one can beat our ace student,
Patrick!"

"Hi honey. Sorry to have missed your party,
Susan, but Saul and I received an award at our Bowling
ceremony."

"What was the category?"

"We won for Best Couple Over 60!"

"Congratulations. Although you both could pass
for forty-somethings!"

"Just for the compliment, breakfast is on the
house!"

"In that case, I'll have my usual with an extra
side of fruit!"

"Patrick's going-away party went well, I take
it."

"It was so much fun, Rose! I went with a Greek
toga theme, you know since he is going to off to
college and all. Everyone came in togas. We served
Greek food- kabobs, pita, hummus, stuffed grape
leaves, spanikopita, souvlaki, baklava. It was so

yummy! We had our own mini Olympics with competitions
in horseshoes, potato sack races, one-legged races,
three-legged races, diving, swimming. By the way your
nephew, Bobby, was the big winner!"

"Of course he was! He gets his physical prowess
from me!"

"No doubt, Rose. But of course, my too smart for
words nephew, Patrick, took home all the prizes for
the trivia contests.   I have to say the funniest
part of the evening was when my poor little Myles lost
his toga, and of course, he was going commando!"

"Awww."

"Yes, his cousin, Justin, stepped on his toga
during
the three-legged race and off it came. He was such a
good sport though. He just busted out some exotic
dance moves and gave us a full-frontal show. No idea
where he got that from!"

"Aunt Rose, I need to head out for a while. I
have to go to UCLA and fill out some paperwork for the
coming semester."

"No problem, Bobby.   Seeing as you are an
Olympic champion, you should take the rest of the day
off."

"Aww, thanks! You're the best aunt.   Cool, I
can go hang out with Sophie."

"Tell her, her mom says 'hi,' please."

"Sure, Susan. I'll probably see you at your
house later."

Bobby leaves.

"Young love, isn't it grand!"

"At any age, love is grand.   Now that Bobby is

gone, I can ask you, did you get the plan in effect?"

"I think so. Speaking of the plan… Hey Cherise."

"Hey Susan, Rose, Nico! Plan is in action."

Before Cherise can say more She walks in.

Sits. Orders. Coffee. Cinnamon roll. Stationary and pen out. Writes.

Dear Molly,

What a strange weekend!   But good, I guess. Nothing much happened Friday or Saturday, just hung out at home mostly, did a little cleaning and some shopping.   There are so many places to shop here. I am spending all of my money before I even make it. But luckily I finally have a roommate.

Coffee arrives.   Blows. Sips.

About 3:30 pm on Sunday, I was home watching television when the doorbell rang which surprised me as I wasn't expecting anyone.   When I opened the door, there was this really cute little woman. She apologized for just stopping by unannounced, but said she was in the area and wanted to know if I was still looking for a roommate. She said she saw my ad on Craigslist which was weird because I thought my ad had expired about a month ago. Anyway, she looked really nice, and so I let her in to look around. She rented the room. She seems too good to be true. I think I may have found a California BFF- don't worry you will always be my number one BFF.

Cinnamon roll arrives.   Nibbles.

She is really pretty, but no competition because we are complete opposites. She's a little thing- about 5 feet, very petite frame, really long golden brown hair, big brown eyes and the sweetest smile with perfect teeth.

If I didn't know better I'd think I was a lesbian the way I am talking about her. LOL!!! Anyway, she is also so sweet. Her name is Melanie. She is in business school at UCLA. She, like me, has a married boyfriend, but he's a doctor. We talked about that for a long time and she was so understanding about my situation. It made me feel really good to be able to talk to someone who understands. She said she and her boyfriend meet in hotel rooms a lot, so she actually will be gone a lot of the time. She actually moved right in. Apparently she had been couch surfing for the past two weeks. We stayed up all night long talking about our boyfriends. Okay, so maybe Jack isn't officially my boyfriend, but he will be. Have you ever known me to give up?!!!

Really excited about my new roommate. Nothing else new except my eyes have been a little blurry the past couple of days, maybe it's stress, who knows!

What's new with you? Is mom really going to get an eye lift? Can't believe dad is going to pay for that!

Talk to you soon!

Miss you!

Your tenacious sister...

P.S. Guess what- Melanie is going to get me some positive pregnancy results from her boyfriend. Isn't that awesome!!! That should buy me some time.

Finishes coffee and muffin. Pays check. Packs up. Leaves.

"Operation Get-The-Bitch-Out-of-Dodge is in

motion!!!! Thanks Cherise!"

"My pleasure, Susan!"

CHAPTER 47

Shit! Shit! Shit! I cannot believe Maggie just
came in with a positive pregnancy test! Should I even
believe her. I told her I wanted to go with her to
the doctor! WTH am I going to do?!!!! Relax Jack!
Okay I know, I'll just call the doctor myself to
verify the test. Why is there no doctor's name on
this result? That is odd. Let me just call Maggie
in here and ask her.

"Maggie, please come to my office asap!"

"Sure baby!"

Baby! I am not her baby, her honey, her
sweetheart, her sugar-pie! And God please don't let
me be her baby daddy! Oh My God, I am watching too
many Maury Povich commercials!

"Ready to celebrate, Jack?" Says Maggie as she
saunters into Jack's office with a big, sexy grin.

"What is the name of your doctor?" Jack cuts
straight to the point.

"Oh my God, Jack, are you still questioning my
pregnancy? Here feel my tummy. You can feel your
baby in there."

"I am not touching your stomach, Maggie! I just
want the name of your doctor! Now!"

"I don't know, Jack! Dr. something …man!
Kleinman, Goldman, Newman…"

"Kindly! Maggie! Go back to your office and look
it up! And then come back here and tell me
immediately!"

"Aye, aye, captain!" Maggie gives a hand salute.

If she does not come back in 5 minutes with the

doctor's name, I swear I am going to harm her!!!

"Here, Mr. Skeptical, his name is Dr. Jackman and here is his number." Maggie throws down a piece of paper with a number on it.

Jack dials frantically.

"Hello, may I please speak with Dr. Jackman."…"Oh, hello Doctor. I wasn't expecting you to answer the phone. My name is Jack Martinelli. I am calling regarding Maggie Papadopoulos. You saw her the other day for a pregnancy test."…"No, I am not her husband. I was just calling to verify the results."…"I see. You can't give them to me without her approval. Well, she is here right now."

Jack covers the phone.

"Maggie, get on the phone right now and authorize the doctor to speak with me!"

"Yes, sir!!!" Takes phone out of Jack's hand while giving him another hand salute. "Hi, Doctor. Yes, this is Maggie Papadopoulos. You saw me the other day. I am the architect from Chicago."… "Oh, that's very nice. I enjoyed meeting you, too!"… "Please feel free to tell Jack anything he wants to know. He is a little bit overwhelmed right now with the good news and all."… "Thank you. See you in a couple of weeks for my check-up." Smugly hands phone back to Jack.

"Hi. This is Jack again. I just wanted verification that these results are accurate."… "I see. And there is no way there could be a mistake?"… "Hmm, hmm. Okay then. Thank you very much!"

"Please leave, Maggie. I need some time to process this."

"What is there to process, Jack? I am having your baby! This is awesome news!!!"

"This. Is. Not. Awesome. News. Maggie! I don't want this baby! I don't want you! I don't want my life ruined!"

"Well, you should have thought of that before you made love to me!"

"I never made love to you, Maggie! If anything, we had sex and that is it. And I don't even remember that!"

"Whatever, Jack! We are having a baby and I hope we can stop this tension and get back to where we were. It's not good for the baby."

"Maggie, please go and let me think."

"Fine, Jack. I'll call you later. Maybe we can go out to dinner and celebrate."

Maggie sashays out of Jack's office.

Is that girl nuts or what!!! How can she still act as if this is a blessing. Dinner?!!! How much more clear can I be that I don't want to go out with her. Alright, Jack, settle down! Most importantly what are you going to do about Susan. Should I tell her tonight? Oh my God, I can't tell her tonight. Tonight we are leaving for Palm Springs for the weekend. The kids will be there as well as Susan's grandma. I have to get out of here! Maybe by next week this nightmare will be over.

CHAPTER 48

Oh my god! I don't know if I can do this anymore. Jack was so miserable this weekend. I felt so awful. Maggie must have shown him her fake pregnancy results on Friday. He came home in such a foul mood. He even threatened to cancel our last get-away weekend to Palm Springs before the kids go back to school. That is so unlike him. And that would have been such a pity. Despite Jack's mood, we had such a good time. It was awesome to see Grandma doing so much better since her fall. The kids had such a great time too. I think I got a little too much sun. But oh well. I don't need to stay wrinkle free, I'm already married! Ha!!!

How long can I go on letting Jack believe he is the father of some non-existent baby? Just a little while longer or else the plan to get Her back will not be able to go forward. And she needs to feel some pain. Jack would never allow us to have our little fun. He is much too honorable. He would just fire her and tell her to leave. That is not enough! She must pay!!!!

Oh, must get ready for Debbie and Dave! So excited they are doing so well! So happy they are available for an impromptu BBQ! Who cares that I am exhausted from driving back from Palm Springs this morning. Maybe I should invite the rest of the family over too. Yes, I'll do that. Jack is probably going to kill me. I'm sure Debbie and Dave are all he can handle while carrying around this burden. But, oh well, life must go on and so must the traditional last

family BBQ of the summer. I hope everyone can come at
the last minute. Hey, I'll call the Eggsactly gang
too. Better get moving.

CHAPTER 49

Susan can't believe how empty Eggsactly is when she walks in on Thursday morning.

"Hey Rose! Did you close down or something and forget to tell me? There is no one here."

"Hey honey! We had a power outage about an hour ago and everyone left. We still don't have any power. All I can offer you is a piece of room temperature apple pie."

"Sold. So I'm going to be all wrinkled from tanning too much and now fat!"

"Never! You don't age, Susan! You are a true beauty!"

"Aww, thanks Rose. Thank you for coming Monday. I had so much fun at the BBQ."

"Thank you!!! Saul and I had a great time. It was like being back at a college party with all of the budding romances and people making out!"

"I know! Debbie and Dave, Cherise and Eddie, Bobby and Sophie, Drew and Marion, Nico and his new little hottie, Me and Jack, You and Saul! So fun! Oh my god- that corn, red pepper, feta salad you made- to die for! I loved it!"

"Thank you! It was so easy! I'll give you the recipe."

"Ciao bella!"

"Hey Nico! Thanks for coming Monday. Who was the new hottie?"

"Oh her! Not so hot when I got her alone. You Americans, you like to talk a lot. I couldn't even get a kiss! Can you believe a guy like me couldn't get a kiss!!! What is wrong with this world! In my country, we kiss first, talk later! I should have known when I first met her, it was in the frozen food section at Whole Foods!   Lucky for me, this town is full of hotties! Susan, you not ready to take me on yet, are you?"

"Not quite yet, Nico! I'm still pretty much in love with my husband, but I'll let you know."

"Yes, yes, the husband!   Looked like things were pretty smoking between you two the other day."

"Smoking indeed!"

"Did the kids get off to school okay? Today is their first day back, right?" Rose inquires.

"Yep.   They all were ready on time. Miracles of miracles! And they all seemed pretty happy to be going. Didn't want to question it too much and jinx it. Both Jack and I drove Sammy and Miles to school."

"That Jack really is a prince."

"He really is. And no one is going to ruin my fairy tale!"

"Too bad you don't have a moat! Oh shh! Here She comes." Rose warns.

Sits. Doesn't even notice the lack of customers. Orders.

"Hi. May I please have banana waffles, side of bacon, cinnamon roll and a glass of carrot juice?"

"Sorry, dear. We lost our power. I can get you the carrot juice. It might be a little warm though. I can see if some of the ice hasn't melted yet.   You can also have a piece of apple pie, room temperature, of course. Sorry, we ran out of cinnamon rolls earlier."

"Oh, okay. The juice will be fine. I'm not that hungry anyway."

Pen out. Stationary out. Writes.

Dear Molly,

How are things? Things are okay! Having a roommate has been great. The situation with Jack still isn't resolved. He insists on getting a second opinion from another doctor and going with me to the appointment. I don't know how I am going to keep putting him off.   I might just have to have a miscarriage a little earlier than planned.

Juice arrives. Drinks. Scrunches nose.

Remember I told you that my eyesight has been blurry, well it is getting worse, and I think my hair is falling out. I'm really very worried. I told Melanie, and she said her boyfriend could come over to the apartment and examine me.   Imagine a house call in this day and age. I think I will take him up on the offer because you know how I hate going to the doctor. He is supposed to come on Sunday. I'm excited to meet him. Melanie says he is really cute and nice. The only negative is that he is married. I so get it!!!! Oh BTW, I am drinking carrot juice, you know how they say carrots help with eyesight!

Finishes juice in one gulp. Makes sour face.

Anything new over there? How was Billie's birthday party? I can't believe he is six years old and I missed his party. Did he get my present? He still likes Wii right? Gotta go, the page is so blurry!

I'll let you know if I miscarry this weekend and what the doctor says.

Love,

Your Blind/Bald Headed Sister

Pays. Packs up. Leaves.

"I almost feel bad about what we are doing."

Rose raises her eyebrows.

"Almost!"   Susan smiles.

CHAPTER 50

YES! YES! YES! Should I really be this ecstatic about someone having a miscarriage? Probably not. But, oh well. I have my doubts that Maggie was really pregnant anyway.

I think there really must be a God! Thank God I did not tell Susan about Maggie. Not that I didn't try. Thursday I told Susan I needed to talk to her before we went to bed. Then I went to the restroom and the next thing I knew she was fast asleep. Weird! She never falls asleep before me, and she always wants to talk. Then Saturday morning I was about to tell her when we woke up when the phone rang and it was Debbie calling to tell us that she and Dave are moving in together. I certainly couldn't ruin Susan's good mood after that. You'd think she has a personal investment in Debbie and Dave being together. She was so happy. I guess that is just how Susan is and one of the reasons I love her so much. She truly is happy for her good friend's good fortunes. She cares so much about the people she loves. She is such a selfless person.

Anyway, then Sunday night I was going to tell Susan when Maggie called crying, insisting I come over and threatening that if I didn't come right away she would tell my wife everything. How could she call the house phone!!! What a close call! When Susan handed me the phone saying it was a girl from work named Maggie, I nearly lost it. I almost threw up everything I had eaten since the beginning of time. I hated lying to Susan and telling her I had to go to the office to pick up some drafts, but I guess it was worth it. All's well that ends well, right?!

What a mess Maggie was! I still don't quite believe she was pregnant, but she certainly put on a good show when I went over there. She looked awful when she opened the door, eyes all bloodshot from crying, hair disheveled, half up/half down, torn sweat pants, a 1970's concert t-shirt and dirty feet. It was almost pathetic.

Gosh, the moment she opened the door she fell into my arms crying, telling me she had a miscarriage that afternoon. Not wanting to be too much of a jerk I helped her to the couch and sat her down. She wouldn't let go of me, so I did let her put her head in my lap while she told me what happened. I hated the way she kept pulling my hand down off the back of the couch to rest on her stomach. Man, does she have a wrestler's grip or what!!! The way she described the stomach pains and gushing blood was very realistic though. However, if it was real, why she didn't go to the hospital, I don't know. Her explanation that her roommate's doctor boyfriend examined her at home is a little strange, but whatever. Who cares! I am off the hook.

And this "rare disease" she says she now has, what was it? Oh yeah, "Magooavalas Syndrome." I have never heard of that, blurry to loss of vision and hair loss. She is probably making that up, too. How can she even think I would accompany her to some specialist in New Mexico. She really is whacked. But she's not my problem anymore. Whew!!!

I really hope I made it perfectly clear that

206

whatever she thought was going on between us is over. Completely over!!! She needs to stop harassing me!! NOW!!!

Back to life as I knew it pre-Maggie! Yes!!!

CHAPTER 51

Thank goodness Jack won't be affected by our Get-the-Bitch-Out-of-Dodge plan anymore. I am certain She must have had her "miscarriage" last night. Jack must have gone over to her house last night when he told me he was going to the office to pick up some drafts he forgot. He never forgets anything. Boy, what a different mood he was in from when he left to when he returned. He left like he was about to walk the plank and came back as if he finally reached the end of the rainbow with its pot of gold and all. What nerve that Girl had calling our house! She really has no shame. Poor Jack looked like he was about to throw up when I told him a girl from work named Maggie was on the phone for him!

I felt so sorry for Jack all weekend. I knew he was trying to tell me about Maggie several times. Gosh was it hard dodging that conversation. I couldn't believe he actually thought I was asleep on Thursday night after he told me we needed to talk. I never fall asleep before him and especially wouldn't if he told me we needed to talk. That is so not me. How could he have bought that!

Thank goodness Debbie called Saturday morning. She really saved me and didn't even know it. How awesome is it that Debbie and Dave are moving in together. I bet by the end of the year they are engaged. Maybe I'll offer to have the wedding at our house. That would be so much fun! Oh my goodness, I can totally imagine it, tealights in the pool, an aisle of roses leading up to the altar which I'll put under the big oak tree, everything in pure white, who cares that it is the bride's second marriage, white chiffon covered tents, the tennis court could easily be turned into a dance floor, maybe Michael and Rachel could get Michael Buble to come perform. I think they know him. Oh my god, I can make this the wedding of this century as my wedding was the wedding of last century!   Oh, I am so excited. Now I just need to get Dave to propose. Not a problem. Dave and Debbie are perfect for each other. They should have been together all these years. This is wonderful! Wait until I tell Jack!   Now that he doesn't have to worry about fathering Her baby, he can relax and have fun! Yay!

Boy did he relax last night and boy did we have fun! WOW! When he got home from "picking up his drafts," it was all I could do to make him wait until the kids went to sleep. If he had had his way we would have made love right in front of all four of them on the living room floor. Man was he good last night!   What stamina! He certainly knows what I like!   4 times! We haven't done it that many times in one night in… gosh, I don't know how long… maybe since before Samuel was born. I think I am walking a little bow-legged this morning.   All the better to ride my stallion! Where did he learn those new moves? I didn't even know my body could still bend like that. Thank god for yoga! And those hands!   Maybe I should take out an insurance policy on those hands. They are one of a kind!   Oh my, did someone turn the heat on in here. I am getting awfully hot!   Hope he is as amorous tonight.   We have a lot of making up to do

since we've had this She thing hanging over our heads.
Wow, I better start thinking of something else
otherwise I'll never get anything done today. I'll go
call Debbie and tell her about her wedding!

CHAPTER 52

She is already there when Susan enters Eggsactly the next morning. She is already writing furiously when Susan sits down next to her. A cup of coffee and a bagel are sitting at the top of Her stationery.

"You're late, honey!" Head nod motioning towards Her!

Head nod in understanding back. "Hey, Rose! Yeah, I know. My husband stayed home this morning and we uhm, uhm, made up for some lost time, if you know what I mean!"

She doesn't pay any attention to the conversation going on next to Her.

"Of course, I know what you mean. I'm sixty something honey, not dead. Saul and I still get it on you know!"

"No doubt!" Wink!

"I'll have the usual, please."

Susan picks up her oversized bag and pretends to look for something as her eyes are fixated on Her letter. Susan reads quickly to catch up.

Molly~

I've got good news and bad news. First- the good news. I "miscarried" this weekend. I just didn't know how to keep it going with Jack pressuring me to see another doctor and to go with me. It actually worked out pretty well. I would have liked a little more time to get Jack used to the idea and for us to get a little closer, but I can feel he is coming around.

211

I called him Sunday night hysterically crying. I didn't even have to fake it, I really was crying, but that is related to the bad news which I'll get to in a minute. His wife answered. Don't like her voice at all. She sounds like a little girl, all squeaky and high-pitched. Yuck!

Susan drops her sunglass case on the counter and sneers to herself. Rose looks over. Susan snarls her lip at Her. Rose retreats to the kitchen with a frightened look.

Anyway, he was more than happy to come right over. As soon as he got to my place he saw how upset I was and helped me to the couch. It was like in the movies, I put my head in his lap and he rubbed my tummy where our baby had been, well, would have been if I had been pregnant, but he didn't know that. It was really sweet. He just sat with me. I can so feel that he was really upset about "the loss." He sat with me for so long. He tried to tell me again that our relationship was over, but I know he didn't mean it. I could see it on his face. Plus, when I told him about my other real bad news he looked so concerned.

Alright now to the bad news, remember I told you that my roommate's boyfriend was going to examine me to see what was wrong because I've been having blurry vision, which has gotten worse, and hair loss, which also has gotten worse. Well, he, Dr. Quackenbush, examined me and I have some rare disease called "Magooavalas Syndrome." It is so rare I could only find one website on it. Apparently it is some chromosome defect that mainly affects women of Greek descent between the ages of 25 and 35. If not treated immediately it can lead to complete blindness, complete loss of hair as well as frothing at the mouth, seizures and night sweats. I haven't experienced the frothing or the seizures- thank goodness, but last night I was sweating profusely! I asked Melanie if she was hot and she said no, she was perfectly comfortable. Thank goodness she was there with me. She is so comforting.

I'm freaking out!!! Dr. Quackenbush, Melanie's boyfriend, gave me this strict regimen to follow for the next two weeks to keep the disease under control until I can see the specialist. Apparently there is only one doctor in the United States that deals with this, and she is in New Mexico. The earliest appointment she had was for two weeks away. I'm going to go crazy! I'm really scared!

For the next two weeks I have to drink 8 oz. of carrot juice every 2 hours, even during the middle of the night. Remember before I even found out about my disease, I already started drinking carrot juice on my own to help correct the vision loss?- Well, maybe it has already helped some. Anyway... I also have to massage my head with olive oil every morning for 15 minutes, stay completely out of the sun and avoid fluorescent lights, battery operated watches and cell phones, apparently the radioactive waves from the cell phones accelerate the disease (guess I will only be calling you from home for the next couple of weeks), take 3 of these horse size pills that smell like rotten eggs every 4 hours, drink this awful tasting mixture of I don't even know what, 3 times a day (by the way- which costs $100 for a 3 day supply and I can only get it from Dr. Quackenbush because he gets it straight from the specialist), run for one hour every night, apparently this stimulates some kind of endorphin that helps minimize the symptoms and no shaving! Not shave- are you kidding me??? I'm Greek- direct descendant of the monkey. At the end of two weeks, I will be able to be cast as the next King Kong!!!!

I hope I can get rid of this disease. I don't want to be blind, bald yet hairy, frothing, sweaty and convulsing!!!

I called mom this morning and told her. She offered to come take care of me and go with me to New Mexico, but I told her it was okay. I know she has the eyelid lift surgery scheduled for next week and I don't want to ruin that for her. She deserves it and don't repeat this, but she needs it. Oh my God, last time I saw her she looked like a shar-pei! I don't even know how she sees out of her eyes there is so much droopy eyelid. Oh my goodness, I hope it's not hereditary! Gosh, I could not stand it if I looked like that! Don't tell mom! I love her and all, but I clearly got my looks from Dad's side, the Greek side which apparently also gave me this horrendous syndrome!!!! But at least I look good, for now anyways! What am I going to do if I lose all of my hair? Thank God, I have a beautiful face and rocking bod!!!

I really want Jack to go with me to New Mexico! I know you can't meet me because that's when you and Jerry are going to Hawaii for your second honeymoon. Don't even think about cancelling, you deserve it. Just like mom deserves her eyelift surgery! Don't worry about me, I'll be fine, all alone, bald, blind, frothy, sweaty, convulsing.

Anyway I did ask Jack to go with me. Even though he said he

couldn't, I am hoping he changes his mind. Maybe if I look really pathetic

he'll find a way to go.   I just know he cares about me. I can't understand

why he is fighting it so much, especially after hearing his wife the other day.

She sounds so scrawny and weathered.

Susan harrumphs loudly!!

I know everyone at the office says she's cute, but they are probably

just trying to be nice to the boss' wife.

"May I please have a glass of carrot juice?"
"Right away."

Just ordered my carrot juice! Yuck! I think two chunks of hair fell

out while I was sitting here writing this letter! Gonna finish my juice and

then go to work, even though I am so tired from being up every 2 hours all

night drinking the carrot juice. But I have to go to work. Now I really need

the money! The treatment for this disease is so expensive, but it will be

worth it once it is gone. Oh and by the way, I asked Dr. Quackenbush if

there was any way to detect this syndrome early, so you and Sarah can go

get checked out, but Dr. Quackenbush said he didn't think so. It's too rare

and new. He told me I should ask the specialist. I'll let you know if there is

something you should do to make sure you and Sarah don't have this.

Guess I better get going! I'll call you later from home, so as not to

aggravate my syndrome! Hope all is well with you!

Love,

Your disintegrating sister

Downs juice. Sips cold coffee. Eats one last
bite of bagel. Packs up. Leaves.
"She so deserves everything that is coming to

her!!!"   Susan also packs up and leaves but not
before saying good-bye and kissing everyone.

CHAPTER 53

What is She doing here before me again! Wow, She looks horrible! She must have had a terrible 7 days since I saw her last. Haha! Maybe I am taking this too far. Nah, She deserves it. Wonder what the oompa-loompa has to say for herself today. Her cat burglar uniform- black bandana covered head, black leggings, black turtleneck, big dark sunglasses cannot conceal how awful She looks! Yay!!! Plan is working! Double yay She is sitting right next to my seat. Susan quickly claims "her" seat. Quick nod and smile to Rose, Nico and Bobby. Rose automatically brings Susan her usual.

"Thanks, Rose."

"Sure, honey."

Conspiratorial smiles are exchanged.

Why is She taking so long to start writing? Come on hussy, start scribbling! I want to read how your weekend was!!! Finally!

Pen out. Stationary out. Sip of previously ordered carrot juice. Bite of cantaloupe.

Molly,

Life is so unfair!!!! I look like a mess! I know it is hard to believe, but it is true. Your once stunning sister looks like an oompa loompa!

Oh my god! Oompa loompa!!! Did we just think the same thing? Scary! We cannot be on the same wave length!

I AM ORANGE!!! Yes, you read that right! ORANGE!!!! I am almost completely bald, blind and now orange!!! This is awful! I think drinking all of that carrot juice has turned my skin orange. Thank God I only have one more week of this until I go see the specialist. I still haven't convinced Jack to go with me. But I will!

This past week has been so miserable. I am running into things all of the time. Everything is so blurry. I have bruises all over my legs and a black eye from walking into a lamp post that Melanie had moved to get more light next to the dining room table. I tripped over a pair of Melanie's thigh high f*** me boots she had left in the kitchen and my coffee table which Melanie had also moved and didn't put back when she was looking for an earring she had dropped. During the middle of the night, as I was going to get a glass of water, I actually completely fell over Melanie's suitcase she had left on the floor in front of my bedroom door- don't really know why she did that. She said she was packing and didn't have enough space in her room to lie it on the floor. Why she didn't just put it on her bed- I don't know. Maybe because it was too heavy. She really is very tiny. She and her boyfriend are going out of town this weekend. Come to think of it- why was she packing so early- it's only Tuesday and they aren't leaving until Friday and only going for four days to a beach resort in Cabo- it's not like she is packing for a month or needs that many clothes for a beach vacation. Weird! If I didn't know better I'd think she was intentionally trying to hurt me. But that's impossible! She is the sweetest girl ever! She has been so understanding- listening to all of my problems with Jack and this new disease. I couldn't ask for a better roommate, even if she is rearranging the house and causing me to constantly injure myself. Each time she has *apologized profusely though. Maybe I should just get a white cane until I get my sight back.*

"Drew, Marion, so nice to see you here this morning! I thought you left for your Alaskan cruise yesterday."

"Hi honey! Great to see you too! Thank you so much for coming to our 60th anniversary party on Saturday. We had such a great time! Your husband is such the charmer! And yes, we were supposed to leave yesterday, but the trip got cancelled because of some bomb threat. Hi Rose, Nico, Bobby!"

"Hi everyone!" Drew chimes in as he quickly snags the last table right behind Susan's seat at the counter.

"Buongiorno Marion, Drew!" Nico calls from the kitchen.

"Hey!" Bobby yells out.

"Hello to my favorite Chicken dancing couple! What can I get you?"

"Yes, we are the Chicken Dancing queen and king! I'll just have some fruit and cottage cheese. Drew, what do you want? Remember the doctor warned you about your cholesterol."

"Yea, yea, I know. I'll just have some pancakes and a side of bacon."

"Drew!!!"

"What? I'm not having any eggs!"

"Fine. Don't come complaining to me when you have another attack!"

"Fine woman!"

"Your party was so much fun! I loved meeting all

of your family after all of these years!"

"Thanks, honey! They loved meeting you and Ja..,
your husband, too! Rose, you and Saul can certainly
cut a rug!"

"Thanks, Marion. We were just trying to keep up
with you and Drew. Where did you learn to dance like
that?"

"Well, we've been dancing together for 60 years
now. Actually we were semi-professional when we were
first married back in the 50's. We won the regional
championship 3 years in a row for the Lindy Hop."

"That is so awesome! What great memories! And
you still have it! Oh by the way, your daughter's
house is beautiful. Does she do interior decorating?
If not, she should."

"Aww, thanks. I'll tell Patti. She actually
does do some interior decorating for friends. She's
always been our creative, artistic one. She'll love
the compliment."

"Please do let her know. And if I decide to
redecorate anytime in the near future, I will
definitely give her a call. Anyway, back to your
cruise- what happened?"

"Apparently the cruise ship got a phone threat
about some bomb on the ship yesterday morning. They
immediately cancelled the voyage. You know with all
the tightened security these days, the cruise line had
to cancel the trip to look into the threat. Turns out
it was bogus, but it was too late to let all of the
passengers know. So we got half of our money back and
re-booked for next week. Luckily for us, there was a
cancellation for next week and we were free. I feel

sorry for all of those people who had to schedule time off of work and now can't go on their vacation."

"That's awful! I just don't get the perverse pleasure these whack-o's get in ruining other people's lives! People they don't even know! It's just sad!"

"Yes, it's terrible. But on the bright side for us- we got a partial refund and still get to go next week. And now get to have breakfast with you and you can update us!" Wink, wink!

"I love your positive spin on things, Marion. And an update will be forthcoming shortly, just as soon as Elvis leaves the building." Smiles all around from the group- Susan, Rose, Marion, Drew and even Nico who was listening as best as he could over the noise from the kitchen. Bobby is headed out the door.

"See you everyone! Got to get to school!"

"Bye, Bobby!"

"Bye, Bobby"

"Ciao amico!"

"Have a great day! See you tomorrow!"

"See you tonight for dinner, Bobby? Sophie said you were coming over."

"Yea, I'll be there. Thanks, Susan!"

Strangest thing just happened- well, maybe not the strangest, but odd- this couple just came in and I overheard this customer (the typical rich-stay at home-skinny-soccer mom type who is here all of the time- does she not have a life?!- oh and she is the one who spilled that glass of water all over the place that one time, remember?) comment on the couple's 60th anniversary party and how beautiful the daughter's house was.

Coincidentally, yesterday I overheard Jack talking to his secretary and telling her about how he went to a 60th anniversary party over the weekend for friend's of his wife and that it was held at the daughter's house. What a coincidence, huh? Couldn't possibly be the same people! That would be too strange! Can you imagine if I have been sitting next to Jack's wife this entire time?!!!! Wouldn't that be beyond bizarre?!!!! But, I know she can't be his wife. This woman is so.... I don't know... just dull. Everything about her is dull- her hair, her body, her face, the way she talks- Dullsville with a capital D!!!! OMG- I just realized the busboy called her "Susan." That's Jack's wife's name. Can't be the same one. Susan is a common name. Must just be a coincidence. Right?

"By the way, Marion, Dave, my husband said to tell you the next time I saw you, thank you again for the wonderful time at the party. So- thank you from Dave, my husband!" Said slowly and with exaggerated enunciation!

I guess it is not her. Apparently her husband's name is Dave which she just said repeatedly as if she were talking to 5 year old retards! I know, I know- retards is not politically correct- but whatever! Oh my gosh, I have to go. I'm going to be late for work. I need to get some Jack time, so I can convince him to go with me next week. Call you later!

Love, Your Oompa Loompa Sister!

Packs up. Pays. Leaves.

Immediately Susan lets out a loud yell!

"I hate that that that thing!!!!! She called me dull! Oh, I'll show her dull! And to think I felt a little sorry for her! She gets no sympathy!"

"Believe me, Susan, you are not dull! All the men in my country would give up spaghetti for a year for one date with you!"

"Awww, I love you, Nico! Thank you so much!"

"So what's with the orange skin?"

"Drew, you noticed?"

"I may be old but I'm not blind. She looks like an oompa loompa!"

"Oh my god, that's what I said! And she said! Someone may have added a little cheap self-tanner to Her daily moisturizer. Ooops! Thanks, Melanie!" Conspiratorial wink and glass raise to the absent Melanie.

"Wow, that really does the trick. She is orange! Melanie is really doing a great job. Isn't she, Susan?"

"She is a god-send, Rose! I'll have to thank Cherise again the next time I see her. Melanie has been executing the plan perfectly!"

"And how are you pulling off the baldness and blindness?"

"The baldness is a result of a little or a lot of Nair in Her hair conditioner."

"What is Nair?"

"Thanks for asking, Nico. I don't know what it is either."

"Drew, Nico, Nair is a creamy hair remover. When added to hair conditioner it slowly makes the hair on your head fall out! As for the blindness, Melanie has been replacing Her daily contact lens' with a lower prescription. Each day the prescription is lower so when she puts on her contact lens' it appears that she can't see as well as the day before. Luckily Melanie's boyfriend Mario, aka Dr. Quackenbush, is an Ophthalmologist so he has easy access to tons of free samples of contact lenses."

"Wow! She really is falling for it!"

"Yep! She is, Marion! Oh, and the night sweats she is experiencing is caused by a little adjustment to her bedroom thermostat which gets re-set each morning, so that she has no clue that it is going up in the middle of the night to 95 degrees."

"Brilliant! How long do you think you can fool her?"

"Probably a long time as she doesn't seem like the brightest light on Broadway; however, after her trip to New Mexico next week to visit our "specialist", she should be cured. Melanie will move out. And stage 2 of Operation Get-the-Bitch-Out-of-Dodge will commence."

"Perfect. I actually spoke to the "specialist" today and she is all set to go. She is really looking forward to this."

"Thanks again, Drew, for setting that up."

"No problem. It's great to have friends in low places!"

"Oh shoot, I'm late. I have to go to pick up Myles and Sammy. They are having back to school night tonight, and so they get out early. See you all! Marion, Drew, if I don't see you before you leave- have a wonderful vacation!"

"Thanks sweetie! Hope the "treatment" goes well. Can't wait to get back and hear how it went."

"Can't wait to report! Ciao everyone!"

CHAPTER 54

Jack, why are you such a sucker!!! You almost caved! What is wrong with you??? How could you have almost fallen for Maggie's pitiful oompah loompah desperate plea to go with her to New Mexico! Sucker! Thank God I came to my senses before it was too late.

Gosh, she is so pathetic looking- orange, bald, squinty eyed, disheveled. How could she even ask me again to go with her? I have made it perfectly clear how I feel about her. Of course, I am no monster- I don't want her saddled with some rare disease, but I don't want to be part of her life. She needs to get that. She'll be fine going to New Mexico all by herself. Oh my God, why am I feeling the slightest twinge of guilt. She'll be fine. She's a big girl!

Okay, I don't care how sick she is… how crappy she looks… how alone, sad and pathetic she is- she just needs to leave me alone and take care of herself!!!!!! I am not her keeper.

And to think I almost agreed to go with her. Almost- until she talked about how after the treatment she hoped she would be well enough so that we could make love again! What is she crazy?!?! She doesn't know when to quit. When she first came into the office I felt really sorry for her. She reminded me of a homeless puppy. Her saying she was all alone and really scared was just a ploy to get me to go with her. I don't think she is scared or all alone. Why doesn't someone from her family meet her there. I know she has a pretty tight-knit family. Whatever- it is not my problem!

This is ridiculous- go home. You are not going
to get any more work done here today. Go home and
make love to your beautiful, fun, not crazy wife!
Done! I'm outta here!

CHAPTER 55

No one is there when Susan enters Eggsactly two weeks later.

"Hey, Rose! No one is here yet? Hey Nico."

"Ciao bella!"

"Hi, Susan. Sorry, honey. No one. No customers. It's been a very slow morning. Oh, I'm sorry, there was one customer here when we first opened. Matthew McConaughey."

"Shut up! You are lying!"

"Honest to God. I don't know many new celebrities, but I do know Mr. McConaughey. He is one very hot man! He came in here all hot and sweaty asking for a Protein Smoothie to-go! I think he had just gone for a run! Be still my heart. I think I still am having palpitations. If only I were a couple of years younger and a few pounds lighter, he would have been all mine!"

"His loss, Rose! Definitely his loss! But you are right- he is HOT!!! He is one of my five!"

"One of your five?"

"Yes, all married couples have a list of 5 celebrities that they are allowed to "be with," if you know what I mean, if the opportunity arises, without any marital consequences."

"Wow, I didn't know that and yes, I do know what you mean! Gosh, all these years married to Saul and I could have "been with" Clark, Frank, James, Jimmy and Sammy."

"I'm assuming- Clark Gable?"

"Yes."

"Frank Sinatra?"

"Yes."

"James Stewart? Cagney? Dean?"

"Actually it was Jimmy Stewart and James Garner."

"Oh, okay. And Sammy…?

"Sammy Davis, Jr."

"Really?"

"Oh most definitely. The glass eye always got my engines running. It was so exotic!"

"My five are Matthew, George Clooney, of course, Hugh Jackman, Hugh Grant, love the accent, so I'll have to forgive his one little "indiscretion" and Gilles Marini."

"Gilles?"

"The hot Dancing with the Stars guy"

"Oh yeah! I did watch that season. He can salsa all over me anytime, too!"

"Rose!!!!"

"Oh, look who's coming."

"Finally! I thought She would have been in last Thursday. The "treatment" was scheduled for last Tuesday."

She enters! Still looks like a hot mess! And She's BALD!

Susan gasps!

Sits. A seat away from Susan.

Orders. Coffee. Cinnamon roll with extra icing. Side of sausage. A stack of pancakes. Fumbles in purse for pen and paper. No more fancy stationary.

Susan spills water.

"Oh shoot, Rose. Sorry. I just spilled my water. Oh no, it's about to drip on me. I'll just

scoot over to this seat." Susan surreptitiously
scoots right next to Her.

Begins writing furiously.

Dear Perfect Sister,

OMG!!!! I cannot believe I have survived. What a friggin nightmare this week has been! And now to top it off, the ditzy, dull soccer mom I mentioned before, just spilled water all over the place... AGAIN!!! And is now sitting right on top of me. If I didn't know she was married, I'd think she was hitting on me. She is constantly staring at me and sitting right next to me when there are dozens of other seats in here. Whatever! I think I overheard the restaurant owner say once that they should put a plaque on that seat with her name on it because that woman only sits there. Freak!!!

Anyway, back to me! I cannot believe I didn't get to talk to you all week. Okay, so before I left for my "treatment" I asked Jack, again, to go with me. I went into his office with my puppy dog, sad face and looking all pathetic, which wasn't a big stretch since I was/am bald, blind and orange, and begged him to go with me. I almost got him to go, too. I just know it. But then I had to go too far and mention making love again. I know he would have wanted to, but I just shouldn't have said it out loud. First, he was all sympathetic and asked me how long we would have to stay and started looking on the computer for flights, but then once I mentioned making love, he turned all cold and said he couldn't go. So, bottom line, I went by myself. Scariest thing I have ever done.

I don't know what Julia Roberts loves so much about Santa Fe, but to me it was creepazoid!

Scarfs down muffin!

So I arrived in Santa Fe on Monday night. This big, burly, hairy, balding man with a handlebar moustache was waiting for me to take me to Dr. Schmekel's house (strange name, huh?).   He didn't say much the whole way there, but he did manage to get lost in what I am sure was the Santa Fe hood!   Did I fail to mention that he drove an old beat up Chevy with the passenger side windows broken- both passenger windows. So I am sitting in the back with the window open, freezing, while we are passing group after group of tattooed, shaved head, grilled teeth, baggy pants wearing teens who I am sure are all packing iron!!!!   SCARY!!!! (By the way, you know what a grill is?- they are colored braces rappers are wearing these days- real attractive! HA!)

Finally, after about a two hour "scenic" ride through the most destitute areas of Santa Fe, we arrived at what I can only describe as a haunted house. Seriously, it was like out of a Stephen King novel. The house was at the end of a dark, dirt road with no other houses around it for miles. It was made out of the typical grayish planks of wood that make up all haunted houses. Windows were broken, tattered curtains flew in the wind. No lights were on as we pulled up. The driver, who never even told me his name, didn't even turn the car off when we got there. He just slammed on the brake, ordered me to get out and then sped off.   I lugged my bag to the porch and knocked on the door. No response. I knocked again and again and again. I would have rung the bell, but of course it was broken. I think I waited on the porch for at least 20 minutes before the door was slowly opened. Of course, I don't really know if it was 20 minutes as I didn't have

230

a watch on because of the no battery operated jewelry restriction of my get-well regimen. What stood in front of me, can only be described as a witch!!!!

Dr. Schmekel was about 4'10", about 80 lbs, with long stringy grey streaked black hair, a long pointy nose and wearing a floor length black long sleeved dress- no joke! She really looked like a witch- only thing missing was a big, black pointy hat! In Dr. Schmekel's raspy, foreign voice (I think maybe- German), she told me to follow her which I did. We went down a long, dark corridor until we came to a door that led to the basement. She told me to go down. Then she explained that I had to stay down there for forty eight hours without food, drink or light, so as to cleanse my body and prepare myself for the complete cleansing treatment ritual. I began to question her, but before I knew it she was gone and the door was locked. Of course, I began screaming, but she didn't come back- not for forty eight hours.

Gulps coffee. Susan snickers.

In the darkness, I felt around and found a cot with what felt like a paper thin sheet and an empty pot. Just a cot and a pot! At least I had a pot to piss in!!!! Literally! Needless to say it was the most miserable forty eight hours of my entire life- even more so than when I was nine and got my tonsils out and had to miss Little Hank's birthday party. Oh, did I mention that I think she uses the basement as a spare refrigerator?!!! It must have been 40 degrees in there! By the time the little witch came back I was constipated, frozen, stinky, exhausted and dehydrated!!!! Then the "ritual" began!

I had just finally fallen asleep when Witchy-pooh came back with a little kerosene lantern and ordered me out of bed and into a folding chair she had placed in the center of the room. Even though the light was rather dim, my eyes still stung as they had not seen any light in 2 days. I started to argue with her and confront her about leaving me down in the basement like a prisoner for 2 days but was silenced quickly when she gave me an evil cold stare that looked like she may have just cast a spell on our entire family. Then she declared in her raspy Bratwurst freaky voice that she did not have time to listen to my complaints or arguments and that if I didn't want her help I was free to go, but warned that this disease was at the stage where it was going to start progressing more rapidly and she was the only doctor in the country who had the cure. I was trapped! I couldn't do anything, but obey, and you know I am not good at obeying!

So... I got into the chair where Witchy-pooh shaved my head!!! Yes, you read that correctly. I am now bald. Thank god for my beautiful face! Luckily, I can pull it off like Natalie Portman! She explained that what hair was left on my head was contaminated and would only spread the disease to any new hair, so we had to remove it!

Then she gave me an apple cider vinegar rub down. She rubbed down places where no one should go!!!! This she explained would detox my body and pull out any impurities. Next, I had to sit in a tub full of ice for 15 minutes to "shock my body into releasing any additional toxins." After that, I had to hang upside down for twenty minutes in some make-shift apparatus to "circulate the blood flow and allow [my] own body inhibitors to fight off the disease."

Following that I was told to lie down on this massage table. I actually sighed with relief thinking that finally I was going to be treated with some tender loving care- OH NO!!! Witchy-pooh started chanting and rocking her body back and forth while moving her hands up and down, slowly over my body, without actually touching my body. This I was told was to "cleanse my chakras." WTF!!!!! Then she started pinching me- all over! I am sure she pulled off a couple of layers of skin!

Crams pancake in mouth.

Next Witchy-pooh wrapped me in cellophane and I had to stand in a corner for an hour. After that I had to jog in place for 45 minutes, and then drink 10 glasses of water every hour for eight hours. Finally I was allowed to sleep for a WHOLE 3 hours. When I was woken, abruptly, I was finally given some food of which can only be described as poison! I have no idea what it was, but it was lumpy, green and smelled like a mixture of rotten cabbage and burning flesh and there was a lot of it. I was told that I needed to finish all of it! How I did not throw-up- I do not know! Finally I was given some "medicine"- again more poison, I think. Witchy-pooh then had me pee on a stick which she "read" and said I was cured! Big, burly no name driver came and took me back to the airport. He was late, so I missed my plane and had to pay a cancellation fee plus the difference in price for the next flight- $575!

Susan laughs!

Little Miss Scrawny Soccer Mom is really getting on my nerves!

Anyway, once I got home, I had to start Witchy-pooh's 72 hour prescribed "after-care treatment to ward off any potential lingering infections." For the next 72 hours, I was instructed to stay in bed, except to go to the restroom, and to rub Greek yogurt on my body three times a day. I also had to drink some other potion four times a day- again more poison that tasted and smelled like gasoline and fish with the consistency of raw eggs with bits of pig intestines. At the end of the 72 hours I had to rub down my body with castor oil, then take a 15 minute ice bath, then light some candles and take some finger nail clippings outside and offer them to the healing Gods. No seriously- that was what I was told to do! And yes, I did it- without question!

I actually do feel better. I even kind of like my baldness. It's so easy and I really do have a stunning face. It really stands out now.

Oh, guess what else- my roommate moved out. No notice. Nothing. I came home from New Mexico to find she was gone. She had totally moved out! Nothing was left behind. So strange. I called her cell phone and it was disconnected, so I called her boyfriend, Dr. Quackenbush, and that phone was disconnected, too. Very bizarre! After all my health care expenses and now having to come up with the entire rent, I am totally broke. Thank goodness for mom. I called her this morning and told her about my experience. She reminded me that she had that eyelid surgery last week. She said she had some complications while on the operating table and they had to revive her. Whatever- as if her experience can even measure up to the one I've just experienced. She also said she isn't happy with the results so far. Apparently one eye is higher than the other. Have you seen her yet? No matter how badly they botched the job, her eyes could not look worse than they were! But anyway, she is sending me some money!

Well, gotta go! I'll call you tonight- I can talk on my cell phone again- Yay! You can tell me about Hawaii! Hope you had a good time!

Love,

Your Cue Ball but Still Beautiful Sister

Finishes pancakes and coffee. Packs up. Pays. Leaves.

"OMG!!!! Did you see that????"

"Oh my, honey. You think, maybe, Drew's "specialist" went a little too far?"

Long pause.

"Nah!"

Another long pause.

"Yeah, you're right!"

Uproarious laughter from Susan, Rose and Nico!

"Stage 2 of Operation Get-the-Bitch-Out-of-Dodge ready to begin!"

"Really? You don't think that was enough?"

Long pause.

"Nope!"

Another long pause.

"Me either!"

More laughter!

CHAPTER 56

Two weeks later, the whole gang coincidentally is
at Eggsactly when Stage 2 of Operation Get-the-Bitch-
Out-of-Dodge goes into effect.   The gang has a lot to
catch up on.   Susan is filling in Marion, Drew, Eddie
and Cherise on Little Miss Wanna Be Homewrecker's
"specialist" visit. Marion and Drew already know some
of the experience as Drew spoke with his friend, the
"specialist." Marion and Drew are telling everyone
about their fabulous cruise experience including all
the food they ate, the weight they gained, the
wonderful people they met and the beautiful sites they
saw.   Lots of chatter is going on when Eddie taps his
water glass with his knife and announces he and
Cherise have some news they want to share.

"Everyone, I want you all to know that this
weekend I became the happiest man alive when this
beautiful woman sitting next to me agreed to be my
wife!"

Silence. Shock. Cheers! Applause! Laughter!
Congratulations all around!

"Oh my God you two! That is so awesome! All
this time we have been talking, how could I have
missed that huge ring on your finger, Cherise? It's
stunning! Eddie, did you pick this out all by
yourself? Cherise, how did he propose? Did you know
he was going to ask you? When is the big day? Do you
need any help? I am great at planning parties. You
can get married at my house if you want. How many
people are you going to invite? Have you picked out a
dress? I know a great cake maker. Flowers- I've got

the perfect girl. Oh my god, Cherise, you are going
to make such a beautiful bride. Oh, and Tyler, have
you told him yet?"

"Wow, Susan, thank you! You're more excited than
my own parents! Okay, one question at a time."
Cherise breathes.

"Since Susan already asked all the questions, let
me just say congratulations! You two make a beautiful
couple! I wish you all the happiness in the world!"

"Drew and I second that! Don't we, Drew?"

"Yes, dear! Congratulations you two. If you
    have a
marriage half as happy as Marion's and mine, you will
be all set!"

"Awwwww, Drew, thank you, sweetie! Glad I
married you, too!" Peck. Peck.

"Complimenti, I miei due amici belli!
Congratulations, my two beautiful friends!"

"Awwwww, thank you so much everyone! I'm going
to cry all over again. I think Eddie had enough of me
crying this weekend when he proposed!"

"Never, baby. As long they were tears of joy! I
was so touched that you were so touched!"

"Ohhhh, this is why I am marrying this man. He
is so sweet to me! I love you, Eddie!"

"I love you, too, baby!"

"Okay, back to Susan's questions. Yes, Eddie
    picked
the ring out all by himself. Of course, I may have
mentioned a couple of times, or more, [he-he] that I
like antique looking platinum rings. But it was all
him! And I love it! It's perfect!"

"I know it's not huge, but it's the best I could do on a P.E. teacher's salary."

"I love it, Eddie! But honestly I would have said yes if you had proposed with a plastic ring you got out of a gumball machine!"

"Really? Bummer! All that money to waste! Give it
back and I'll get you a really special plastic one with a really shiny fake glass stone!"

"Get your hands off my ring! You're never getting it back and I am never taking it off!"

Lots of laughter! Happy couple kisses!

"Okay next question- I was really surprised. I mean we had sort of talked about this being forever, but never like really seriously. The way he did it was so sweet! On Saturday, we took Tyler to the playground. Eddie suggested we have an obstacle course race and whoever won would get a prize. So the three of us- Eddie, Tyler and I- raced through the playground. We had to go down the slide, across the monkey bars, over the jungle gym, through the wooden barrels, hop the hopscotch, and finally jump over a low bar into the sandbox. Of course I won, which I think was planned. In the sandbox was a little blue box…"

"A blue box! You mean a Tiffany blue box?" Susan interrupts.

"Well, I couldn't let my rising star wear anything but a Tiffany now could I?"

"They must be paying P.E. teachers a lot more these days!"

"Drew, that's rude! Don't be impertinent!"

"It's okay, Marion! Maybe this particular P.E. teacher does a little trade swapping on the side and has made a nice little profit, so that I can keep my bride here in the custom she will get used to!"

"Eddie, I think you and I need to talk. I could always use a little cashola!"

"Me, too, Eddie!"

"Me, three, Eddie!"

"Me, four, Eddie!"

"Anytime, Drew, Rose, Nico, Susan! Let me get married

first, then we can work on your stock portfolios. Sorry, Cherise. Please finish telling everyone about the wonderful way I proposed."

"It was, sweetie."

Kiss. Kiss.

"Okay, so anyway there is a blue box in the sandbox, and the next thing I know both Eddie and Tyler are down on their knees and Eddie is saying, 'Life is full of obstacle courses, honey, good and bad, and I want you to be my playmate through all of them. I love you! The past seven months have been the best of my entire life. Will you do me the honor of being my wife and step-mother to Tyler?'"

Wipes away a tear.

"Then Tyler says 'Yes, please be my mommy! I love you, too!'"

"Wow, baby, you memorized that word for word."

"Of course I did. It was the happiest moment of my life so far. Plus, remember I'm an actress!"

Laughter.

"Of course I said 'yes' through all my tears.

Then Tyler started yelling for me to open the box. I did, and this beautiful, perfect ring was inside. And here we are. No other plans have been made yet. But, Susan, I will definitely keep you in mind for lots of help!"

Smiles. Hugs. More cheers. More laughter.

As everyone is chattering away, She quietly slips in. Then He walks in. He sits at the end of the counter. She sits next to Susan's seat; although Susan isn't sitting there as she is sitting with the group at the corner table.

Orders. Carrot and cucumber juice. Omelette with avocado and tomatoes. Cinnamon roll.

"Hey you just ordered my drink!"

"Excuse me?"

"Carrot and cucumber juice is what I was going to order."

"Well, I'm sure you still can. They probably have more than one glass." OMG, why did I just say that. That was so rude. And he is so HOT!

"Ouch!"

"I'm sorry. That was rude! I have just been having a
hard time lately, and I guess I am taking it out on the world."

"Sorry to hear that! I would expect that someone as beautiful as you would only have smooth sailings!"

"Hardly. But thank you for the compliment. Now why would you be ordering carrot and cucumber juice? It's gross!"

"You're welcome! And you're right, it is gross. I wasn't really going to order it. I was just looking for something to say to you. I must confess, I followed you in here. I saw you walking on the street and was star struck. You are just so stunning! I just needed to meet you. So here I am. Hi, I'm Joey!"

Offers His hand. She takes His hand.

"Wow! Thank you! That is the best compliment I've received in long time. Hi, I'm Maggie!"

"Maggie- what a beautiful name! So, are you married, seeing someone, living with someone, too busy to date, not interested in dating…"

"Uhm, not married, not seeing someone, not living with someone, not too busy to date and you know what- I think I am interested in dating."

"Awesome answers! Would you be interested in dating me because I certainly would be interested in dating you?"

"I do believe I am interested!"

"Great! Not to rush off, but when I saw you, I just quickly parked illegally and ran in here, so I do have to go, plus I am late for a meeting. So, uhm, how should we do this- shall I take your number or shall I give you my number… What's better for you?"

"How about if we exchange numbers?"

"Perfect. Very much looking forward to seeing you again, Maggie. It has truly been a pleasure."

Both write their phone number on a napkin. Exchange napkins.

"Thank you! I look forward to seeing you again, too. It was my pleasure, Joey! Now go, before you get a ticket. I'd hate for your first memory of me to be you getting a parking ticket."

"It would be worth it! I'll call you later!"

"I'll be looking forward to it!"

Off He goes with a wink to Eddie.

During this entire exchange the gang has been watching inconspicuously with bated breaths.

A big sigh of relief from the whole group when He leaves with Her number.

Carrot and cucumber juice is served.

"Here you go, honey. Didn't want to interrupt you when you were talking to that guy."

"Oh, yeah, thank you! He's hot, isn't he?"

"Most definitely. Your omelette will be right out."

"Thank you!"

Pen out. Plain paper out. Writes.

Hello Beautiful Sister,

I think things may just be turning around. I am sitting here in my regular diner wearing a bandana on my head to cover up my peach fuzz when this HOT, HOT, HOT guy comes in and starts flirting with me and asks for my phone number. So HOT! About 6' with a body made out of stone- rock hard! And a butt!!!! OMG! What a biteable ass! Piercing green eyes, wavy black hair, full luscious lips, creamy caramel skin. I just wanted to lick him!   Anyway, he said he actually followed me in here because he saw me walking on the street and thought I was so beautiful. Even bald, I still have it! The best part is, I was actually interested. I may finally be kicking Jack to the curb. He lost his chance with me. Definitely his loss!

Omelette arrives. Eats ravenously.

I know you are thinking you cannot believe I am a wearing a bandana on my head – so 70s!   Actually it doesn't look too bad! Anyway, it's almost

Halloween, so maybe people just think I am dressed up early.   Guess what

else, I am still drinking carrot juice, but mixing it with cucumber juice

because I read it is good for your hair. Hopefully by the time I have a date

with Mr. Hottie (his name is Joey, by the way – isn't that a sexy name?) I

will have some real hair and not this peach fuzz.   But who cares, he already

thinks I am beautiful!   Well, I can't really tell you anymore about him

because I don't know anything else. He said he'd call later. I hope that

means tonight! I'll keep you posted. I can't believe how excited I am about

him already!

Anything new over there?

Talk to you later – hopefully after I talk to my new guy!

Xo, Your Beautiful Sister

Finishes omelette and juice. Packs up. Pays.
Leaves.

"OMG, Eddie, he is hot! You were right!"

"I told you so, Susan! Told you if anyone could
make a woman swoon and forget another man, it was my
brother. I've never met a girl my brother couldn't
have – even if she was otherwise attached. It's been
his blessing and my curse. Can't tell you how many
women walked over me to get to my brother."

"Awwww, poor Eddie!"

"But now it doesn't matter because I now have the
perfect woman here agreeing to marry me. And best part
is, she already met my brother and still wants me."

"That's right, sweetie. Your brother can't have
me! You're all I want! To me you're the hot brother!"

Eddie and Cherise kiss passionately.

A group chorus of "ahhhhhhh…"

"You don't think he'll really fall for Her
though, do you? That would totally ruin our
Operation."

"Oh, no need to worry about that. My brother is
not a one-woman man. He is having way too much fun
sampling many varieties."

"Perfect! Thank you so much for getting him to
do this."

"No worries. He was totally up for it."

"Thanks everyone for helping me with this
mission."

"Our pleasure." Marion says on behalf of herself
and Drew.

"I haven't had this much fun being evil since
junior high school." Cherise admits.

"I love your American ways. In my country, you
would just go to her house and drag her into the mud
until she promised to stay away from your man." Nico
educates everyone on the Italian ways.

"You're like a daughter to me. I have to protect
you!" Rose says with a bear hug.

Conversation goes back to Eddie and Cherise's
wedding. Soon everyone leaves with the promise that
they will meet back up soon to see how the Operation
is going.

CHAPTER 57

Susan walks into Eggsactly two weeks later, still a bit groggy from all of the Halloween festivities. The place is fairly quiet on this brisk November day, only a couple of tables are occupied.

"Good morning, Rose, Nico! Where's Bobby?"

"Morning, Susan. Bobby took the day off to finish a paper that's due on Friday."

"Oh yeah, he said might do that when I saw him the other day!"

"Buon giorno, Susan!" Nico yells from the kitchen.

"Did you both have a good Halloween? We missed you at our party."

"Sorry Saul and I couldn't be there, Susan. I'm sure it was fun. Saul and I were the hosts of our bowling team's annual Halloween Bowl-a-thon. We won the games and the costume contest! We went as Adam and Eve!"

"Oh my God, I would have loved to have seen you two."

"Yes, we were quite the sight! I think we won for bravery more than anything else."

"I'm sorry I couldn't make it either, Susan. But my cousin is visiting and wanted to check out some hip Hollywood clubs! I think we did, but I can't be sure. The night is all a blur. I'm still drunk! And I think there is still some woman in my bed!"

"Oh my goodness, Nico!!!! Well, our party was great! As usual! Jack and I went as Mr. and Mrs. Brady. Myles and Sammy went as werewolves and Jessica and Sophie went as vampires. We had our own little Twilight tribute. Of course, the evening wouldn't have been complete without a least one accident from Myles. He almost drowned while bobbing for apples. But of course, Jack to the rescue. And Myles being Myles was over it as soon he stopped choking- no harm done. Oh look who's coming!"

She walks in smiling from ear to ear looking more beautiful than ever even with her barely-there hair.

Sits right next to Susan even though there are plenty of other stools available.

"Good morning! It's a wonderful day, isn't it?" She cheerily greets Susan.

"Uhm, good morning. It is a wonderful day!" Susan hesitantly responds.

Is this the same woman who has ignored me for months and been nothing but self-centered?!?! I guess the Operation is working.

"Good morning, ma'am! May I please have a cup of tea and the American Breakfast with the eggs over easy and an English muffin."

"Right away, honey." Rose saunters off not believing the personality transformation.

Deep sigh, that can only be explained by love. Pen out. New stationary out. Begins writing.

Dear Favorite Sister (okay, so you're my only sister, but you're still my favorite!),

Life is grand!!!! I cannot believe I haven't talked to you in two weeks. The past two weeks have been a whirlwind- pure heaven.

Remember that guy I told you I met here- oh yeah, you don't know

246

where here is- I'm at that cute little coffee shop again. Anyway, I have been

with him every night for the last fourteen nights, except for two- once when

he had to tend to his sick brother and once when I had to go with Cliff to

look at a new site in Vegas and didn't get home until after midnight and had

to be back at work at 7 for another site inspection in Anaheim.

Breakfast arrives. Eats some.

Okay, so here is the scoop- Joey called me right after he left me the

first day we met- even before he got to his car- and asked if we could get

together that night. Even though I usually require a guy to ask me out at

least 3 days in advance for a first date, I agreed to go.   He said I should

choose where we go because he would go anywhere- he just wanted to spend

time with me. I chose this trendy little sushi restaurant in Santa Monica.   It

was really quiet though. I guess because it was a Tuesday night. Anyway, we

closed the place down. Then we went for a walk on the beach. It was

freezing- well not by Chicago standards but by LA standards. He was so

charming, attentive and SEXY!!!! He carried my purse. He offered me his

jacket. He put his hand gently on my back as we walked across the street.

He constantly told me how beautiful I am- even with my bald head- he said

he found it sexy- hope he'll still think I'm sexy when I have hair.

Eats more.

We stayed out until 4 in the morning.   We kissed on the pier with

the waves crashing down in the background.   Even though I really wanted

to, I didn't invite him in when he dropped me off because I thought we

should wait before we had sex. In fact, we still haven't made love. Joey says

he wants to wait, so I'll know that I am really special and that when we do it, it really will be "making love." How sweet is that! But I must tell you, I am dying to jump him. He is so HOT!!!!!

Anyway, like I said, I've seen him every night since then, except for the two I mentioned- most of the time we just stay in and cook or order take-out. I am so into him, I don't care what we do. I just want to be with him. He's slept over at my place 4 times, but we just cuddled and kissed. I haven't seen his place yet because he says he is too embarrassed because it is a mess. With his traveling so much, he says he doesn't have to time to clean or organize. I really don't care where we are, I just enjoy being with him. Can't wait for Jack to meet him, he'll be so jealous! Okay, so I am not completely over Jack yet, but close- really, really close.

Loud guttural sounds from Susan.

The reason Joey travels so much is because he is a physical therapist for professional athletes. He travels with different teams during the seasons. Luckily he is scheduled to be in town until the end of the year. Even though we have only been dating for two weeks, we've already discussed the fact that we will both be sad when he has to go back out on the road. But, he said we'll deal with it when it gets closer, which gives me hope.

I really think he may be "The One." I can't believe how hard I am falling so soon. I can't wait to make love to him. TMI?

Okay so what's new with you? Are mom's eyes any better?

Love,

Your revived sister

Finishes breakfast. Places stationary carefully in envelope. Packs up. Pays. Leaves.

248

"'Operation Get-the-Bitch-Out-of-Dodge' is in full force!"

"Awwww, I'm so sad I'm going to be losing a customer!"

Rose, Susan and Nico laugh!

CHAPTER 58

6:45 a.m. Saturday, the ringing phone wakes up
the whole Martinelli household. Susan answers it
first. All Susan can hear is crying. Loud crying.
Not sad crying. Happy Crying.

"We're, we're, we're preg, preg, pregnant! It
wasn't me at all! I wasn't a dried-up old lady! It
was his, Larry's, decrepit sperm. They couldn't even
swim in the shallow end!!! Susan, WE'RE PREGNANT!!!!"

"Debbie, is that you?"

"Shut up, Susan. You know it's me!!! Dave and I
are going to be parents. We are so excited. Not that
we know what we are going to do with it. You're going
to have move in and be our nanny. Start packing,
baby! Oh yeah, and we want to get married right away.
So start planning. Anything you want. I know you'll
do a terrific job. Nothing too big. Just Dave's
family, my family, your family, all of our friends and
co-workers and anyone else who wants to come. Susan,
I'M PREGNANT!"

"Oh my God!!!! I'm so happy for you and Dave.
Jack, Debbie and Dave are pregnant. Jack says
'congratulations!' Okay, so let me get this straight.
I'm going to be your nanny and your wedding planner,
right?"

"Right! And don't forget maid-of-honor!"

"Really, you want me to be your maid-of-honor?
Awww, I
am so touched!"

Susan tears up.

"Of course you are going to be my maid-of-honor,

silly! And Dave wants to ask Jack to be his best man! I'm so happy, Susan, I could just cry."

"I think you have the crying covered, Deb! This is so awesome. If only you and Dave had gotten together way back when. Oh well, at least it is happening now! So, tell me how it happened."

"The pregnancy? You should know, Susan, you have four of your own!"

"Don't be silly! You know what I mean. How did you find out? How did Dave propose?"

"Well, I missed my period and I've always been regular, so this morning I took a pregnancy test, four actually, and sure enough they all came back positive, two lines. Dave was with me the entire time. So after the fourth reading, Dave got down on one knee in the cramped bathroom and said that he has loved me secretly from afar for over twenty years and now he wants to shout it from the rooftops and let the world know he is mine and I am his and the baby is ours. He said wants us to be legitimate. He asked me if I would do him the pleasure of making him the happiest man on earth by becoming his wife and mother to his children. Children!!! Not even one. He wants more! He grabbed some dental floss and tied it around my finger as a make-shift ring. He promised to get me the biggest and shiniest ring possible. But I don't care. I am happy with the dental floss! I just want Dave and this baby! Oh, of course, I said 'yes.' Then I called you!"

Susan is now in tears.

"Awww, that Dave- he's a keeper! Okay, we need to get

moving. When do you think you want to have the
wedding?

"As soon as possible. I'm thinking the first
Saturday in December. That's a month away. Can you
do it?"

"No problem! Do you want to have it here at my
house?"

"Would you mind?"

"Mind? That would make me so happy! Okay. I'm
on it! I already have ideas! Want to go dress
shopping today?"

"Definitely. I'll pick you up in two hours!"

"I'll be ready! Give Dave a big hug and kiss for
me, please!"

"Will do. Dave- Susan and Jack say
'congratulations,' and Jack said he'd love to be your
best man! He will, right, Susan?"

"Of course! Jack- Dave wants you to be his best
man, you'll do it, right?"

"Right." Jack has just been lying in bed next to
Susan this whole time hearing her half of the
conversation. He is still a bit groggy from being
woken up so early on a Saturday. Likewise, Dave has
been standing next to Debbie this whole time hearing
her half of the conversation.

Debbie and Susan spend the day wedding planning.

CHAPTER 59

The next few weeks are completely hectic with Susan planning her traditional Thanksgiving Martinelli/Klein feast and Debbie and Dave's wedding. Jack's entire family, his parents, his brother, Mark, his wife and 2 kids, his sister Eleanor, her husband and 2 kids, always flies out for Thanksgiving and stay with Jack and Susan. It's always a big extravaganza.

Susan loves all the party planning, but she is feeling totally consumed, so much so, that she has almost forgotten about Operation Get-the-Bitch-Out-of-Dodge. Almost. Until she sees Her the Tuesday before Thanksgiving. Even though Susan has lots to get ready before Jack's family arrives tonight, she still goes to Eggsactly for two reasons 1) for a little breather before all the chaos begins, fun chaos, but chaos never-the-less and 2) to wish Rose, Nico, Drew, Marion, Eddie and Cherise a Happy Thanksgiving. They had all planned on meeting there for a little celebration breakfast. Bobby isn't there as he is doing some last minute Thanksgiving dinner errands for his Grandma Lily, Rose's sister. He'll celebrate the holiday with his family for most of the day, but then go over to Susan and Jack's later in the evening to be with the Sophie.

Everyone gathers at Eggsactly at 7, a little early for Susan, but the only time Eddie could make it before he has to go work at school, as he has morning recess duty. Jack took the kids to school, so Susan could make it on time.

Everyone shares what they will be doing for the

holiday. Rose and Saul will go to Lily's with Bobby.
Drew and Marion will be spend it at their daughter,
Cathy's house with her husband and kids and their
other two daughters and their husbands and kids.
Nico's cousin is visiting, and they are going to Vegas
for the weekend. Eddie and Cherise are flying out
tomorrow morning to Minnesota, Cherise's hometown. It
will be the first time Eddie meets Cherise's parents.
They are both excited but nervous. Apparently
Cherise's dad, Julio, has already made some nasty
comments about the 12 year age gap between Eddie and
Cherise. Susan is confident that once Papa Julio
meets Eddie everything will be fine. Who could not
love Eddie!!! He is so wholesome, honest, kind,
sincere and completely head-over-heels in love with
Cherise.

Everyone is so caught up in the holiday
festivities that they all almost forget about
Operation Get-the-Bitch-Out-of-Dodge. Just as
everyone is about to leave, Susan asks Eddie if he has
heard from his brother.

"Oh yeah. Joey called me last night to wish me a
good trip, good luck with the parents and a Happy
Thanksgiving. He said the Operation is going along
smoothly. He said he has Her eating out of his hands.
Shouldn't be too much longer."

"Perfect. I do feel a little bad, being that she
doesn't seem to be a problem anymore, but then I
think- nah, she still needs to pay for what she did.
Jack did come home from work last night in a little
bit of a funk, and so of course, at first I thought
She must have pulled one of her pranks again. So I

254

asked him why he was so blah, and not that he would
tell me if it had something to do with Her, but he
just chalked it up to being overwhelmed at work, his
family coming to town and the destruction of our
house, so we can throw Debbie and Dave the perfect
last minute wedding. I did tell you all that my best
friend, Debbie, and Jack's cousin, Dave, are pregnant
and I am throwing them a wedding at our house in two
weeks, right? You all must have met them at one of
our parties. Anyway, everything is a bit hectic right
now, but all good, so I can totally see why Jack was
in a mood. But then he made up for it! Oh yes he
did. Let me tell you he still has it. We didn't get
to bed, well I should say to sleep until after 3 a.m.
TMI?"

Susan giggles. Everyone else laughs too,
although it really is a little TMI, especially for
Drew and Marion!

"Okay, back to the Operation- Eddie, please tell
Joey thank you and to keep moving forward."

"Sure thing, Susan. Well, I got to get to work
and Cherise has a lot of packing to do. Happy
Thanksgiving everyone! See you in a few weeks."

Everyone begins a chorus of "good-bye," "Happy
Thanksgiving," "Safe trip," "Good luck with the dad,"
"See you soon."

Susan reclaims her usual spot at the counter. She
decides to hang out for a bit longer and drink her
tea. Luckily she does this, as not 10 minutes after
the gang leaves, She walks in.

Plops down next to Susan. Orders coffee. Pen
out. Plain paper out. Begins writing.

Molly,

I'm so sad I am going to miss Thanksgiving with you and the family this year. Are you really mad at me? I'm sorry! I just really, really want to spend Thanksgiving with Joey. His family is going out of town, so he'd be all alone if I left, and also after what happened last night I really need to make this work with Joey. Plus, after all the expense of my Magooavalas treatment I can't afford to come home right now. Flights are so expensive around the holidays.

Soooooo, Joey and I finally made love! OMG!!!!!! I have never experienced anything so amazing. He touched places that not only did I not know could be touched, but that I didn't know would feel soooooooooooooooooooooooooooooooooo good!!!! What an amazing tongue, penis and fingers he has! Sorry- I know TMI! It happened on our one month anniversary, last Friday night. Joey is actually the one who remembered that it was our one month anniversary. He showed up at my place after work with flowers and a card. The card said, "The past month has been the best of my life! I now realize how empty my life was before you, and now I can't imagine my life without you. I hope you feel the same! I'm all yours- Joey" He had made reservations at this totally awesome restaurant in Malibu, Geoffrey's- coincidentally the one where I followed Jack and his ball and chain.

Susan grimaces- loudly!

It was great being one of the couples dining, rather than just sitting at the bar watching my man and his wife and longing for my man to realize that I am the one.

256

After dinner, we went for a walk on the beach. We made out in the sand. I think I still have sand in certain crevices you don't want to know about. We didn't fully consummate our relationship until we got back to my place though. Joey drew us a bubble bath and lit candles. I think we were in the tub over an hour just caressing, massaging and sudsing each other. Finally he carried me to bed and that's where I went to Heaven! Again- OMG!!!! He slowly and tenderly kissed and touched me- everywhere! Finally when I was just about to explode he entered me. It fit like a hand in a glove- and not like OJ Simpson's!!!!

Susan is blushing and wants to take her eyes off of the letter but just can't! Water! Yes, I need some water! Susan dips her napkin in her water glass and dabs her temple. Susan is feeling the heat.

Okay, okay! I know, again TMI!!! I love you so much, I almost want to let you borrow Joey for one night, so you can experience the bliss and see what I am talking about- but that would be weird, right? I know Jerry cannot be anywhere near as good as Joey, especially with Jerry's beer belly- sorry, but you know it's true. I know, I know- it's what's inside that counts- blah, blah, blah...

Susan herself is thinking she might like to borrow Joey for one night! Wow!

All right, so you are wondering what happened last night, right? So I decided I would give Jack one last opportunity to be with me before I completely devote myself to Joey. I know after everything I've just told you, you must think I am crazy. Joey is great and all, and absolutely amazing in bed, but there is still something so special about Jack. Maybe it's the challenge. I've never had a guy turn me down before.

Last night, I had to stay at work late to make sure I got everything finished before the long weekend. As I was leaving I noticed that Jack was still in his office. Everybody else had left. It was just the two of us. So, I went into his office and shut the door. Of course he tried to shoo me away, but I quickly got him to soften up when I started apologizing for my past behavior. I told him all about Joey- well not all. ☺ I told him I was sorry things got so messy between us, and I just wanted to be friends. He finally lightened up. He said he accepted my apology and he was really happy for me. Then he started asking all of these questions about Joey. What did he do? Where did he live? Are we serious?   All of the sudden, I realized he was jealous.

"Oh my God!!!" Susan accidentally says it out loud!

She looks over, but then resumes writing.

The look in his eye just broke my heart. I could tell he was hurting but trying to put up a brave front. After we were talking for a while, he left the office to go get a fax he was waiting for. When he came back, there I was- lying on his office couch- completely naked! I just couldn't leave without giving him one last opportunity to have me. I must tell you, I was shocked by his reaction! I thought for sure he was going to jump all over me. But, no!   In a disgusted voice he told me to get dressed and leave! I swear that guy is made of stone!!!   I don't know what his problem is because just moments before he was clearly jealous of my relationship with Joey and then when he gets the chance to have me, he lets me go! Whatever!!! I'm done!

258

Who needs someone who is so wishy-washy and who obviously can't make up his mind about what he wants! It's so over! I am so totally and completely Joey's!!!

Hope you understand why I REALLY need to spend Thanksgiving with Joey. I'm sure next year we will all be spending it together- you, Jerry, Billy, Sarah, mom, dad, me and Joey. Maybe even some of Joey's family will fly out. Speaking of which, I haven't met his family yet. He has one brother who is a single dad with a little boy. His parents are retired and live in Palm Springs. That's about 2 hours away from Los Angeles. I haven't been there yet, but it's supposed to be an old time fancy schmancy desert resort area. I think Bob Hope used to have a place there.

Oh just saw the time, gotta go to work and finish up what I didn't get done yesterday. We have tomorrow off, so I really need to get it done. Wonder if Jack will be there. Bet you he's kicking himself for passing me up. He really will be when he sees me today. I look so HOT! I bought this totally sexy white skirt suit. The jacket is tailored perfectly to my big boobs and small waist. I look good! Eat your heart out, Jack Martinelli!!!!

I hope Joey realizes how lucky he is to have me. I think he does- that's part of the reason I am so into him. He constantly is telling me how beautiful and wonderful I am and what a lucky guy he is to have found me. Okay gotta go! I'll call you later!

Love and miss you!

Your totally blissful sister

Susan quickly orders tomato juice. Rose brings it immediately. Susan takes a drink and then chokes spewing juice all over Her new "sexy white skirt suit."

"Oh my God. I am so sorry! Here let me get that!"

Susan starts wiping Her suit with a yellow paper napkin leaving a yellow stain mixed with the red juice stain.

"Stop! Stop! Stop! Oh my God!!! You are just making it worse! I cannot believe what a klutz you are! This is unbelievable! I just bought this suit! It's ruined."

"I really am sorry. Here let me give you some money for the dry cleaning and I'll pay for your breakfast. It's totally on me."

"No, actually, it's on me!!! You idiot!"

Susan hands Her a $100.00 bill. She grabs it. Throws her stuff into her bag. Leaves. She cannot get out fast enough.

"That may have been the best $100 ever spent!"

"You are bad, Susan. Bad!" Rose shakes her head.

"Molte male il mio amico! Very bad, my friend!" Nico smiles.

"I know!" Susan grins ear to ear.

"Oh, Rose, I'm sorry. I may have just lost you a customer!"

"No problem, honey! But I have a feeling She'll be back. Who can pass up my cinnamon rolls. I think she may be addicted."

Susan fills Rose and Nico in on That Girl's latest escapade. They all agree that the Operation must continue with full force.

Susan finishes her tea and prepares to leave.

"Rose, Nico, hope you both have a Happy Thanksgiving. Nico don't go too crazy in Vegas!"

"Thanks, sweetie! Hope you have a great one, too! See you next week!"

"Grazie, bella! No worries. Nico knows how to have a good time and still stay safe! Besides my cousin will be there to protect me. He is a bouncer back in my country. You have a good one, too!"

Kiss. Kiss. Kiss. Hug. Hug. Hug.

CHAPTER 60

Last night after Maggie finally left, Jack sat alone in his office for a few minutes to compose himself.

Just when I thought I was done with Maggie, she goes and pulls another one of her stunts! That girl is unbelievable. How could she possibly think I was asking her questions about her new boyfriend because I was jealous?!!!! I was just trying to make sure they were serious, so I could finally relax and know she will no longer be a problem. Crazy!!!

I certainly deserve a medal of loyalty though. Oh my God, no matter how much I am in love with Susan, I could not help but notice that girl has one rocking hot body, not to mention her stunning face! Wow! For me to turn that down when it is being offered to me on a platinum platter, I am one committed husband. If only I could get credit for it from Susan. But no, Susan must never know!

Damn with a body like that, what is that girl doing pursuing me so fiercely?!?! I would think she could have any man, with the exception of me, that she wants! What is her obsession with me?!!! I guess I should feel somewhat flattered. I hope she finally got the message! Well, if she has to undress for me one more time to try tempt me, I guess I can handle it. Twist my arm!!! LOL! I am only human!

Honestly though, no matter how many times she gets naked in front of me, I swear on my kids lives that I will never cheat on Susan! Even though, truth be told, while I am here in my office all alone, the visual was not too hard on the eyes and I wouldn't mind seeing it again! In fact, it was quite pleasing! Get a grip, Jack! Go home and make love to your beautiful, sweet, not crazy, mother of your children, hilarious, kind, caring wife! That's exactly what I am going to do! I'm outta here!

CHAPTER 61

The Thursday, the week after Thanksgiving, Susan barely has time to stop into Eggsactly, but makes it in, just for a cup of tea on her way to the florist to finalize the flowers for Dave and Debbie's wedding that weekend.

The whole gang is there again. Everyone shares how they spent their Thanksgiving. Drew and Marion had a wonderful time with their entire family. Their youngest granddaughter, one of Patti's daughters, announced she is getting married.

It must be in the air!

As expected, Cherise's parents loved Eddie! They are very excited about the marriage.

Nico thinks he may have accidentally gotten married in Vegas. But no worries, Italians are known for being great lovers and having many wives, per Nico.

Rose and Saul enjoyed their time, too. Rose's sister, Lily, Bobby's grandma, always makes the best stuffing and corn bread casserole.

Susan's, of course, went off without a hitch- as all of her parties do. Jack's family, as always, had a great visit! Patrick regaled everyone with stories about his first semester at Harvard. Jessica, Sammy, Miles, Piper, Justin, Dustin and Jack's two nieces, Francesca and Gianna, and two nephews, Antonio and Giovanni entertained with a homemade skit about the first Thanksgiving feast. They created their own Indian and Pilgrim costumes, complete with feather headdresses, loin cloths, felt hats, coifs, shifts, ruffs, cuffs, petticoats, aprons, breeches, garters and stockings. Sophie kept to herself until Bobby arrived for dessert, and then together they enjoyed the entertainment provided by the other kids.

As the gang is sharing their holiday stories, She enters. She makes a thorough scan of the room. Clearly looking to see if Susan, aka the klutz, is there. As soon as She spots Susan, She makes a beeline for the corner table as far away from Susan as possible. Susan, Rose and Nico share a private giggle which they will share with the rest of the gang when She is out of ear shot.

As the gang continues visiting, She gets into her usual routine, albeit, at a table rather than at the counter where Susan can peer over her shoulder.

Orders. Latte. Cinnamon roll. Bowl of cereal. Side of bacon. Pen out. Fresh stationary out. Begins writing.

Susan watches Her out of the corner of her eye. Dang, how I am going to read her letter now?! That Bimbo is sitting too far away. Oh well. I'll figure out something.

Hello Precious Sister,

Life is grand! Sorry I haven't talked to you since I spoke with you briefly on Thanksgiving Day when you were in the middle of your "disaster." I spoke with mom last night and she said you were able to salvage the turkey, and everything turned out nicely, even though I wasn't there.   She said I was really missed.   I missed you all too, but I had a great time with Joey. Things are really moving along nicely.   We had such a romantic

Thanksgiving. He slept over on Wednesday night and prepared a turkey. He does this thing where he cooks the turkey for 24 hours in a paper bag. Oh my God, it was so yummy! He made everything- yams, mashed potatoes, green beans, monkey bread, corn relish, pumpkin pie. I didn't lift a finger. He is an amazing cook. After we ate, we went for a walk down to the beach. When we got back he gave me a full body massage and then.... well, you know!!! ☺ It was so sweet. Again, he told me how thankful he is to have me in his life and he hopes that this is the first of many, many Thanksgivings and holiday celebrations together. I told him how thankful I am to have him in my life too. Especially after the whole Jack fiasco- didn't tell that part to Joey though. I really am thankful to have him in my life. He is so wonderful! He just may be my soul mate!!!

He spent the entire weekend at my place since neither of us had to work. We just hung out together, made love, over and over again, ate, gave each other massages, watched tv. It was great. So comfortable, yet exciting at the same time. I really think I am falling in love with him. I am pretty sure he feels the same way. I don't know what I am going to do when he goes back on the road in January. I am not a long distance relationship kind of girl. I mentioned this to Joey and he said we would talk about it this weekend. I wonder what he is going to suggest???? Do you think he is going to propose this soon???? I think I would say "yes" if he did! Oh my God!!!!!

Thanks again for understanding about Thanksgiving!

What's new with you? Hope to talk soon! It's just so hard now that I *spend all my time with Joey.*

Love you,

Your Thankful Sister

She places the letter on the side of the table. Eats her breakfast that has been sitting there for 10 minutes. Nico is talking on the phone when he comes to clear away Her dishes. Click. She doesn't even notice that the cook has just bussed her table. She is too lost in her own world.

Packs up. Pays. Leaves.

"Here, Susan, you might want this."

"Your phone, Nico? Why would I want your phone? I have a cell phone. But thank you!"

"Look at it, mi amico!"

"Oh my God! How did you get this?"

"I'm good, Susan. I'm real good!" Nico slyly smiles.

"Okay, everyone. Look at this- Nico took a picture of Her letter on his cell phone. Apparently, the Operation is going as planned. She is in love. Awwwwww."

Laughter all around.

"She thinks he might propose this weekend."

A chorus of "awwwws."

More laughter.

"Spoke with Joey. He said 'full speed ahead.'"

"He isn't really falling for her, is he, Eddie?"

"Oh God no! He did ask me to tell you 'thank you' for all the sex though. I guess she really is good in that area."

"TMI!" Marion is up on the lingo!

More laughter from the group.

"Not for me! Please dish some more!" Drew is up on the lingo too!

More laughter.

"As far as falling for her though- no way! I told you Joey is not a one woman man. Plus, according to Joey, She is quite the clingy one! Not his favorite quality. But he is playing along."

"Please tell him I said 'thank you,' again! I really appreciate it."

"Sure. No problem. What were and Rose and Nico laughing about, by the way, when She first walked in?"

Susan catches the gang up on her last encounter with Her and the spilled juice. Susan gets a standing ovation from the gang for her quick thinking and sly execution!

The gang wraps up their conversation and then they all leave to continue with their day, well obviously except Rose and Nico who work there! Susan barely has enough time to make it to the florist on time, but it was worth it, as she thoroughly enjoyed her time with everyone and was happy to see how the Operation was coming along according to Her. Not that She knows about the Operation.

CHAPTER 62

Saturday night, Susan climbs into bed exhausted after all of the guests leave from Debbie and Dave's wedding. Jack is already fast asleep.

Fabulous!!! The wedding was fabulous! I can't believe I was able to pull that off on such short notice. It was perfect. Everyone loved the shotgun wedding theme. Debbie's dad was such a trooper to carry the shotgun with him down the aisle as he escorted Debbie to the altar. Sophie and Jess did a great job on the banners, "Marry Her or Else!" Dave's fraternity brothers, Tommy and Andrew, were awesome as small town sheriff and deputy, a la Andy and Barney. So much fun! I should be a wedding planner. Maybe in a few years when the boys are in middle school.

Debbie looked so beautiful and Dave so handsome. They will definitely have their happily ever after. Just like Jack and me! I love this man so much!

Jack slightly stirs as Susan runs her fingers through his hair.

I am so lucky to have Jack! This year has been a bit trying at times with all of Her antics, but that will be over soon. Then Jack and I will be back to our happily ever after. Nice way to end the year!

"Good night CB! I love you!"

Jack manages to mumble, "Night LG! Love you, too!"

CHAPTER 63

Susan still pooped from the weekend does, however, make it into Eggsactly on Tuesday. The diner is completely full except for Susan's seat which Rose was holding for her. No sooner is Susan sitting in her spot when She glides in. As luck would have it, the gentleman sitting at the counter stool next to Susan finishes his breakfast and leaves. With no other choice, She sits next to Susan. Susan expects a cold reception from Her, given the tomato juice episode, but She surprises Susan by politely saying "hello."

"Hi." Susan responds somewhat dumbfounded. "Please let me apologize again for getting tomato juice all over that wonderful suit you were wearing."

"No problem at all. It's just clothes."

Susan is almost at a loss for words.

"Were the cleaners able to get out the stains?"

"I really don't know. I haven't had a chance to take it in yet."

"Oh no! You can't just let it sit there. It'll set and you'll never be able to get it out."

"Really- no worries. I'll just buy another one. Life is more than about clothes."

"Wow! Well, okay. If I owe you more money, just let me know. I'm in here all of the time."

"Don't give it another thought. All is good! Enjoy your breakfast!"

With that She orders. Coffee. Cinnamon roll. Pen out. Paper out.

Susan and Rose give each other a look of utter

confusion. Is this the same girl? Have aliens taken over this woman's body? Where is the snotty homewrecker that used to be housed in this body?

Dear Beautiful Sister,

I'm just floating on air! I am soooooooooooooooooooooooooooooooo in love! Yep- in love! This weekend Joey asked me to go on the road with him. He is going to Canada to work with some hockey team right after the new year. It's not a wedding proposal, but it's a start. He told me I should just give up my apartment, sell or store my stuff and go with him. He said he would totally take care of me and I don't have to worry about anything. I'm told him YES!!! OMG! I can't believe I am going to do this!

Coffee arrives. Sips.

I already gave my landlord notice. Luckily I was on a month-to-month lease, so I won't be penalized. I started packing last night. I'm just going to ship whatever I can't sell to mom. She said I could store the stuff in the garage. If I don't sell my new couch, you can have it if you want. It's totally cool and much better looking than that old thing you have in the family room. But if you do take it, please make sure the kids and Jerry don't spill anything on it. Oh forget it- I don't care- let them spill whatever they want on it. I AM IN LOVE!!!! AND HE LOVES ME BACK!!! He told me so when he asked me to go with him on the road! Of course, I burst into tears! Happy tears! I wish you could have heard the way he said, "I love you!" It was so honest and sincere. I could really feel his love! He is so totally into me! And not like boring, clingy Vince. Joey is so perfect! He is hot, exciting, adventurous, romantic, charming, sincere, loyal, generous, good with his hands and other parts... LOL! Things are finally falling into place!

Cinnamon roll arrives. Takes big gooey bite.

Speaking of falling into place, OMG, did he ever fall into place! He brought over this sex manual, you know like the Kama Sutra. Have you ever tried "The Melody Maker" "The Reverse Cowgirl" "The TV Dinner"? If not, you should! I'm still hot!!!!   I'll send you a copy. Tell Jerry he can thank me later!

Another big gooey bite.

I know you are thinking – what about my job. Well, it's only an internship, and if things work out with Joey the way I think they will, I won't need or be able to work because I will be traveling around with him most of the year.   I'm so excited!!! I'm going to give notice to Cliff today. I'll give him 2 weeks, so I can go to the office Christmas party. Apparently the office throws awesome ones. Joey said he'll go with me which will be great! Jack will be so jealous! I just know it! Oh well, his loss!

Can't wait to see you at Christmas. Joey is coming with me by the way! Can't wait for you to meet him. You'll love him!   We fly in on the 23rd. We are only staying until the 28th because Joey is taking me to Aspen for New Year's Eve. Isn't that so romantic?! I just know he is going to propose!   I'm sooooooo happy!!! Speaking of Christmas, anything special the kids want? I know Joey will buy it. He is so super generous!

Miss you! Love you!

Xoxoxoxo,

Your So In Love Sister

Finishes breakfast.   Packs up.   Pays.   Leaves.

272

"Operation Get-the-Bitch-Out-Of-Dodge is almost complete! Here's to the New Year free of the slutty, stalking, conniving homewrecker!"

Susan and Rose clink glasses.

CHAPTER 64

I can't believe tonight is Jack's Christmas party. Oh my gosh, I hope I didn't make a mistake orchestrating this Operation. I really hope She doesn't make a scene or figure everything out before it is all completed. Nah, She won't. She's not that bright. But who am I kidding?! I do hope she makes a scene and everyone sees what an evil, conniving tramp she is!

Oh, I can't wait to wear my new dress. Even with the age difference, I am going to give Her a run for her money. I look HOT in that white dress. She is not the only one who can wear white after Labor Day and look sexy. Look out, Bitch, we'll see who is frumpy and plain! I hope Jack and I even make it to the party. Once he sees me in that figure clinging number he may just ravish me on the staircase. Thank goodness all of the kids have sleepovers tonight.

Okay here it goes- six inch crystal studded stilettos, back bearing angel white gown, diamond hoops, here I come.

Get ready to be floored CB!

CHAPTER 65

"LG, come on. We're going to be late."

"Coming CB!"

Boy, I hope Maggie isn't there tonight. I really don't feel like having to make the introductions between her and Susan. She shouldn't even be there, she already gave notice. Thank God!

What a happy day it was when Cliff told me Maggie was quitting to go travel around with her new boyfriend! Well, I guess at least if she is at the party, she'll be there with her new boyfriend. I wonder if I should warn him about her psychotic stalking tendencies. Nah, it's his problem. She is no longer my problem! Whew!!!! What a scary year! To think how close she came to ruining my life. Put it out of your head, Jack! It's over! Yes!!!!

Susan appears at the top of the stairs.

"WOW!!!! Really WOW! LG, you are f***ing HOT! Thank God the kids are gone. Come here!"

Susan slinks down the stairs to Jack's trembling arms.

"You still take my breath away, baby!"

"Mission accomplished then, baby!"

Slow, soft, tender, yet hot kisses filled with love and lust accompanied by equally slow, soft, tender hands that need no direction take over the scene. Lots of mmms, ohs and ahs follow.

"We…Mmmm…Need…Mmmm…To…Mmmm…Stop…Mmmm."

"Really? You really want me to stop?" Jack asks breathlessly as he nibbles on Susan's neck.

"No…mmm…not really. But we have to, ahhhhh… or

we'll never make it…mmmm…to the party." Barely said
as Jack's hand slides up Susan's exposed thigh.

"Who cares about that party! We can have our own
private little party for two." Jack whispers as his
other hand glides down Susan's bare back and skims
over her perfectly toned butt.

"Sounds wonderful, but, baby, mmmm…you know you
have to…mmmm…be there. Mmmm… You're one of the
partners. Ohhhh…"

"Are you sure, LG?"

"Not really, but let's….ahhhh… go and then….ohhh…
come back and you can continue where you leave
off…Mmmmm…"

"Alright, if you say so. But be prepared to not
get any sleep, baby."

"Promise?"

"Pinky swear!"

One last long hot steamy kiss and they leave.

CHAPTER 66

The party is in full force at the beachfront Loew's hotel in Santa Monica. It's a beautiful clear night. The ocean sparkles in the moonlight. Everyone is having a good time- drinking, dancing, laughing, karaoke-ing. Phil puts on a Santa outfit as he passes out the employees' holiday gifts. She arrives fashionably late. Ironically, She is wearing all black. A long, figure hugging black gown with a train. Quite the contrast to Susan's all white cocktail dress. Jack sees Her the minute She walks in with Joey. A big sigh of relief. She is with her boyfriend. Maybe she won't even say hello. No luck. She makes a beeline straight for Jack dragging Joey along the way. Susan's back is to Her as She approaches.

Loudly, "Merry Christmas, Jack." Double kisses to each cheek. "Jack, this is my boyfriend, Joey. Joey, this is my ex-boss, Jack."

"Nice to meet you, Joey."

"Likewise."

"So, where is your wife, Jack. Can't believe all this time I've worked here I haven't met her."

Susan turns. Their eyes meet. Maggie hesitates. There is something familiar about this woman. Where have I seen her before? Hmmm… I know it will come to me. I guess she cleans up well. She is not quite as plain as I thought from the picture I saw.

"Maggie, this is Susan, my wife. Susan, this is Maggie, an intern. Maggie will be leaving us this week."

"Hi, nice to meet you." Maggie holds out a limp hand.

Susan takes Maggie's hand with a Hulk Hogan grip. "Pleasure is all mine. You look so familiar. Don't we know each other?"

"Uhm, I doubt it. Ouch! Do you mind letting go of my hand."

"Oh, sorry. Sometimes I just don't know my own strength. I just know I know you."

"I really don't think so. I just moved here less than a year ago and you've never been in the office when I am there."

"Hmmmm… Oh. My. God! Aren't you the Letter Writer?"

"Excuse me?"

"Don't you go to Eggsactly and write hand-written letters?"

"Oh my God! It can't be! You're the clu-ut-utz cu-cu-customer that spilled tomato juice all over my brand new white suit!" Steam begins to seep out of Maggie's ears.

"Uhm… yeah, I was kind of hoping you had forgotten about that. Sorry about that again."

Jack is staring in disbelief. Susan knows Maggie! Oh. Shit. Susan spilled tomato juice on Maggie's suit. WTF? That's not like Susan.

"You two know each other?"

"Well, we don't exactly know each other, baby. Maggie, that's your name, right? occasionally comes into Eggsactly, and she is always writing these letters on this beautiful stationary with a very fancy pen." Susan turns her focus right to Maggie. "I must admit I've been tempted to take a peek at those letters. You always seem so intent. You barely look up from what you're writing.   I always assumed you were writing to a boyfriend."

"Uhm, no, my sister." Maggie barely mumbles.

"Awww, how sweet. You two must be close. Rose, you know the owner, and I kind of made up a game trying to guess about what you were writing. Sometimes you came in floating on air and then there was that terrible period when you looked so- how should I put it- uhm, let's just say not your best. We should sit down sometime and compare our stories with what really was happening. It would be such a hoot!"

"Definitely. Such a hoot. Well, it was nice meeting you. Jack, thank you again for everything. Joey, let's go dance."

"Oh no, again the pleasure was all mine! Happy Holidays!"

"Bye, Maggie. Joey, a pleasure."

Joey is unable to respond as he is dragged off to the dance floor.

CHAPTER 67

The party is in full swing. Finally the
speeches begin just as Susan knew they would. Every
year Cliff makes a speech thanking all the employees
for their hard work, and then gives a special thank
you to any employees or interns who will be leaving
the company. Cliff announces that Maggie will be
leaving the firm and wishes her all the best. He asks
if she would like to say something. Of course, she
does. As she walks to the podium, someone (Susan)
steps on her train and rips her dress. She shrieks,
but then composes herself as she gets to the mike.
She gives Susan an evil eye. Susan shrugs with
innocence. "I want to thank Cliff and Jack for this
wonderful experience! It has been awesome. I have
learned so much here, but it is time to move on and
start a new phase in my life. Please let me introduce
you to my boyfriend, Joey, soon to be fiancé, I'm
sure. Wink. Wink." Nervous laughter all around.
"Come on up, Joey."

"Uhm… Maggie, that's probably not a good idea."
Joey sounds so sincere. Wink. Wink.

"Oh come on, sweetie. Let everyone see how lucky
I am to get you. Please come say 'hi'."

"Seriously, not a good idea, Maggie." Joey being
all polite and sheepish, as if the entire plan wasn't
for him to get on stage and make a speech. Maybe he
should be an actor.

"Please, baby. Come tell everyone how much in
love you are with me and how we are going to travel
the world fixing injured athletes and making love at

every national monument."

"Yeah, about that Maggie…" Joey makes his way to the mike.

"Here's the thing…." All eyes are on the two of them.

"It's been great and all. But, I just don't think this is going to work out after all. I think I am just going to hit the road myself. But, hey, thanks!"

"What? What? What do you mean, 'hey, thanks'? Please stop joking. This is embarrassing." Her voice is beginning to rise.

"Yeah, no joke. You're pretty and all, but I need more. You know someone with some substance and ambition and morals."

"Seriously, stop Joey. This isn't funny. People are going to think you are serious." Her voice is rising more.

"I am babe. But, good luck to you and all."

"What the f***?!?! Are you serious? You are in love with me and told me so. You asked me to go on the road with you and said you would take care of me."

"Yeah, my bad. Sorry!"

"Sorry????? That's all you have to say? Sorry? Are you f***ing kidding me?" Now she is trembling and looking out over the crowd of party-goers when someone catches her eye. All of the sudden she gets this bizarre look. " 'Melanie?'… 'Dr. Quackenbush?'… 'Witchy-Poo… I mean Dr. Schmekel?'… 'Mr. Big Bad Cop?' … 'Mr. Weasley Cop?'… Why are you all here?"

Melanie, "Dr Quackenbush" aka Mario, Witchy-Poo/Dr. Schmekel, "Mr. Big and Bad Cop" aka Toby and

"Mr. Weasly Cop" aka Raymond, all look around baffled.

"What are you all doing here? Melanie, why did you move out without telling me? Dr. Schmekel, why are you in California? Mr. Big and Bad Cop, Mr. Weasley Cop, what happened to the police station?" The group looks around at each other as if they have no idea what She is talking about.

"I know you all. Why are you all here?" It only takes moments for the light to go on. "Oh my God!!! You did this to me!" Finger pointing straight at Susan. "You, you, you, the clutz! You did all this! It was all a set-up! You blinded me, balded me, dyed me orange, had me arrested. It was all you!!" She lunges at Susan. Jack and Cliff grab her just in time and all hold her back.
She continues rambling and freaking out and yelling at Susan. Susan stands there looking all innocent and doe-eyed as if she has no idea what She is talking about.

Somehow the "paramedics" arrive. (Thanks again, Drew!) She is sedated and carted off in a straight jacket.

As the gurney is leaving the building Jack looks at Susan for an explanation. Susan just winks and says "Merry Christmas."

CHAPTER 68

Molly,

Help!!! I am stranded! The wife set me up!!! I am in some whack-o holding cell. I don't even know what state I am in. The wife kidnapped me.

I am trapped in a single white room with a teeny-tiny bathroom off the side. There is only a cot, a milk crate and a folding table full of food. On the wall is a banner saying, "5150 Holding Cell" written in what appears to be a Sharpie.

Help!!!! I can't get out!!!!

The Christmas party was a nightmare. It started off great! I looked fabulous. Right when I saw Jack I went up to him to show him what he was missing. He was standing with his wife, but her back was to me, so I couldn't see her at first. When she turned around, I was a bit baffled. I knew I had seen her before, but I couldn't place where. Then she said told me she is the clutz from the diner. The one who spilled tomato juice on me. She didn't say clutz, but.. She said she noticed I was always writing letters and had thought about taking a peek at them. Can you imagine?!?! Well imagine it, because she DID! She had to have read my letters. She totally knows everything and set me up! What a bitch!!!

Anyway... I quickly pulled Joey out onto the dance floor because it was so awkward. Cliff gave me a nice farewell send-off, so I went to the stage to say thank you and gush about Joey. Then guess what happened- Joey dumped me- in front of everyone! Yes, he dumped me. Can you believe it?!?! I was so embarrassed and in shock, I was trembling. And then, as I was looking out over the crowd I saw my old roommate, Melanie, her boyfriend, Dr. Quackenbush, the witchy-poo doctor from Santa Fe and the two cops that arrested me and took me to jail. It was all so weird. That's when I realized she set me up. The wife set me up! I started screaming at her, but she looked all innocent and no one believed me. Someone must have called the paramedics because I was drugged and the next thing I knew I woke up here.

I was all groggy and started stumbling about. Then I found her letter! It was all a scam. Joey was part of the set-up. It wasn't real. He didn't love me. The proposal was a phony. I am all alone who knows where, jobless, homeless and boyfriend-less! Help!!!! I don't deserve this! I am too good of a person and too beautiful! Help! Get me out of here!
Your kidnapped innocent sister!

CHAPTER 69

Dear Wanna-Be Homewrecker~

I do hope you are enjoying your time-out. Think of it as a 72 hour hold to find yourself and re-group! Lol! You need this time. I hope you learned a lesson.

Do some soul-searching. A car will come get you in 3 days and take you to the airport for your ticket back home to Chicago. You can torture the fine people there.

Don't worry, I've provided you with plenty of food until then. I've noticed you are quite the hefty eater. Your back side has noticed too! Just sayin'.

Anyway, I really hope you will come out of this a better person, you couldn't get worse, and realize we are all not pawns in Maggie's chess game!

I am not going to press charges for drugging my husband, but if I ever see you in California again, beware!!!!

Merry Christmas,

Mr. Married Boss Guy's Wife

CHAPTER 70

"Merry Christmas, CG!"

"Merry Christmas, LB"

The look that passes between Jack and Susan is one of silent understanding. The Homewrecker/Letter Writer is never mentioned again.

They make love with the passion and love that has been there from the start.

Everything is Eggsactly as it should be.